PRAISE FOR NATURE'S

"*Nature's Bite*, the third of a medical mystery series by Dr. Mark Anthony Powers, weaves the grim realities of climate change, fascinating medical detail, and presidential politics into an intricate plot filled with twists and surprises — as well as delightful wry humor."

> — Cat Warren, author of the NYT bestseller *What the Dog Knows* and Professor Emerita of English North Carolina State University

"*Nature's Bite* begins with a tick bite, on the derriere, of the President of the United States. He's got Alpha Gal Syndrome, and Dr. Phineas Mann, an almost-retired pulmonologist and beekeeper, can't suppress a grin. Dr. Mann's grin disappears in this climate-fiction thriller when men in black pound at his door. What does the FBI want? Is Dr. Mann's past back to bite *him*?
During a summer of withering heat, Dr. Mann's life is upended by storm cell-like events, unpredictable and potentially lethal, like the warming earth itself. The calm against malevolence, Dr. Mann's family and his passion for bees and beagles will warm the heart of the reader. For fans of *Migrations* by Charlotte McConaghy and *The Water Knife* by Paolo Bacigalupi, nature's bite will sting, but leave the reader hopeful and, as if donning a beekeeper's suit, armed to fight for change."

> — Sara E. Johnson, author of the Alexa Glock Forensic Mysteries

"Mark Powers' *Nature's Bite* gives us a scary glimpse into an alternate future in which a narcissistic president retains power. He shows us all too convincingly how mismanagement of climate policy and public health can have dramatic and far-reaching negative consequences on our health and the environment. He beautifully illustrates the potentially life-altering effects of clinical trials research and why strict regulations are needed. Throughout this harrowing ride, Mark uses his knowledge of medicine and beekeeping to skillfully educate the reader on the basics and nuances of these disciplines. A fantastic read!"

> — Loretta G. Que, M.D., Professor of Medicine, Duke University and Interim Chief of Pulmonary, Allergy, and Critical Care Medicine

"In *Nature's Bite*, Mark Powers keeps the story moving with a steadily moving plot and characters that are consistent and well-drawn throughout the novel. The concluding episodes are especially strong. They are fast paced, made realistic with ample medical detail and credible dialog, and an absolutely killer characterization of a former President, whom everyone will recognize — a delightful veer into satire."

— Rosemary Waldorf, Mayor of Chapel Hill, North Carolina 1995-2001

"In the third installment of Mark Anthony Powers' medical thriller series, Dr. Phineas Mann is back, and this time tangled up in an effort to save democracy—and biodiversity—from the whims of a feckless demagogue. Powers deftly imagines a not-too-distant future in which a tyrant attempts to puppeteer science, risking the fate of our ecosystem. Powers shines a light on alarming planetary and social implications of unchecked power in a page-turner that is both frightening and delightful to read."

— Alexis Luckey, Executive Director, Toxic Free North Carolina

"Powers does an excellent job weaving together a band of nuanced characters as they discover the truths of a not-so-far removed alternate reality. Devastating climate change, roving bands of political thugs, heart-wrenching medical scenarios—I certainly didn't expect to laugh out loud at the final plot twists, but *Nature's Bite* delivers the perfect balance right through to the end."

— Ashley Troth, Ph.D., Extension Agent, Consumer and Commercial Ornamental Horticulture, North Carolina Cooperative Extension

"While this political thriller offers an alternative to contemporary history, Powers' book neatly captures the 'biting' impact of climate change along with the absurdly divisive political response, as if ripped directly from news headlines. An engaging read by a percipient author."

— Thomas Stevens, artist and gallery owner, Mayor of Hillsborough, North Carolina 2005-2019

NATURE'S
BITE

A NOVEL

NATURE'S BITE

MARK ANTHONY POWERS

HAWKSBILL PRESS

www.hawksbillpress.com

Edited by Dawn Reno Langley, President of Rewired Creatives, Inc.
Book design by Christy Day, Constellation Book Services
Cover art by istock
Author photo by Amy Stern Photography, www.amystern.com

ISBN (paperback): 978-1-7370329-4-6
ISBN (ebook): 978-1-7370329-5-3

Printed in the United States of America

For Andrew

APRIL

"...all of this with the global warming and...a lot of it's a hoax. It's a hoax. I mean, it's a money-making industry, OK? It's a hoax, a lot of it."

FUTURE POTUS AT A 2015 RALLY

"Looks like the climate crisis literally bit the president on his ass." Phineas Mann offered his wife a mischievous grin and rubbed the sweaty roots of his meticulously groomed snow-white beard. He continued perusing the April 11, 2024 Apple News story on his iPad while he arranged the once weekly delivery of snail mail by addressee into short, precise piles next to his cell phone. Perspiration evaporated from his temples and neck in the 80-degree air conditioning. The short walk from his office to the hospital parking deck after work was hotter than he remembered this early in the spring.

Iris raised her glacier blue eyes from her laptop and studied him over her reading glasses. She was seated across the dining room table from her husband, as they always were after a workday. She tossed her silver braid over her shoulder from front to back and leaned into her chair. "You'll need to elaborate, I'm afraid. I don't have a clue what you're talking about."

"He has Alpha Gal Syndrome."

"Does 'Gal' mean he has a new name for the First Lady, or does he have yet another mistress?" She accepted her three envelopes and altered her posture, exaggerating raising her slender torso up straight and throwing her shoulders back, her standard signal to her husband that he again slouched under the weight of his day.

"It's a medical syndrome. He's allergic to mammalian meat. If he eats it, he gets terrible hives." His grin grew into a broad smile. "And you know how much he loves a cheeseburger. He eats one now, and he'll have the 'mad itch'. That's gonna put him in some bad mood."

He noticed her signal and corrected his posture, trying to forget the burden of his recent month covering the Intensive Care Unit service as a 70-year-old Professor of Medicine teaching and supervising tired interns and residents, a knowledge-hungry fellow, and four panicky medical students. Always a stressful rotation, it could never reach the levels of May 1998, when someone poisoned one of his patients with arsenic. He wondered over the years where the suspect, the nurse Angela Portier, escaped to after she incited the patient's racist son into a monumental act of domestic terrorism. The racist was captured, found guilty, and remained in Central Prison. Angela Portier was never located.

Decades later, there'd been Phineas' exhausting and terrifying intensive care work during the coronavirus pandemic, also easily among the top three of the most trying times of his life. And it lasted, and lasted, and exhausted his younger colleagues and crushed senior citizens like himself.

Iris stared at her screen and tapped her keyboard. "I don't see the article...So, Dr. Mann, what's the treatment?"

"Avoidance. He can eat fish and poultry, anything with fins and feathers. No red meat."

"Doesn't he also gorge on KFC?" she asked.

Phineas turned off his iPad and folded his reading glasses. "Not sure.

Might be an investment opportunity for my IRA. If that's so, chicken stocks are bound to get a bump as word spreads—or even better—Impossible Foods—and word is they're going IPO."

"Impossible Foods?" She studied him with a blank expression.

"They make the Impossible Burger, a bioprocessed plant-based hamburger. I tried one at a meeting in Toronto last year. It's pretty good, especially with cheese."

"So why do you say the climate crisis bit him on the ass?"

"Alpha Gal Syndrome can develop following the bite of a Lone Star tick, a blood sucker that crept north from Texas with global warming. The article says the President found a tick on his 'thigh' (fingers making air quotes) after a round of golf at his Washington DC course...He probably picked it up when he kicked his ball out of the rough."

"Aww...poor baby. Pretty ironic. Maybe punishment from Mother Nature." A wry smile followed a twinkle in her eyes, a familiar sign that she'd created an amusing insight. "So, climate change caused the ticks to spread north, and the ticks reduce the number of people who can eat beef, and beef cattle contribute to climate change by belching and farting methane." She punched her fist into her palm. "Mother Nature might be beginning to fight back."

"He's claiming the ticks were put there by Democrats with ties to a deep state, and he's demanding an investigation by the FBI and DOJ. They're probably DNA testing the tick as we speak."

Iris shook her head slowly and let out a long sigh. "What has this country come to?"

Phineas' cell phone began vibrating and 202-877-8339 appeared on the screen. "No one I know. Probably a robocall from another Super PAC wanting money." He watched it go to voicemail then hit the play button and speaker icon. He'd forgotten the volume was turned all the way up.

"This is the FBI. We are at your front door and are about to ring your doorbell."

DING DONG.

Iris' jaw muscles clenched and created dark shadows in her cheeks. She locked startled eyes with Phineas, as he whispered, "I'd better see who's there."

Through the foyer door's windowpane, two men in black suits tracked his approach. One was stocky and one taller and lean. They pressed their badges against the glass for his inspection. Both read "FBI" at the top and "Special Agent" at the bottom.

WTF? Phineas stood inches from the men, staring at them through the transparent barrier. Their foreheads glistened in the evening swelter. The drying sweat in Phineas' damp shirt gave him a sudden chill. He cracked the door open. "May I help you?"

The lean agent sported a black crewcut speckled with grey. He held his badge up again. "Dr. Phineas Mann?"

"Yes."

"I'm Special Agent Meyers and this is Special Agent Richter. We'd like to ask you and your wife a few questions." His words were delivered in monotone through thin lips. He dabbed his sleeve at his shiny brow.

"Should...should we have a lawyer?"

Richter's suit stretched over muscular shoulders and upper arms. "Not if you haven't broken any laws." His five o'clock shadow lined his cheeks with a bristle darker than his light brown hair. "May we come in?"

They pushed through the door and the heat rushed in around them. Phineas had to step back. "What...what is it you need to ask me?"

Their black suits pressed shoulder to shoulder with him in the Mann's small entry room. Richter extracted a handkerchief from his hip pocket and began to dry his face and neck. "Is there a place where we can speak with you and your wife?"

Iris squeezed in against Phineas and surveyed the unexpected visitors with a withering stare. The two men immediately stood taller and held up their badges as if they were protective shields. Meyers lowered his far enough to expose his face. "Iris Mann?"

"Who's asking, and why are you in our house?" She sounded defiant and more irritated than worried. Barefoot and standing tall, her probing stare was almost level with Myers' eyes.

"Special Agents Meyers and Richter, Ma'am. We've been sent to ask you and your husband a few questions."

"You can ask. We may answer." Iris pivoted away from them as she uttered, "We've had a long day. Let's get this over with. And close the door. We can't air condition the planet." She marched back to the dining room table and shut her laptop. Phineas and the two suits followed. She settled into her seat. "You might as well sit down."

The pair scurried to the vacant wooden chairs. Richter pulled the seat next to Iris farther from her wrath, to create a buffer zone. He extracted a leather-bound notepad from his suit jacket's vest pocket and flipped it open. Then he retrieved a gold ballpoint pen and clicked it three times. "I'll start with questions for Dr. Mann."

Phineas looked warily at his wife. She squinted at Richter. "Which Dr. Mann?"

Richter's stony face flinched. "Sorry. Dr. Phineas Mann."

Phineas hid his amusement. *He really stepped in it that time.*

Richter turned to him. "Let me confirm that you are Dr. Phineas Mann, Professor of Medicine at UNC in the Pulmonary Department."

"Division. Pulmonary Division. In the Department of Medicine."

The agent jotted a note. "And that you came to UNC from New Orleans in 1986 after multiple murder charges against you were dropped." His speech remained flat through the word 'murder'.

Phineas glared at him and considered how or whether to respond. He passed beyond annoyed to alarmed. *That again?* Was that always going to follow him like an original sin—but never with the possibility of cleansing by baptism?

"If you don't want to comment, you can just correct errors we might have, after I state information in our records." Richter broke the uncomfortable silence. After more writing and not eliciting any response, he continued the interview without a break in his flat expression. "Your salary is currently in large part supported by a grant from SynMedical Biopharma for the Phase 3 trial to study a novel asthma drug, SYMBI-62022. Your National Institutes of Health R-01 grant support recently ended."

Phineas' efforts to keep quiet failed. "Your big boss has cut NIH funding so much, almost no one gets research support, except from pharmaceutical companies." Anger replaced alarm. "He doesn't want anyone to advance basic science. We might learn something that doesn't suit him." He wondered if he'd regret his outburst. His last NIH funding application was denied days after he sat on a national panel and discussed the health effects of climate change. He'd reported on how increasing temperatures and air pollution were causing more severe asthma cases and more hospitalizations for emphysema patients. CNN included clips of his comments in their news programs that night.

Richter stopped his note taking and stared at Phineas. "You and your wife have had dual Italian citizenship since 2020. Do you plan to move there?"

This is getting really creepy. "Why do you ask?"

"Just confirming our information."

"I learned from a colleague that it was available to me through my Italian grandfather, so why not obtain it? I thought we might want to visit there more after we retire." He hadn't informed Iris that he was considering an actual move to Europe, if leadership in the United States didn't improve.

"Thank you, Dr. Mann." Richter nodded to his partner.

Meyers produced a similar notepad and pen. "Now, Dr. Iris Mann, PhD, I just have a few questions." His tone softened in an apparent attempt to be disarming.

Her narrowed eyes continued to search his.

His head drooped into a defensive posture. "You're a tenured Professor in the UNC School of Social Work." He waited for a response. She offered none. "Your salary is now mostly supported by your teaching activities. Your NIH grants ended two years ago, leading to a cut in your salary."

She shifted in her seat. Her lips squirmed ever so slightly, suggesting to Phineas that she was trying to not respond, before she did. "Once again, your Commander-in-Chief doesn't want my research to reveal why sick people aren't getting necessary health care after he eliminated their Affordable Care Act coverage and raised the age for Medicare eligibility."

Meyers clicked his pen twice and appeared to make a check mark on his pad. "Your son, Jacob, age 38, is an unmarried writer and an entomology professor at North Carolina State University. I just learned that's the study of insects. Until a few years ago, he had been receiving generous royalties from his bestselling debut novel and its film rites."

Jesus Christ! Phineas glared at Meyers. *Leave our children out of whatever crazy shit this is.*

Iris' head jerked back like she'd received an electric shock. Her mouth fell open.

Meyers' face stayed blank, as if he wanted to show his questioning was strictly business. "Your daughter, Martha Mann Hernandez, age 33, is married to Felipe Hernandez, and they have a two-year-old son, Mateo. She studied political science at UNC and has a master's degree in public policy from Duke. She works in Governor Cooper's administration and is running for Congress from North Carolina's 13th district after winning the Democratic nomination in the primary election."

Deep furrows crossed Iris' forehead. "What are you really here for?" Her words rolled out like hot asphalt on a highway.

"We'll come to that. Do we have everything correct, so far?" Richter answered.

Neither Mann responded. Two statues.

"I'll take that as a "Yes." Only two more." Meyers held up an index and middle finger in a 'V'. "Then you'll be rid of us—for now. You're both Democrats. Correct?"

"And what's your party?" Iris shot back then squinted at him. "Is that why our last NIH grant proposals were turned down?"

Richter now held up his index finger. "One final question." He turned to address Phineas. "Dr. Phineas Mann, if called upon, will you serve our country?"

"I'm—I'm a bit old for that." Phineas was caught off guard.

"It wouldn't be in combat."

"Ask me then."

Richter stood and rolled his bulky shoulders forward and back. "Thank you both. We'll be in touch when we have more need of you."

Meyers lifted his lanky frame upright and audibly cracked his neck. "We can show ourselves out."

Phineas escorted them to the front door. He couldn't stop himself from offering an "arrivederci" as they filed out. He heard two car doors slam and watched their heavy black sedan disappear into the darkness.

Iris hadn't moved from her seat or reopened her computer. She appeared tired and pissed off. "What the hell was that?"

⌒

"That's the last of it, Ma'am." The burly twenty-something man from the moving company handed Marie Porter a clipboard for her signature. "Anything heavy you want us to rearrange while we're still here?" He stole a glance at her tall, slender frame. His expression hinted at skepticism.

She handed him and his scrawny, surprisingly strong younger brother each a fifty-dollar bill. Her new job paid well, and she felt generous. "I'm good. Thanks for not breaking anything."

She waited until she could hear the truck's diesel engine turn over before she restrained her thick chestnut mane into a wavy ponytail and surveyed the piles of boxes in her brand spanking new downtown condo's living room.

Back in Durham! The painful memory of her mother's and her abrupt departure twenty-six years ago surfaced almost as fresh as the day they'd left—the hurried packing of all that would fit into her mother's compact car and the endless driving west. With less than two weeks remaining in the sixth grade, Marie wept most of the trip. Her two years in Durham were a highlight in her younger life, before the series of small towns they inhabited with each of the private duty nursing positions her mother could arrange for sustenance. Sometimes those jobs meant she and her mother had to live in the patient's house and crowd into one room. But her mother's fragile clients always died after a while, and the two travelers had to find a new sick person to nurse. In a new town. With a new school.

Until Chinook, Montana. Her last three years of high school. Three good years. She made friends there, good friends. Track and cross-country teammates. Then her mother was off to a new town, and Marie was off to college.

Montana State University required Marie to learn how to learn. After freshman struggles and away from her hovering and smothering mother, she flourished there, enough to gain her entrance into the University of Washington's medical school. She'd been admitted through a backdoor, the WAMI program for students from Washington, Alaska, Montana, and Idaho. At that time, in a moment of pride, her mother let slip that Marie's father was also a doctor, all Marie knew about him for most of her years—until a few months ago when her mother named him, as she neared death, a miserable death from widespread breast cancer.

Marie's work as a salaried internist/hospitalist on inpatient services engaged her at first, but the weekly variations in her work schedule and long nights on the wards grew old quickly. Then the coronavirus pandemic struck and tested her endurance over two brutal years. Finally, months ago, during the trying days and nights of watching her mother die, Marie decided that since she wasn't forming long-term attachments to patients in her work, she ought to investigate a career in the booming pharmaceutical industry. Maybe she could enjoy a 9 to 5 schedule while she was still young and single. The job at SynMedical Biopharma rose to the top of her short list of offers once she learned that it would be based back in Durham, North Carolina, and her first duties would be to help supervise an exciting Phase 3 trial of their promising new asthma drug, the final study before the challenging FDA approval process.

There were no promising new miracle drugs for her mother.

Her mother had been proud enough of her breasts to sometimes display cleavage and reveal the silver cross her father gave her as a teen during his lingering death. Then a rampage of rock-hard lumps and masses deformed those breasts and only briefly regressed after the first toxic doses of chemotherapy, treatment that sapped her mother's usual energy and sent her greying hair into the bathroom trash in great clumps. As her balding mother slowly died, she blamed the President for canceling the Affordable Care Act, causing her to skip regular mammograms and wither into an agonizing death.

But did her very private mother ever have health insurance, or were her assurances just lip service to satisfy her absent doctor daughter living two western states away? Her daughter who now felt guilty that she was too busy to confirm that her mother was indeed insured and had indeed been getting recommended tests. Marie only learned of her mother's dire finances after she began slipping away, claiming all the while that she was waiting for Medicaid approval, claiming the second term Republican President had canceled her prior coverage.

Frustrated as her mother's deterioration accelerated, Marie had offered to find out why Medicaid hadn't come through to pay for needed treatments and support.

"I never finished registering," her mother finally confessed. She'd stared off into the distance.

"Why not?"

"If I fill out all the lines on the application, they'll connect me to one of their bygone criminal databases." Her voice was little more than a whisper.

"Mom, what are you saying?"

"Why do you think someone like me, a university-trained registered nurse, would take lousy jobs and move us around from small town to small town?" Her eyes shone as she met her daughter's stare. "I've been a fugitive since we left Durham."

Marie had known only that a scratch on her Louisiana birth certificate renamed her from Portier to Porter before her fifth-grade registration in Durham, an alteration she gave up trying to get her mother to correct. That was Marie's first glimpse of the document. She saw the box for the father's name that stated only "unknown" and asked her mother once again if she'd tell her who he was. Instead of her mother calmly deflecting her inquiry as she always had before, that time the look of pain and shame on her mother's face shut Marie down so completely, she never asked about him again.

But in her mother's last hours, she unloaded a lifetime on her daughter, including her father's identity.

Marie pushed the boxcutter through the packing tape and sliced open her first box of possessions and collected memories—the one that contained her mother's ashes.

⌒

As the red sun hung less than a finger's breath above the western horizon, Phineas donned his thickest beekeeping jacket and probed the zippers with his finger to convince himself each one was fully closed. Salty perspiration trickled down his cheeks and into the corners of his mouth. Ignoring it, he held up a roll of duct tape. "For this colony, you'd better put on your jacket *and* gloves, Jacob."

"Duct tape? Those must be some really mean bees." Jacob scratched his dark brown lumberjack style beard while he inspected the numerous scattered splotches on his XXL jacket, baggy on his lean six-foot six-inch frame. The splotches were evidence that Jacob explored the insides of scores of hives at North Carolina State University almost daily for his honey bee research.

"Looks like that jacket is getting a lot of use—and could use a cleaning." Phineas readily identified the majority of the stains—bee poop.

Jacob chuckled. "With climate change, we have to monitor the hives more often to try to prevent swarming. Swarms are happening earlier each year, and when one of our hives swarms, it eliminates that colony from a research study."

"This colony's got the meanest bees I've ever seen. By far." Phineas tore off ten-inch strips of the tape to seal the bottom of each pantleg to his heavy boots. "I'm worried that the hive has been usurped by an Africanized swarm. That's one of the reasons I called you. You can let the state inspector know what you think." He tore off more tape and bent to apply it to Jacob's pants. The denim had already begun to soak up his son's sweat in the 95-degree April heat.

Jacob held out the other leg. "Still the Dad." He finished closing his jacket's zippers and gloved up.

Phineas pulled on his long goatskin gloves and checked them for defects. He lit the hive smoker and stuffed it with pine needle fuel then shook out a jumbo-sized black plastic trash bag. "After you get the sample bees you need, I'm putting this hive down while most of the foragers are inside it. I don't want them to take over one of my other colonies, and I don't plan to live with them, no matter what the tests show, especially when your inquisitive two-year-old nephew is visiting."

"Ready?" Phineas raised his silver flat metal hive tool like a sword.

"Let's go." Jacob led the way to the apiary with long strides.

After several puffs of smoke at the hive entrance, many of the bees lounging on the landing platform scurried inside. Phineas blocked the entrance with a strip of wood. "One less way for them to attack us."

He gently pried off the outer cover. A soft 'pop' came from breaking the bees' sticky propolis seal, followed by an instant change in the buzzing volume. Bees poured through the central ventilation hole of the inner cover. Dousing them with plumes of smoke barely slowed their exit. When he lifted the inner cover, guard bees lined the tops of frames and pointed their stingers his way. The alarming roaring surrounded them and sounded like a jet engine. Heartbeats pounded in Phineas' temples.

Numerous bees took flight then crawled across his jacket's face screen, obscuring much of his vision. With so many angry stinging insects mere inches from his face, he forced himself to stay calm. Their undersides' anatomies were on close display—except for one whose wings were fully visible before they unfolded from the *back* of its thorax. He shouldn't be able to see its back, unless...It shot from left to right *inside* his hood.

Shit! There's an opening in my jacket! All I need is Africanized bees stinging me up my nostril or in my ear canal! Phineas fought back panic.

"Jacob, there's one inside my hood." Sweat dribbled into his eyes and he lost sight of the intruder. As a guess, he grabbed a handful of the right portion of his screen and squeezed. The rogue bee tumbled down the screen, its guts hanging from its abdomen, and settled next to Phineas' chin whiskers.

As a young man, part of the attraction of beekeeping was the adrenaline rush of an excited hive. As a seventy-year-old, would it one day be the end of him? His knees weak, he turned to his son, as much for comfort as for assistance. Jacob tugged the rings on Phineas' jacket's zippers together at the base of his neck. "Dad, you left a space about the size of a bee's head. Should be tight now. I'll press on, so we can get this done."

He relieved his father of the hive tool and lifted a central frame from the top box. "Only honey and pollen. No brood. Let's go down a level."

Phineas pumped clouds of smoke into the next level and at the bees in front of his face. He felt a sting on his thigh, and a hand-sized cluster of bees immediately gathered there on his jeans. He smoked them and scraped off the stinger. The banana smell of alarm pheromone dominated the more pleasing and comforting background honey aroma.

Jacob lifted another frame from the second level down. "Plenty of brood here—and we got lucky. Here's royalty." He held the frame for Phineas' inspection, just long enough for him to see the queen scurry into a corner, dragging her long abdomen. Jacob removed a screened queen cage from one of his many jacket pockets and skillfully picked her up between his index finger and thumb and jailed her. Using the rim of a small jar from another pocket, he scraped bees off the frame's surface to collect them. "Okay. I've got enough workers. Let's close up before this whole colony detonates." He quickly reassembled the hive while his father pumped stream after stream of smoke. Hordes of bees covered their face screens and explored their jackets and pant legs for openings to flesh.

Jacob pointed at his knee. "Could use some smoke here. One got me through the cloth." He scraped the spot with the hive tool. "You wanted to put the bag on this hive?"

Phineas shook open the trash bag and slipped it over the back of the hive. "If you lift the rear then the front, I'll slide it under. Once we get it in place, I can seal it later, when these angry girls have returned for the night." He removed the wood strip blocking the hive's entrance then pumped smoke along it, hoping bees would go back in. Wrong. A vibrating phalanx began exiting it. He shoved the entrance blocker back into place and felt the crunch of bee exoskeletons being crushed.

With the execution bag in place, Jacob started to walk away. "They're focused on trying to get at the queen. Ouch! One just got her stinger through my glove." He raised the cage over his head. A golden melon-sized cluster of bees covered his fist. "I could put her back in the hive, and they'd follow, but I'd like to keep her...I've got an idea. Can you fill a large bucket with soapy water?"

Phineas jogged to the garage, trailing a haze of bees. He filled a pail from the hose bibb, then added a splash of car wash soap. When he returned with it, Jacob sealed the queen cage in a sandwich sized Baggie he'd pulled from another of his many jacket pockets. Within seconds, the bee cluster over his fist and Baggie constituted the bulk of the attacking bees. He plunged his gloved hand and bagged queen into the suds, counted to twenty, and removed it. Most of the clinging bees remained submerged or struggled, drowning between the surface bubbles. The few remaining on his fist fell off and staggered on the ground. He unzipped the Baggie to give the queen air. But soon, a smaller contingent of airborne worker bees gathered around the bagged queen, again attracted by her pheromone. Jacob repeated the dunking procedure. "You should close off the bag covering the hive now, before any more escape from the ventilation hole and come looking for their queen."

Phineas left his son long enough to twist a wire over the bag's opening, sealing the colony's fate. Heat and carbon dioxide would build up and the doomed bees would enter their eternal sleep. He'd harvest their honey later, their golden legacy.

Jacob held up the open Baggie again, attracting most of the attacking bees to his gloved hand. He sealed it and, for a third time, drowned those remaining of the queen's loyal subjects.

"I may have to write this technique up for the *American Bee Journal*. If it hadn't worked, we'd have had legions of furious bees trying to sting us for the next hour." He located a magnifying glass in another of his jacket's pockets. "Now let's have a look at their wings." He held out the jar and turned on the battery powered light that illuminated his lens' perimeter.

"I really appreciate your help on this." Phineas watched with pride. After a rocky pre-adolescent year, Jacob had evolved into a serious student then an easy-going man whose visits Iris and he cherished.

"No problem, Dad." He glanced over at his father. "I'm hoping you can do a small favor for me."

"I hope I can. What do you need?"

"A dog sitter for about ten days, while I lecture at Cornell and then at the Eastern Apiculture Society."

Phineas felt proud but disappointed. He missed having a dog and thought he'd enjoy sitting for one. Yet, if he'd known his son was speaking at such a prominent beekeeping event as the EAS, he'd have signed up to attend. "Since when did you get a dog?"

"One of our post-Docs is overseas as part of her grant, and she twisted my arm. Looks like I've got her two-year-old beagle for a year."

"Good thing I put deer fencing around the backyard." Phineas peered over Jacob's shoulder, through the magnifying lens, and tried to see what he could of the bees' anatomic details. "We should clear it with your mother."

"To be fair, I have to warn you about something. She's a real alpha bitch."

"I hope you're talking about the dog."

Jacob snorted. "Hah! Of course." He put down the magnifying glass. "I think their wings are consistent with Africanized bees. I can't say more without microscopic measurements, but the vein pattern and dimensions look like it to me. And their slightly smaller body size is suggestive. We'll confirm with genetic testing through the state inspector. He told me they've already had a few cases in 2024 where European bee colonies were usurped by Africanized colonies."

"Damn climate change." Phineas accepted the lens and squinted into the jar of bees. "Only a couple of years ago, our winters were too long and cold for them to make it in North Carolina."

"And there's something else, Dad." Jacob took a deep breath and let it out slowly. "I'm considering taking my research north, back to Cornell."

"Really? It was pretty cold and miserable when I was an undergrad there, and when you were on Cornell's baseball team. I remember having to listen to complaints from you about pitching in upstate New York's weather."

"Well, it's warmer now, and their bee populations are way more stable than they are in North Carolina. My old mentor is still monitoring their feral populations, and they have an isolated research lab up in the Adirondacks. If they ask me back to Cornell, I should go. I'll know more after my trip." Jacob grinned. "And I got a call from my old baseball coach there. He wants me to work with his pitchers if I take the faculty job there." Cornell had pulled out all its tools to attract Jacob back.

"Imagine how different your life would have been if you'd signed with the Orioles after they drafted you." Phineas thought back to how much he enjoyed watching Jacob play ball, and how he missed it after his son's college career ended. Iris and he would sorely miss Jacob once he moved.

"Dad, you know the odds of making it out of the minors were slim, and even if I did, I'd still need a career after baseball. Going on to grad school was the right decision. My destiny was to make a living with my head, not my arm."

"I know you're right, but there weren't that many who threw in the 90s back then—and had good off-speed stuff." Phineas surveyed his suit and pants for stray bees. "What does Claire think of moving to Ithaca?"

"We're not together anymore. She moved out." Jacob took off his gloves and wrung out sweat.

"Oh. Sorry," Phineas mumbled. He looked for pain on his son's face and, not finding any, began inspecting his son's protective covering for more bees.

"No need to be. We'd been drifting apart for a while, and Ruby literally put the finishing touch on it."

"Who's Ruby?"

"The beagle. One night close to bedtime, I was focused on a paper I was writing, and Claire decided it was time for Ruby to relieve herself. So, she led her to the door and told her to go out. Ruby poked her nose out into the pouring rain and started backing up. Claire gave her a shove and told her, 'Go on, Ruby. Go pee.'" The beginning of a grin emerged, just visible through Jacob's hood's screen. "Ruby looked Claire in the eye, squatted, and peed on her foot, then immediately circled back to her pillow. I couldn't stop laughing. Claire got pissed off after she was pissed on—and I thought it was funny. Still do, but...well, that did it." His tone abruptly shifted from amused to melancholy. "She left the next day."

Phineas shook his head at the telling story. "Definitely an alpha bitch—and I'm still talking about the dog."

Jacob ripped off duct tape and peeled his jacket off his soaked tee shirt then extracted a dry NCSU entomology tee shirt from his gym bag. His bee gear went into a stainless-steel compartment in the bed of the NC State Department of Entomology's red pickup truck before he secured the jar of bees and queen cage on the passenger seat. A worker landed on the queen cage. He pinched her. "Hope that's the last one."

"Ouch! It wasn't." Phineas began scraping the back of his bare hand. "Jacob, there's one more thing I wanted to bring up."

"What's that, Dad?"

Phineas began a second inspection of his jacket and pants for loose bees. "Your mother and I got paid a visit by the FBI a few days ago."

"WHAAAT?"

"They seemed to know everything about our family, even you."

"Why? And *me*?" Jacob's face shifted from puzzled to distressed, and Phineas shared his son's feelings.

"Obviously, they haven't contacted you. We have no idea why they mentioned you and Martha. Maybe her running for Congress as a Democrat? But they seemed to focus more questions on me."

"What'd you tell them?"

"We had nothing to tell. Your mother did give them a piece of her mind though, and a comment about their Commander-in-Chief." Phineas inspected the raised pink spot on the back of his hand.

"I'd expect no less from her." A brief knowing look preceded Jacob depressing his bushy eyebrows in concern. "She didn't increase their interest in us, did she?"

"I doubt it. She was just jousting with them. It was at the end of a long day."

"How'd they end it?"

Phineas grinned and shook his head. "Asked if I'd be willing to serve my country, if called." The question had created a mystery that lingered in his thoughts during each quiet moment since that night.

Jacob cleared his throat. "Aren't you a little old for that?"

"Hah! What I said. Just thought I should mention it, and that you might want to be careful what you email or say on your cell. They could be monitoring us."

"Creepy. Really creepy, especially not knowing what's behind it."

For a moment, the two men were silent in thought before Phineas blurted, "You said a mouthful!"

Jacob's stomach let out a growl. "Speaking of mouthfuls, you pickin' many veggies yet?" He glanced at the raised beds in the garden.

"Yup. They're coming in earlier than they used to. Already have peas and greens, and of course, radishes."

"It's good that you've kept your garden producing full tilt. Looks to me like produce offerings in stores have been slim without anyone to work the crops and pick 'em—or enough pollinators to fertilize them." Jacob closed his truck's bins. "Well, I guess that's it."

Phineas finally mustered the nerve to get out of his stifling protective jacket. "I don't see our president reversing himself on immigration any time soon. His base loves his damned wall. And I used to be somewhat skeptical when beekeepers claimed that without bees and other insects, food production could fall by a third or more, but the empty shelves and sky-high prices suggest they were right." Phineas reached up to put his hand on Jacob's shoulder. "Thanks for your help, Son. Got time to come up to the house and give your mother a hug and have some spaghetti with Bolognese sauce?"

"Always." More stomach growling.

⌒

They found Iris at the dining room table hunched over her laptop. She tilted her head back to take in her son's sweat-dappled face. "You guys need to cool off."

Jacob leaned in for a peck on her cheek. "Whatcha' doin' Mom?"

"Changing all my damned passwords. Making sure none of my apps are tracking me. Eliminating apps I don't use. Encrypting everything." A tiny kelly-green sticky note covered the camera lens above her screen. "Damned FBI!"

"Dad told me. That's pretty creepy." Jacob turned a chair across from her around and sat cowboy style.

Iris returned her focus to her laptop. "Why can't we lead quiet existences like everyone else? First it was murder charges in New Orleans, then a racist terrorist here, and now who knows what. And we don't have a clue this time." Her fingers pounded the keyboard.

Phineas shrugged helplessly and poured Jacob a tall glass of ice water. Then he filled most of a two-gallon pot with water and set it on a burner. He dumped in a handful of salt and splashed in a dollop of olive oil. A

Tupperware container of Bolognese sauce went into a saucepan. "Jacob, what kind of pasta do you want?" He retrieved a generous salad from the refrigerator and began mixing a balsamic dressing.

"How about linguini? Or spaghetti will be fine. So, Mom, what about the Internet of Things? What about your social media presence?"

She stared at her laptop. "Never wanted an Alexa or Echo. Got rid of Facebook and closed Twitter. Internet of things in our old house? Hah! Are you kidding?"

"How old is your 'fridge? Your other appliances? Your thermostat?"

"Never hooked any of them up to the internet," she grumbled.

"You sure?"

"Hell no." His mother squinted up at him.

"How old is your router?"

"Just ordered a new one. Should arrive in two days. Already figured out a difficult password for it. Until it gets here, everything will be in airplane mode, except when I really need it. Here." She pushed a scrap of paper across the table. "It'll be on the back side of the garage door opener, next to the ceiling, when you need it."

The mouthwatering bouquet of tomato, onions, garlic, and oregano filled the house's open kitchen and dining area. Phineas dumped two handfuls of linguini into a roiling boil. "Sounds like my digital life just got more complicated."

Jacob had extracted his cell phone from a front pants pocket and scrolled down it with his thumb. "Shit."

"Jacob!" His mother arched her eyebrows.

"Sorry, Mom. NPR just announced that the President is calling for massive tick and mosquito spraying across the U.S."

"Why?"

"Seems he picked up a tick playing golf on one of his courses—and now he can't eat red meat. He must be really pissed. Tweeted that he was protecting citizens from dangerous bugs. Says he wants to give a tax credit for insecticide spraying."

"Do you think spraying for mosquitoes will have *that* much impact?" She pressed her lips together.

Phineas groaned and stirred the sauce. "Hell yeah! Now Jacob's bees and mine will be foraging on plants covered with more poisons—not to mention the more important devastation of native pollinators—and insects in general. And the birds...and reptiles that feed on 'em. Why doesn't someone explain to him that bugs are at the bottom of nature's food pyramid?"

"Someone may have tried, but then they'd have gotten fired for disagreeing—or bringing up science," Iris replied.

Phineas captured a noodle on his pasta fork and hurled it at the refrigerator. It fell to the floor. He retrieved another noodle from the pot and tasted it. "Pasta's not there yet."

"Do you *have* to do that?" Iris frowned at him.

"Not really, but it's still kind of fun." He and Jacob grinned at her like ten-year-olds caught in a prank.

She shook a finger at them. "You boys! So, Phineas, what's going on with your bees?"

"We had to put a hive down. The colony seems to have been replaced by Africanized bees."

"Phineas! You have killer bees in *our backyard*?" Iris' hands fell to her lap as she stared up at him.

Jacob murmured, "Mom, beekeepers prefer the term Africanized Honey Bees to killer bees. And there haven't been *that* many cases of them usurping North Carolina hives—yet."

"Yet." She squinted at her son. "That name sounds like some entomologist's euphemism." She returned her focus to Phineas. "You finally ready to give up beekeeping, especially since we have a toddler running around the yard on a regular basis?"

"It's the damn climate change. I promise I'll keep a close eye on the other three hives...They seem okay so far."

Jacob studied his cell phone's screen. "Have you looked at the president's face lately?"

"Not a face I care to look at. What are you seeing?" Phineas extracted another strand of linguini from the pot.

"It looks even rounder than the last time I saw it, which was a while ago. And less orange."

"Let's see." Jacob held up the phone so Phineas could see it. "You might be right. Maybe they put him on steroids for his alpha gal allergy."

"Alpha gal?"

"The red meat allergic reaction that came after his tick bite."

Iris closed her laptop. "This president on steroids. Now that's a frightening thought."

The light on Phineas' office phone flashed twice then buzzed. He pressed the intercom button. "Yes, Grace?"

The shared division administrative assistant and "master of all necessities" answered, "Your four o'clock appointment, Dr. Porter, has arrived. Shall I show her to your office?"

"Sure. Thanks." He tightened his loose tie, stood, and quick checked to be sure his fly was up. He'd once, long ago in a hurry, missed that during an interview. Ever since, checking it was reflex.

As the door cracked open, he walked around his standard state-issued desk to greet Marie Porter. "Phineas Mann. Nice to meet you. Welcome to my humble workstation." Her brown eyes were level with his and about the same shade. She bore no signs of make-up, and her thick mane of wavy brown hair fell halfway down her back. A charcoal jacket and skirt conformed to her tall and athletic physique. Her grip was firm, nails short and unpainted. A sword on her hip would not seem out of place.

She released his hand and glanced out the seventh-floor window behind his desk. "Humble? At least you have a view when you want it. And your walls aren't plexiglass like mine, so your co-workers can't keep an eye on you."

"The privacy *is* helpful for catnaps during my tiring months on the ICU service." Phineas pulled out one of two chairs from under the front of his desk. "Please have a seat." He circled back to his ergonomic webbed desk chair, his one extravagance, and gestured at the thick open binder on his desk. "I've been reviewing the Phase 3 trial protocols for SYMBI-62022." He felt a twinge of embarrassment that she caught him with the paper document and not the computer version.

She settled into the chair and focused on his open binder. "Then we're probably at the same place. I just recently came on board and have been studying it too."

"So, tell me about yourself." He leaned back into form-fitting mesh.

"Not much to tell. I'm an internist. Worked on an inpatient medical service as a hospitalist, until I started with SynMedical recently. While I learn the ropes, I'm also trying to read as much as I can on asthma research." She offered the bland statements like she was reciting.

"That all sounds good...Just curious...What made you decide to take the big step of leaving clinical medicine?" What would make a young doctor leave patient care to work for a drug company?

"Thought I'd give something with a more humane lifestyle a try." She blinked twice and paused, then met his gaze. Her demeanor softened, as if an internal heat had welled up and melted her veneer. "The last few months at my hospitalist job were tough. My mother was dying—and that took a lot out of me. After she passed, I had no one...I mean no reason... to keep me out West. I was ready for a change." She lifted the back of her hand to her eye.

"I'm sorry." He'd gotten more than he'd bargained for.

"No. *I'm* sorry. Not very professional. I just moved here and haven't met many people outside the office—so this is the first time I've mentioned my mother's death." She gave a single clearing shake of her head and sat more erect.

Clearly, she still had grieving ahead of her. The phone's light flashed again. He pushed the speaker button. "Yes, Grace."

"Sorry to interrupt, Dr. Mann. I know you're in a meeting." This time there was more edge in her voice. "Your son's here."

"Can he wait till five?"

"He has a *dog* with him—and it's sniffing my philodendron!" Each word was louder than the last.

Marie's face relaxed. "I don't mind dogs." She seemed relieved at the distraction.

"Can I send him over...now?" the phone's speaker pleaded.

"Marie, you sure you don't mind?"

"I came by mainly to meet you and go over any questions you might have." She reached into a pocket on the side of a compact black purse and extracted a card. "Here's my card. Call, text, or email me anytime. Let me know when you want to meet next." She stood and reached across the desk to hand him the card.

The office door burst open and a chubby beagle, its nose snuffling along the linoleum floor, scrambled through, straining at its leash. Jacob, his arm outstretched in front of him, looked like he was off-balance and being dragged. One hand pinned and balanced a bulky brightly colored paper sack over his shoulder, while his other hand, the leash hand, clutched the handles of a bulging cloth grocery bag. He nudged the door closed with his butt.

"Sorry about the interruption, Dad. I was hoping to drop Ruby off before I head out of town to the conference." Eager to look out the window, Ruby jerked Jacob forward and so close to Marie, that, when she turned, their faces almost met. Unable to get to the window, the frantic dog circled the two humans, lassoed their legs with the leash, and pulled them against each other.

Jacob dropped his end. "Sorry, Miss." His eyes met Marie's, his dog apparently forgotten.

"Marie Porter." She wriggled her arm into the cramped space between them and offered her hand. "Looks like you've got your hands full."

"Jacob Mann." He continued to grasp her hand seconds past the greeting. Ruby rose up and planted both front feet on his leg.

Marie smiled down at the dog. "She wants you to pay attention to *her*. I need be going anyways." She stepped out of the leash's coils.

"Please don't...don't let me end your meeting. Ruby emptied herself outside. She should be okay for a good while."

Phineas came around the side of his desk and bent to pat Ruby. "Well *that's* a relief. I don't want her marking any territory here."

"I've enjoyed meeting you." Marie edged toward the door. "All three of you. Uh, bye." She slipped through and pulled it closed behind her.

"Who is *she*?" Jacob plopped the massive sack of dog food on Phineas' desk, covering the open binder.

"Someone I'll be working with. Someone whose company is supporting me." Phineas restrained Ruby with one hand on her collar and ran his other hand from her head down her back, while she scanned his office with bulging, deep brown eyes. Maybe a firm petting would distract her from further mischief.

"Marie Porter, MD. SynMedical Biopharma," Jacob read as he peered at the business card he spotted on the corner of his father's desk. "Know anything about her personally?"

"Only that she's an MD working for a drug company and doesn't have any family. She just lost her mother. That's why she moved here to take a corporate job."

Jacob's eyebrows arched up. "When I get back in town, mind if I contact her—to apologize?"

"Right...Maybe we should see how things with her company's drug study go before you complicate things for me."

⌒

Marie heard the click of the Tesla Model Y's driver side door unlocking as she approached it. She tossed her purse onto the passenger seat, buckled up, and hit the power button. The friendly dashboard 12.3-inch computer screen came to life and displayed a map of roads leading away from UNC Hospital's parking deck.

Phineas Mann didn't disappoint and measured up to his web presence. Friendly and warm. As tall as she, fit-looking, and well-preserved for a seventy-year-old.

And a very tall son. "Siri, search Jacob Mann."

The image shifted to multiple separate paragraphs and a narrow row of very different facial images. She touched the first, the one with the eye-catching beard. New paragraphs appeared. The first linked to NC State. The second to Wikipedia. She touched the latter and read.

"Born in 1986 in New Orleans." *Just like me.* "Associate Professor of Entomology at North Carolina State University... research in honey bee behavior...Author of a bestselling novel inspired by an event he'd experienced as a twelve-year-old in 1998."

She'd heard of the movie version. 1998. The year her mother yanked her out of sixth grade and fled North Carolina. She touched screen to order the Kindle version of Jacob's novel on her Amazon Prime account. A receipt for the book filled the screen.

"Siri, let's go home." The dashboard lit up and the screen provided high resolution images of everything behind her. Marie rested her hands lightly on the wheel, while the Tesla's computer piloted her in reverse out of the parking space then forward toward the structure's exit and her new home.

She still had plenty of unpacking to do. At least she'd hung up all her work clothes, so she wouldn't be all wrinkled in the office, and she'd carefully arranged her precious high school track and cross-country warmups in her dresser. She'd always be a proud Chinook Sugarbeeter. The Sugarbeeter mascot had a comical sugar beet head and pants that were supposed to look like eggbeaters. A cartoon image of it covered the back of the jacket. In high school, everyone who earned places on varsity teams wore the warmups constantly.

Those Montana teams so many years ago were the years she got closest to feeling like she had a family. The girls she ran with during her last two years of high school were the best friends ever. They even invited her for meals and sleepovers. Ada, her *best* best friend, was Mormon and had seven siblings. Ada's family hardly noticed when Marie camped out in the rambling house on their farm. It was like she was part of them. Family.

To ease loneliness in recent months, Marie wrapped herself in those comforting warmups, even when she had to turn up the air conditioning.

After her mother's death, Marie found the YouTube clips of news videos from 1998, the ones of Phineas Mann and a Black man, Jericho James, as they brought to a halt the UNC Hospital Bomber's deadly plot. Hard to imagine that her mother planted the seeds to this entire crisis by cozying up to and manipulating a racist—the son of Phineas Mann's elderly patient—into a state of irrational fury against the UNC doctors, especially Mann.

Her mother's deathbed confessions to Marie included that she'd slipped the bomber's father small doses of arsenic while visiting the old man in Mann's Intensive Care Unit, leading to acute puzzling and terrifying setbacks that incensed the son. *Arsenic! Her mother—a registered nurse—gave arsenic to a sick man!* At last Marie understood that her mother's sudden fear of being discovered, arrested, and jailed was why they suddenly fled North Carolina—and why her mother took them to a western town near the Canadian border.

Upon hearing the arsenic confession, Marie screamed at her bedbound mother. "How could you, a nurse, do such a thing?"

"Revenge." Her mother coughed and gasped after the word. "For what he and his lawyer did to me on *60 Minutes* after Jezebel. They made me a national laughingstock." Another gasp. "It was years before people didn't laugh and point at me in public—or worse. At every interview, every job I took before we came out West from North Carolina, I heard them whispering behind my back." A raspy cough. "Humiliation followed me everywhere."

Marie could find no words. She'd only stared at her mother in horror. *Revenge?* But a mother's humiliation affected her daughter as well. It sent her adolescent years from town to town and school to school and never allowed her time to settle into one happy place. Should she also desire revenge against Phineas Mann?

Her mother had struggled to continue. "See, I'd worked with Phineas Mann after I was just out of nursing school. Imagined I felt something for him... a crush, you'd say." A brief smile. "I used to like to hear his voice when I paged him at night—and to know I woke up his snooty wife. Hah!" A burst of coughing before she closed her eyes and appeared more peaceful. The narcotics were easing in.

"Then Hurricane Jezebel happened, and we were together for five straight intense days. Seemed longer. No power...no water...no phones. And the heat...Oh, the heat!" Her eyes fluttered wide open and she stared at Marie with cold, dead eyes. "Toward the end, he began giving patients morphine— and they died. I was exhausted. Figured he was giving up, euthanizing them, so I confronted him." She struggled to lift her head off the pillow. "Told him only God decides when someone dies...When we finally got out, I reported him...They charged him with murder—multiple murders."

Hell hath no fury like a woman scorned—or worse—ignored.

Marie might have slapped her mother, if she weren't dying. "I wish you'd never told me any of this."

But her mother lay in the gentle arms of Sister Morphine. "It's just *some* of what you need to know."

⁀

Thank God he had Jacob to help him transport Ruby the demon dog and all her accessories down the elevator and across the parking deck to his weathered, twenty-year-old pickup truck. Jacob tossed the giant bag of dog food into the truck's bed, and they arranged the dog in the passenger seat, then the shopping bag containing her bed pad, toys, and bowls on the floor. Phineas wedged his briefcase behind the driver's seat and surveyed the mess. "How far are you driving tonight?"

"Unless traffic totally sucks, about five hours. I've got a motel reservation, then on to Ithaca tomorrow."

"Back to Cornell." Phineas heaved a mock sigh. "I always enjoy visiting the idyllic campus and reminiscing—at least when the weather's good." They were both alumni, his own Cornell days more than thirty years before his son's.

"Same. Well, see you in ten days. And thanks. I owe you."

"I'll let you know how much, after we see how your mother and Ruby get along." At her name, the dog pulled her nose back from the window and eyed him. "Good girl. Ready to meet Iris?" Phineas climbed in, shut his door, and started the engine. He lowered the passenger window enough for Ruby's snout to protrude, but not enough for the rest of her to slip out. He'd forgotten how much he enjoyed watching a dog's interest in its surroundings. Ruby kept her nose out the window almost every second of the trip home and sniffed with vigor at each traffic stop. When the truck finally crept down the Mann's long driveway, she placed her front paws on the dashboard and stood at attention.

"We're here, Girl."

She whined impatiently.

As soon as Phineas cracked open his door, she bolted across his lap and leapt onto the asphalt. He had to scramble to grab her leash. She sniffed Iris' Prius and immediately squatted and let go a stream next to the driver's side back tire. Phineas reached back in for his briefcase. "You couldn't wait till I got you to the yard?"

Ruby tugged him toward the front steps, where she paused to mark the threshold with more drops of urine.

"Better be the last time you do that!"

Ruby pulled him inside until they reached the dining area, where Iris halted the canine invasion with her expression, the one Phineas referred to as "the look," the one she had perfected on two children and two dogs decades ago. She opened her hand over a large stainless-steel bowl in front of her and allowed a handful of delicious smelling popcorn to dribble back into it. "And what do we have here?"

He unhooked the leash. "Beelzebub, so far. Jacob's postdoc's dog—and our guest for ten days."

Ruby sniffed the air then Iris' ankle and sat next to it. The two females locked eyes and stared into each other. Neither blinked.

Iris threw her shoulders back.

Ruby's lips twitched.

Iris lifted her head and tucked her chin in tight.

Ruby's haunches fidgeted, her tail a rigid anchor.

Iris hooded her eyebrows and bore down.

Ruby's lips separated, revealing spiked teeth. She emitted a menacing growl then a staccato series of barks, each steadily louder—then suddenly, she broke off the dominance contest and raced toward the front door, howling at first, then, as if in response to some internal shifting of gears, she bayed from down deep inside her stout belly.

"I'll text Jacob to let him know how well you two are getting on." Phineas grinned as he placed his briefcase on the table.

"I'd better go see what she's barking at." Iris sighed and rose from her chair. "Might be FBI again."

As soon as Iris stepped into the foyer, Ruby doubled back, leapt onto Iris' chair, and lunged at the abandoned bowl of popcorn. Phineas rescued it with a quick snatch. "Aren't you the clever and diabolical one?"

Iris marched back from the foyer, shaking her head. "There's no one there." She spotted Ruby on her chair. "You little devil! So, that's how you want it, eh? Well, we'll see who gets the popcorn in *this* house."

Phineas stole a glance at Iris' laptop screen. It showed a smiling POTUS next to coal-stained miners. The headline declared that more coal-fired power plants were coming online and that tomorrow the President would visit natural gas wells fueled by fracking in Pennsylvania. Phineas resisted the impulse to scream and pound on the walls.

Lately, he'd only been scanning the news. It was getting harder and harder to watch reports of the President's actions, actions that accelerate environmental devastation and were sending his planet Earth hurtling toward oblivion with Iris, Jacob, Martha, Felipe, and Mateo—sweet and feisty two-year-old Mateo—as its passengers.

MAY

"Since our leaders are behaving like children, we will have to take the responsibility they should have taken long ago."

"Adults keep saying we owe it to the young people, to give them hope, but I don't want your hope. I don't want you to be hopeful. I want you to panic. I want you to feel the fear I feel every day. I want you to act. I want you to act as if the house is on fire, because it is."

GRETA THUNBERG AT DAVOS 2019

This was the hottest Apple Chill Festival that Phineas had suffered through. The annual spring event closed Chapel Hill's main drag for a day of fun, art, and food for over fifty years, interrupted only by the pandemic of 2020-2022. Today, record temperatures forced the perspiring foot traffic to creep from booth to booth. Dogs on leashes panted with their tongues hanging out and lay down on any patch of shade-covered grass or dirt. Their bulging eyes pleaded with their owners for water. Waves of heat rose from every bit of sunbaked asphalt. No one was barefoot.

Iris had again volunteered to register voters at the Orange County Democratic Party's booth, and, at the last minute, once again cajoled and shamed Phineas into rounding up people strolling Franklin Street and its more captivating booths. He regretted his selection of a cotton tee shirt that failed to wick away his sweat and was embarrassed by his drenched appearance. He must look like he was melting, because he was.

He'd handed out all fifty of this batch of blue and white flyers on where to vote and whom the party recommended and figured he'd earned cups of ice water from their booth's team-sized thermos. Iris appeared considerably more comfortable sitting in the shade under the temporary canvas shelter and glanced up at him from helping a college-aged man with his voter registration form. "Need more flyers, Phineas?" A battery-powered fan sent a soft breeze onto her face.

"I need water. Jeesh, it's hot, and it's barely May!" He wrung sweat from his UNC ball cap onto the pavement.

"Dr. Mann, can I treat you to something ice cold and tastier than water?" The woman's voice behind him sounded vaguely familiar. He turned toward the tall young woman sporting butterfly shaped sunglasses. Her long, wavy brown hair cascaded over her shoulders and down her back. It took him an uncomfortable interval to recognize her.

"Marie. Hi." A tank top and snug shorts distracted him momentarily, even as a married senior citizen, and he felt a twinge of his childhood Catholic guilt.

Iris cleared her throat. "Phineas, aren't you going to introduce me to your young friend?" Her tone was icy.

How is it an innocent hard-working older man can get into such jeopardy?

"Iris, this is Dr. Marie Porter. She'll be my contact at SynMedical for the new drug trial we're about to start. Marie, this is Iris, my better half."

"Great to meet you, Iris." Marie leaned toward the booth's table and offered her hand. "Can I get something refreshing for you too?"

"I'm good. I don't want to keep potential voters waiting. I guess you can borrow Phineas, but bring him back soon. We need him to round up more Democrats." After a piercing stare at Phineas, Iris turned back to the young man she'd been helping.

"I support the cause. I can help." Marie's offer was bursting with energy.

"Please do. You might have more luck with the male demographic." Iris handed her stacks of party literature.

A half dozen men ambled into view from behind a woodcarver artist's booth nearby. Two had assault weapons dangling from harnesses, the others wore semiautomatic pistols holstered on their hips. One, barely over five feet tall, wore a yellow-trimmed black shirt that announced his allegiance to the "Proud Boys." Others' shirts, with or without sleeves, displayed various depictions of the Stars and Stripes. Hairy paunches escaped below a few. Red ballcaps or faded durags commanded "Keep America Great" or "MAGA." Some of these "boys" sported unkempt facial hair that revealed unskilled applications of Just for Men Mustache and Beard.

Phineas wiped away a renewed crop of sweat beads. This ragged residual branch of right-wing militias had not aged well. Their usefulness had ended in 2020, after they'd intimidated Democrats to stay away from the polls during the 2020 presidential election. As for the fitter ones, they had subsequently been culled to fill the President's new Anti-Demonstration Force, his domestic gestapo.

Phineas leaned close to Iris and whispered, "You got a plan for this?" He watched her tap the Chapel Hill Police number on her cell phone, the one she'd entered earlier that belonged to an officer assigned to the street fair.

She brought her phone close to her mouth. "We have armed right-wingers at the Orange County registration booth. They look like Proud Boys."

"On our way. Don't engage them," her phone responded just loud enough for Phineas to hear.

The shortest of the ragtag group, the one with the "Proud Boy" shirt must have caught sight of the sign over the Orange County booth. He gestured with his head toward the sign, and a sinister grin emerged. "So, what do we have here? Democrats?" He ambled toward them but halted his approach six feet away and looked Marie up and down. "Well...look what I found. Honey, you should hang out with real men. Why don't you leave these Socialists and come party with us?" The others gathered beside him and nodded hopefully.

Anger made Phineas step closer to Marie. Alarm kept his mouth closed. Provoking unbalanced armed miscreants had come to tragic ends in other cities. From behind him, he heard Iris' voice. "Those guns sure do make you boys look brave and manly." Her tone was defiant. Surprised and unnerved, he glanced back at her. She was still seated at the table but was giving them "the look."

Short Boy focused on Iris then on Phineas then back to Marie. "These your parents, Honey?"

Why did Marie's jaw muscle twitch?

"They still give you a curfew?" Short Boy pressed on. "We can have you home before then."

Marie went to Iris' table and picked up a clipboard with its attached pen. "Sorry, Boys. I already have a date today...Why don't you each write down your names, emails, and cell numbers, so I can find you another time?" She offered her signup sheet to Short Boy. He held his ground, but one of his beer-bellied followers stepped past him and reached for it. Short Boy pushed Beer-Belly's hand away. "You *idiot*. Don't share your info with them."

Two police officers peddled up and arranged their bicycles to form a metal barrier between the militia members and the Orange County Democrats' booth. Two more uniforms arrived on foot and lined up with the others behind the bicycles. Men on both sides dragged their hands to their weapons. In the heated silence, sweat dripped down foreheads to cheeks and off chins onto the pavement.

A Black foot patrol officer, whose badge read "Bradley," finally spoke. "Ronald, we know who you are, and you know the judge here has a restraining order against you setting foot in Orange County. So, why don't you head on back to Alamance County, before I call the whole force for back up, and you get into some serious trouble?" His tone was seeped with disgust for these grown men misbehaving like irritating children.

"Damn liberal Chapel Hill." Short Boy took his hand off his pistol and sneered. "Cops in other places are behind us. Some even belong." He gestured to his followers. "Come on. It's too hot here anyways. There's iced beer at the club house."

"We'll accompany you to your trucks and radio you an escort out of the county," another Chapel Hill Police officer added. "And Ronald... don't come back." The uniforms flanked the procession as it trudged away from the booth.

"Wasn't that nice of them to invite me to their little party?" Marie exclaimed just loud enough for the departing males to hear. "Because the Internet says Proud Boys are a *gay* group."

Iris snorted. Officer Bradley pivoted with his index finger vertical against his mouth to shush her, then covered a grin with his hand while he continued herding the Proud Boys away. Phineas' pounding pulse finally began to ease from sprint levels. He caught Iris' eye and asked, "We get hazard pay for this?" He suddenly also craved ice cold beer but not with the Proud Boys.

She answered, "The hazard is in the White House. Back to work now."

Beer later.

⌒

It was still sweltering when Phineas noticed that Iris and her team were disassembling their booth. He happily handed in his short pile of leftover flyers. Iris would be pleased with his day's effort. "Marie turn hers in yet?"

Iris located the appropriate box and filed his papers. She tucked her chin and squinted up at him. "So, how much will you be working with *her*?"

"She'll just be monitoring our trial's numbers—mostly by email—and facilitating communication with her company." *Was that a hint of jealousy?*

"Well then...No, I haven't seen her recently. Probably gave up in this heat." Iris returned to packing up, and shoved items into boxes with added vigor. "But I do think we had an unusual number of men show up to register, and she *did* come back once for more flyers."

She stacked the boxes on a hand truck and motioned for Phineas to help her fold the table. A wide-eyed look of surprise replaced her business face. "Well, look who's here! We were just wondering if you were still out there toiling in this North Carolina steam bath."

"All gone. Just gave out the last one." Marie held up empty hands. Her hair was plastered to both sides of her shiny forehead, now a prominent rose tint. "But this northwestern girl isn't close to being used to this heat!"

"Your efforts are greatly appreciated. Looks like you got a bit too much sun." Iris' tight face relaxed until she noticed Marie's blossoming sunburn. "We should get you inside somewhere."

Phineas' worry eased. Maybe Iris wasn't going to be upset about Marie working with him

Marie pointed down the street, toward where Chapel Hill became Carrboro. "I saw a bunch of food trucks in a parking lot up there. How about I treat you two to dinner? I have a brand new untested corporate credit card and can expense it." Her excited tone suggested that she'd found a burst of new energy.

Phineas winced. "I doubt that's kosher." He knew that's what his wife would say.

Unconcerned, Marie pressed a finger into her pink shoulder and blanched a spot. "Should have used more sunscreen. Don't worry, I'll just ask you a couple of asthma questions and make it a business meeting. That's what they say to do at work." She flashed an impish grin. "Come on. I'm *dying* to try out my card."

Iris settled it. "Phineas, you go with her and pay for ours. I'm starving and tired. And I need to finish up here. Where should I meet you?"

"I don't know the options." Marie shrugged.

Phineas again wrung out his ballcap, shook it, and returned it to his sweaty head. "The Beer Study is around the corner and has air conditioning. They let you bring in food, if you buy their beer."

"Okay. Make my beverage something light—and my dinner something healthy." Iris' relaxed shoulders and deep sigh suggested that she was finally allowing herself to wind down.

In the refreshingly cool and dim barroom, Phineas and Marie commandeered the last three empty seats at a long table. He slipped sideways into a tight space between drinkers at the bar and retrieved two Kolsch style beers and an IPA, while she guarded their claim.

It wasn't long before Iris plopped into the empty seat next to Phineas and across from Marie. She shook her head disapprovingly. "Humph! They're still using nonrecyclable plastic cups here." She opened her compostable clamshell container and surveyed a mound of vegetables dotted with cashews and tiny ears of corn. "Oooh, this looks good." She speared a mammoth forkful. "Nothing gives me an appetite like registering Democrats to vote."

"I got you a Kolsch—the lightest beer they have." Phineas practiced using the food truck's disposable wooden chopsticks and successfully lifted a slippery pork dumpling.

Iris took a sip and smacked her lips. "This'll do just fine. Marie, thanks for helping out today. I believe we did some good this afternoon, especially after the white supremacists were dispatched. That seemed to rally the good people."

"No problem. I'd been thinking of getting involved once I found my way around—and it *was* exciting there for a bit." Marie's expertise with chopsticks was obvious. She set them down and took a long, slow pull on her beer.

"Want to do more?" When Iris raised her eyebrows, it appeared she sensed a likely recruit.

"I do." Marie set her cup down hard. "This is personal."

"Oh?" Iris tilted her head and peered into Marie's eyes, the look she usually purposed when she planned to extract information.

"The man currently occupying our White House is responsible for my mother's death." Marie's accusation was delivered at a volume certain to be heard and resonated like the squawk of a needle scratching across a vinyl record. Conversations around them came to a halt. Their end of the long, narrow room fell silent except for the sound of cups being set on tabletops. Blank-faced patrons at neighboring tables glanced in her direction, waiting. A few took cautious sips.

"He did away with Obamacare, so my mother stopped getting mammograms—and recently died from breast cancer." She sniffed and blinked. "I'll forever hold him accountable."

Iris reached across the table and placed her hand on Marie's. "Sorry…I understand," she whispered. After an uncomfortable moment of silence, the other drinkers looked away and gradually resumed their conversations.

"How about your father?" Iris had to raise her voice over the rising din.

"They were apart my whole life. I only learned who he is as Mom was taking her last breaths." She looked from Iris to Phineas and back to Iris. Anxiety seemed to flash in her eyes then faded, controlled. "He lives near here—one of the reasons I took this job."

"How did he handle meeting his daughter?" Iris leaned closer.

"He doesn't know I'm his—yet." Marie's eyes were round and her words a stage whisper.

Phineas remained silent and motionless at the unexpected revelations, trying to be unnoticed. At least Iris no longer seemed troubled by his association with Marie.

Iris sat back upright. "Well, I'm sure he'll be thrilled when he meets you." She raised her voice to compete with the surrounding conversations. "If you ever need someone to talk to, please reach out to me—and if you want to do more for the Democratic Party, we can sure use you."

"Thanks. I haven't met many people here yet." Marie extracted a bright red chili pepper from her rice and set it on the back of her clamshell, clearly being careful to avoid a fiery surprise.

"Phineas, are you planning on having your annual honey extraction celebration?" Iris gestured with her fork at a still stunned Phineas.

"I am. The Saturday after I get back from the American Thoracic

Society meeting in New Orleans—that'll be in two weeks." He swallowed a mouthful of ale to conclude his answer.

She smiled back at Marie. "Why don't you come over? You can meet our friends and kids. Our son Jacob always helps out. He's a beekeeper professor."

"I met him briefly at your husband's office, him—and his dog." Marie chuckled.

"Ah, Ruby, the difficult foster dog...So, you'll come?" Iris speared a tiny corn cob and inspected it.

"Thank you, Yes. I'll look forward to it. What can I bring?" Marie sipped her beer and grinned at Iris.

"It's a potluck. Anything you like."

Phineas stared at his dumplings and fried rice. Bringing Marie into their lives gave him a vague feeling of uneasiness. Maybe it was because a significant part of his salary support now came through SynMedical, so he sort of worked for her. And facilitating Jacob's interest in Marie could become problematic. Or was there more? He'd feel better if they kept it all professional, at least until his study was over, and all the drama in Marie's life had settled into the past. He preferred to avoid drama. He'd already experienced a lifetime's worth.

Iris raised a fist in front of his face and knocked on air. "Anyone home? Why so quiet, Phineas?"

"Long tiring day with Proud Boys—and talking to so many strangers— and thinking about all the stuff I've got to get ready for work tomorrow." That was all he wanted to say for now.

~

Damn! Marie kicked off the sheets. The over-the counter analgesic spray hadn't touched the pain of her sunburn which sizzled from her scalp to her ankles. She awakened that morning thinking what a gorgeous, sunny day it was for a spring festival, but all those years in the Northwest hadn't prepared her for the heightened intensity of a North Carolina's springtime sun during global warming.

At least she'd gotten that damned constricting bra off. The straps left indentations on her burnt shoulders that made her wince. She'd learned early in her education that she had to conceal her shape to get male teachers and colleagues to look at her face and not further down. After the 'Me Too' movement, men were more careful with their eyes for a while, but over eight years of a presidential example without consequences, misogyny roared right back again.

Tonight, finding a comfortable sleeping position was impossible. She finally settled on flat on her back, arms stretched out and legs apart like DaVinci's Vitruvian Man and let the air conditioning wash over her fiery bare skin.

Distracting herself from her discomfort by letting her thoughts drift to her afternoon with Iris and Phineas seemed to help. She could sense the strength of their marriage, of his attraction to his wife, and understood why he hadn't responded to another woman's flirtations decades ago in the Baptist Hospital ICU.

She needed to be careful not to disrupt with her urge to be part of the Mann's close family. Being completely alone in the world increasingly weighed on her. Loneliness induced stretches approaching melancholy not soothed by learning a new job and finding her way around a new community. And the melancholy hadn't lifted when, before going to bed, she opened the thin photo album of her childhood to study her mother's face. In most of the early photos, she saw the happy, playful mom. But two of the last shots, taken in their sparsely furnished Durham apartment only weeks before they moved West, caught her mother staring off into the distance, a pre-occupied expression captured on her face.

Could Marie tell Phineas? Could she tell him of her mother's outrageous claim as she was giving up her ghost? That conversation played back in her memory almost nightly since she met Phineas. Her mother had grabbed Marie's hand with icy fingers. "You should also know that Phineas Mann is your father...and he doesn't know it."

"WHAT?" Marie's outcry was volcanic ash shooting out of her core.

"After the winds and rains of Jezebel subsided, we had a long, hard stretch after we lost all power, without any of us getting any rest. When I went into his office for orders, it was pitch black except for my penlight beam." Her mother closed her eyes and tilted her head back. "I found him on the floor in a deep, exhausted sleep...flat on his back...like he was ready for me." A hint of a smile had seemed to emerge with the memory. "Couldn't stop myself...I was under a spell."

Marie could still remember how sick that had made her feel.

But her mother just kept talking. "Over in a flash. He'd tell you it never happened." Her mother coughed and gasped for air. Those were her mother's final words.

Was it possible—that Phineas was so incapacitated by fatigue and in such deep sleep that he didn't resist? Was her mother's bizarre story the truth, fantasy, or a malevolent lie?

For days after her mother's death, Marie forced herself to watch the entirety of the agonizing clips of the *60 Minutes* segments from 1986 that were televised before Phineas Mann's scheduled murder trial. She endured seeing the raw humiliation of her mother, a young, buxom, and secretly pregnant Angela Portier RN, breaking down like a raving lunatic under Morley Safer's leading questions, questions that her mother was convinced were planted by Phineas Mann's slick lawyer.

After Safer's detailed and probing questions about the events around Hurricane Jezebel, he, in a friendly tone, seemed to innocently inquire about how her mother decided on a career in nursing. But those questions led her mother into a deranged ranting tirade about how she, as a teenager, watched doctors allow her father to die when they should have kept him alive and prayed for a miracle for his terminal lung disease, a condition Marie knew *still* had no effective treatment.

The *60 Minutes* segment came to an end with her berserk mother screaming at Safer and charging the camera. Before that show, she was the prosecution's star witness, but she appeared so unhinged on national television, that the charges against Phineas Mann were dropped without trial by early the next day.

Mann must have provided information to help his lawyer craft her mother's public meltdown. Should her daughter also feel anger and resentment toward him for the turbulent childhood she endured?

Are dying people always truthful? Could her mother be believed on the heavy doses of narcotics she consumed in increasing doses? Ironically, the same medications Phineas Mann had administered that led to his being charged with murder.

Was this claim of paternity her mother's one last desperate attempt to pour an enduring round of misery upon him from the beyond? The urn of ashes tucked away in the closet wasn't going to provide answers.

Platters smothered in Cajun delicacies covered long tables that lined the ballroom in Latrobe's on Royal in the French Quarter, the once elegant, now time-worn site for this year's annual UNC Pulmonary Division party at the 2024 national meeting of the American Thoracic Society. The familiar aromas made a famished Phineas salivate.

It had been over a decade since the ATS had hosted their convention in The Big Easy, and Phineas had missed that one, because he had to cover the hospital's pulmonary ward service. Then had come the years of virtual meetings during the COVID-19 pandemic. This would be the first in-person ATS convention since 2019, and it was his first return to the city of his arrest for murder after almost four decades.

He was enduring flashbacks at each familiar city landmark. They'd begun when he stepped into New Orleans' dingy Louis Armstrong Airport early in the afternoon and recalled his hastily arranged flight in 1983, as Iris' father was dying, the event that brought them to the city to care for her grieving mother. The airport hadn't changed.

His Lyft ride into the city today traversed numerous massive concrete abutments supporting the interstate. Phineas tried to spot the one he was evacuated from after Hurricane Jezebel in 1985. He'd been deposited there by a stranger in a flat-bottomed boat powered by an outboard motor. The highway structures all looked alike, and he was so tired that miserable, long-ago day.

His arrival today at The Royal Sonesta Hotel on Bourbon Street felt disturbingly altered. As he exited his driver's Prius, moist heat seared his cheeks. The iconic street still had the familiar reek of rotting garbage but was quiet and almost empty. Gone were the shoulder-to-shoulder audiences for street performers who once staked out their territories on each block. The bars' doors were all closed, it being just too hot to let the precious air conditioning bleed out into the street. Few tourists lingered inside behind those doors, listening to jazz, or ogling sleepy exotic dancers.

Phineas was relieved he only had one block to walk in the heat to the division's evening party at Latrobe's where he studied the culinary offerings. He decided against the soups and salads and went straight to the main courses, filling his plate's perimeter with crawdads, jambalaya, and a portion of blackened redfish fillet. In the center, he added okra, red beans and roasted sweet potatoes then planted himself at an empty table proximal to the dessert displays. He speared a crimson crawdad and lifted it to his waiting mouth.

"Mind if I join you?" He recognized the woman's voice immediately this time.

He lowered the crustacean to his plate and turned to look over his shoulder toward Marie Porter who towered behind him on stiletto heels, shoes that Iris had once labeled 'fuck me pumps' in a whisper about one of her UNC students out on the town in Chapel Hill. Unlike that coed, Marie wobbled, suggesting she wasn't practiced on this version of fashion stilts.

She balanced a small plate of raw oysters on the half shell and a glass of white wine. Her face was almost unrecognizable at first glance in scarlet lipstick and smoky eyeshadow, and her thick hair was now enhanced with highlights and allowed to cascade loose well past her shoulders. The sunburn's peeling on her neck was almost healed. Her usual business suit was replaced with a shimmering white satin blouse, its top two buttons undone, and form-fitting black slacks. He instantly made himself glance back up at her face and did his best to not show surprise at her new glamorous look and her unexpected appearance at the division's party.

"Not at all. Please do. Welcome to New Orleans. I didn't realize you were attending the meeting. When did you get in?"

When she bent to set her plate down, a delicate silver cross escaped from under her blouse and dangled from her neck. Where had he seen a cross like that?

"A few hours ago." She eased into the chair next to him and whispered, "We get to come to your party because we're paying for it. You might notice our people are working your colleagues, trying to slip in positive words about SYMBI-62022." She paused to allow him to scan the room. "We're counting on it being a blockbuster."

Now that she mentioned it, the other fashionable women and dapper young men stood out while mingling with his plainly attired fellow doctors. Not all of the cost of a new drug was research and development.

"And we hope when you talk about new asthma treatments in your State-of-the-Art talk tomorrow morning, that you'll be emphasizing it."

"I'll touch on what we know about its mechanism of action, the early trials, and mention the enrollment for the Phase 3 trial." That would be enough for now. There was no way he would push a drug until the Phase 3 trials proved its efficacy and safety. "And, by the way, thank you for your company's hospitality—for this party." He gestured at her plate. "You're eating light."

"A girl's gotta pace herself. The evening's young."

He studied her feet. "Nice shoes."

Her face flushed through the makeup. "An email from corporate made suggestions on dress for those attending this 'opportunity.'" Her fingers made air quotes. "It might have been aimed mostly at our office reps, but as the new kid on the block, I guessed I'd better comply. So, I had to go shopping."

"You're a doctor, not a drug company cheerleader. You should be able to wear practical—if you want."

"That fatherly advice?" She raised a perfect eyebrow ever so slightly.

Interesting question. Had she met hers yet? "No charge. First time in New Orleans?" He began chewing the waiting crawdad. Its spices ignited his palate.

"First time since I was a kid. I was born here—left when I was ten." Her eyes narrowed. She seemed to be waiting for his response to the information.

But the only response he could give was to stifle a cough and take a hearty swig from his pint glass of Abita Turbo Dog beer in an attempt to extinguish the heat in his mouth. "I...I didn't know that about you. My wife was also born here—and our son."

"What a coincidence!" She lifted an oyster and tipped its juices and flesh between her glossy red lips, then took a sip of her wine, leaving a bright imprint on the goblet.

"Phineas! Glad you saved me a seat." Another woman's voice, this one even more familiar. Gabriella Morales-Villalobos still sported her gray pinstripe suit and practical shoes, designed for long days standing. Her long black hair was restrained in a tight bun. She directed an inquiring creased forehead at Phineas for an instant then placed her plate of food and tall glass of iced tea directly across from Marie. She offered her hand. "Gabriella Morales-Villalobos, colleague to Dr. Mann here."

"Marie Porter, with SynMedical Biopharma. I've started working with Dr. Mann on the new asthma drug he's begun studying for us, SYMBI-62022." Marie gave Villalobos' hand a firm shake.

Phineas realized that fate could now be working in his favor. He'd planned to get the two doctors together to propose a role for Villalobos in the drug's trial. He needed another asthma specialist to help him in his role as Principal Investigator, to substitute for him when he couldn't be there. "Marie is also a physician, Gabby."

Villalobos raised an eyebrow just enough to catch Phineas' attention. She glanced down at Marie's glossy high heels. "So, what's your specialty, and how's life working for a Big Pharma company?"

Marie tucked her feet under her chair and swallowed a sip of wine. "I'm an internist. Worked as a hospitalist till a few months ago, so it's too soon to tell you if I'm living the dream. I'm still learning the trade."

"Marie, Gabby has worked with me on asthma studies in the past. I've shared your drug's information with her, because I'd like to propose bringing her into the study as a co-investigator." The timing felt right to pursue his goal.

"Can I assume you'll be asking for additional funding to cover another specialist's involvement?" Marie asked.

"Gabby has a busy clinic with a large number of asthmatics—and she supervises the fellows' clinic, bringing their asthma patients into our referral base—*plus* she's called in when other doctors have a challenging patient." He'd made his case.

"Sounds like you'd add value, Gabby." Marie lifted another shell and poured the oyster into her mouth, chewed, and swallowed, then dabbed at a dribble with her cloth napkin. "And having a second physician would ensure a constant study site presence if one of you has to be away."

Phineas turned to Villalobos. "Sound good to you, Gabby?"

She shrugged as if no other option made as much sense. "In these times, we academics can rarely say no to precious funding, especially when we have kids in college."

"Let me run it by the people upstairs." Marie sipped more wine. A matching lip print blossomed on the crystal beside the first.

Phineas lifted his glass. "To working together." On their surfaces the women seemed to be opposites tonight, but he suspected their similarities outweighed their differences. They appeared to be sizing each other up but joined his toast.

He swallowed and lowered his pint glass. "Gabby, are you still coming to our annual honey extraction celebration? It's the Saturday after we get back. Marie's planning to be there. Right, Marie?"

"I hope you'll come, Gabby. It'll be good to know someone else, and we can talk some more." Marie was twirling the last of the white wine around the bottom of her goblet.

"I hope I can make it over later in the day. I'll have to make ICU rounds first. Unfortunately, people still get sick on weekends."

⌣

Dawn forced its way through dense haze on the east bank of the swollen Mississippi. Phineas' planned brisk constitutional along the riverside path, aimed at clearing his thoughts before his State-of-the-Art lecture in a few hours, wasn't achieving its goal. He was glad he wore breathable shorts and tee shirt since he was oozing buckets of sweat. At least the countless sorry looking beggars were leaving him alone. He didn't look like he was carrying currency.

The odor coming off the river wasn't the wet and organic smell that he remembered from the 1980s. He, a lover of fine cooking, had always savored the fragrances that come from good food and its preparation. Aromachologist is the word he'd found to aptly describe one who creates those emotion and hunger evoking olfactory blends. But he also knew when a food offering was spoiled—the ammonia smell on seafood, the rot in fruit. The Mississippi now stank worse than spoiled food. Chemical and petroleum smells competed with vapors of decomposing trash and raw sewage. He squinted as the first rays of sunlight illuminated a rainbow sheen on the water's oil slicks merging among the floating islands of waste. Movement on the shore and adjacent floating debris caught his eye. Rats. Platoons of them scurried in random patterns.

Oh, for the Clean Water Act. And for the EPA, and the less spoiled world of the years before the current administration. In 2020 and 2021 there had been an all too brief and modest cleansing of the globe's environment during the COVID-19 pandemic, after travel and economies were forced in an instant to shut down. Activist believers claimed that their infuriated God delivered a plague as punishment for man's destructive stewardship of His precious creation. For a few teasing months after, the air was clearer, and the waterways almost sparkled in places. At that memory, Phineas took a deep breath before an involuntary sigh, and the stench captured in his nostrils made him hurry away from the river.

The world's increasingly foul air exacerbated lung disorders, disorders he'd spent a career trying to control, trying to reduce the suffering they caused. Trying. Asthma was at the top of the list of the afflictions climate change and pollution were exacerbating, and pharmaceutical companies raced to develop new and profitable therapies. SYMBI-62022 was the latest of these and the one with the most promise he'd seen in a decade. Yet, none of the new drugs came to market at costs his patients could afford and tantalized so many, remaining out of their reach.

He needed food before his lecture this morning and salivated at the memory of the delicious beignets he devoured years ago at the Café du Monde. He began threading his way through the body odor of the unwashed hordes crowding around that famous establishment.

Closed! He studied the sheet metal sign screwed onto a boarded-up window.

CLOSED UNTIL FURTHER NOTICE
WILL REOPEN WHEN TOURISTS
WALK THE STREETS AGAIN

Armed men in identical camouflage loitered under the street's few overhangs, claiming precious shade. These government storm troopers were first stationed in big cities with Democrat mayors after the Black Lives Matter demonstrations, then sent back again and again in matching uniforms whenever discontent boiled up. The President bragged that he formed these troops by plucking the 'crème de la crème' of the hodge-podge of local militias for these duties. The Oval Office suppressed reports of the troops' recurrent violent acts, reports often leaked to local underground news sources.

Cameras on each stoplight and at most corner street signs sent facial images to central computers ready to point fingers and trigger detainment of suspects who expressed views contrary to the administration. The President and his henchmen learned methods from their role models, the world's brutal autocratic rulers.

Phineas picked up his pace. If he hurried, the hotel's coffee shop might still have a few knockoffs of the Café du Monde's cherished pastries, his anticipated fuel for his upcoming presentation.

Phineas joined the line at the coffee shop. The black suit, lanky frame, and graying hair on the man at the front of the line were eerily familiar. Who was he? Then the man gathered his paper bag and cup and pivoted from the counter. There was no mistaking him.

Meyers! What's the FBI doing here? And at MY hotel? Phineas' and Meyers' eyes met.

"Good morning, Dr. Mann."

"Special Agent Meyers. What brings you to New Orleans—or is that classified?" Phineas' words caused all heads to turn and stare, first at him, then at Meyers. Was his question ill-advised?

Myers gestured with his coffee cup at the name tag marked 'Guest' that hung from a lanyard around his neck. "I came to hear your lecture, of course." His smile might have been a peace offering, but his answer gave Phineas the creeps.

"When did you develop an interest in asthma?"

"Oh, I've been interested a while. My daughter has it bad." Meyers responded in a less upbeat tone, the tone of a sincere and worried father.

"Sorry to hear that. We'd be happy to see her. Maybe we could help." Phineas' tension eased.

"You got someone who can fix the climate? That'd help her." For a fleeting instant the all-business just-the-facts federal agent transformed into a concerned global citizen before he put his work face back on. "Thanks, but she lives on the west coast." His gratitude felt genuine. "I'll let you know if we need you to recommend someone closer to her home." He glanced at Phineas' shorts. "You been running?"

"A little. The trail along the Mississippi wasn't as pleasant as I remember it."

"Hmph. I know what you mean. I checked it out last night. We've sure made a mess of it." He lifted his paper bag to eye level and began backing out the door. "I'll see you next at the Convention Center—" Meyers halted his exit. "—unless you want to have breakfast together now."

Breakfast with the FBI was not on Phineas well-planned schedule. "Thanks for the invite, but I should rehearse before my talk, and you can see that I need to clean up."

"Got it." Meyers' expression suggested fleeting disappointment. "See you." He vanished into the lobby crowd.

People in the line returned their attention to their cell phones. Phineas stretched his neck to count the beignets behind the glass display. Meyers' surprise appearance and humanity hadn't extinguished Phineas' hunger pangs.

⸏

Plastic seaweed. Marie checked the 'Add to Cart' button, then the 'Check out' button. Her short list also included ceramic renderings of a pirate's treasure chest and a crumbling castle. She hit the 'Order' button. *Perfect.* She knew where on her desk her new purchases would scream her silent statement of 'FISHBOWL'. Maybe she could find a large plastic or helium filled goldfish next.

She glanced around, curious to see if any of her coworkers in the massive office space had been watching her screen through the plexiglass walls of her chamber. Not this time, and not since she'd returned from New Orleans. When she was hired, the human resources representative explained that, after the COVID-19 pandemic, the metal and fabric walls around the old 'open office concept' cubicles were replaced with plexiglass before employees returned to the corporate offices. He explained how plexiglass could be disinfected and that the room air exchange units were converted to negative pressure, so everyone's vapors were now sucked into the ceiling and sanitized.

When she was a hospital-based internist, Marie escaped into the privacy of opaque workroom walls while she completed patient notes and orders. Nine to five at SynMedical seemed a treat at first but feeling like anyone could watch her at any time was oppressive, if she let her mind go there. It wasn't quite the "living the dream" she hoped for, but at least she could see who came and went from all parts of this arena—or corporate sweatshop.

As soon as the man in the suit entered, she recognized him from company emails and the annual report she kept on her standard issue cherry veneer desk. Eugene Schmidt was CEO of the Silicon Valley based powerhouse, Biopharma, that SynMedical acquired in their effort to expand beyond their stale portfolio of conventional drugs into the biologic agents that filled newer companies' coffers with cash. Schmidt was part of this acquisition package and maintained his main office in California, where his company had been founded and was entrenched. She'd heard he kept homes in both states now, both mansions afforded him by the massive windfall of SynMedical's buyout of his vast holdings of Biopharma shares.

His expensive-looking open collar shirt was visible under a tailored suit, and he was clean-shaven, including scalp, except for *that mustache*. It looked like an all-black wooly worm caterpillar had perched on his lip. When she'd Google searched him, she'd seen his Instagram posts and concluded they were otherwise orchestrated by an image consulting firm. But how did they let him keep that mustache? He was moving quickly on top-of-the-line running shoes, navigating the clear tunnels and heading in her direction. She turned her attention to her laptop screen and its trial data, and seconds later, he tapped on her transparent door.

"Come in." She smiled up at him, pivoted in her chair, and began to rise.

"Don't get up." He leaned close and offered his hand. "Eugene Schmidt. I just wanted to come by and meet you while I was in town."

"Nice to meet you, Sir." She settled back into her seat. "What can I do for you?"

He plopped into the one extra chair in the corner across from her. "Call me Gene, Marie. I've been hearing that you're already doing important work. Reports from New Orleans said you dined with Drs. Mann and

Villalobos, and that you looked fantastic and had them fully engaged for well over an hour."

So, I'm being graded on my dining room look and performance. "They're both nice people. We had a productive conversation. I'm working on a proposal to add Dr. Villalobos to the SYMBI-62022 Phase 3 trial. She's already familiarized herself, and she'd be a second investigator in addition to being a strong resource for patient recruitment."

"Excellent idea. I like it. Send it my way as soon as it's finished, and I'll fast track it." He surveyed her desk, empty except for her computer and the company's annual report. "Looks like you're still settling in. No pictures of family yet." The head and tail ends of his caterpillar mustache flexed upward. White roots emerged underneath like tiny insect legs... And the subtle surgical scar, his misguided reason for the worm.

Pictures? There won't be any. "There was only my mother, and she passed away recently. It's too soon to put her picture up."

His smile dissolved. He coughed into his fist once, probably searching for another topic. "So, what have you been doing since you came to North Carolina, besides working?"

Well, that doused his fire. "Not really a lot yet. I'm still trying to meet people and explore."

"Do you play golf? That's a good place to meet folks, and I could have you over to Prestonwood Country Club when I'm in town. Lots of doctors there."

Yuck. "Afraid I never had a chance to take it up. Me on a golf course— could get ugly." *Still, seems nice of him to offer.*

"Hard to believe." Schmidt chuckled. "What do you do for exercise? I haven't seen you in our company gym yet."

"I used to run track and cross country in high school. I'm still trying to log miles outdoors, but you almost have to run before dawn here. It gets hot and muggy so fast."

His expression brightened. "You must have seen the posters and memos for SynMedical's annual 5K in two weeks. Benefits go to lung research."

She'd seen them. She'd been hoping Saturdays weren't going to be work time, and the event didn't start until 9 AM. It'd be sweltering by then for a girl used to the Northwest. "I was just about to fill out the registration."

"Excellent. *I'll* be there—running *and* presenting awards." He rose and took a step toward the door.

She began to stand but hesitated when she realized she was the taller of the two. "It was nice of you to come by."

"It'll be good for your coworkers and the doctors to see you in something other than pinstripes." He glanced up and down her long legs then dashed toward the exit sign.

Would it be a bad career move to kick one's boss's ass in a foot race?

As Phineas prepared for his annual honey extraction, he wondered how much longer he could enjoy beekeeping. What had once been a passion was now a struggle. When he began in the late 1980s, he could count on fifty pounds of honey per hive. Lately, twenty-five was optimistic. And he now had to feed his bees gallons of sugar water soon after the harvest to get them through the overall nectar dearth of the increasingly long and brutally hot summers. While sugar prices had increased, the value of honey had skyrocketed. And honey was a staple in the Mann house. So, he kept at it, despite the heat and sudden violent storms that made his bees so cranky they stung him regularly. And wearing the necessary protective jacket was more and more intolerable in the stifling heat. He was usually soaked to the skin within minutes of donning it, even his new 'breathable' model.

Sources of nectar and pollen now only generated a fraction of his bees' nutritional requirements. As the world kept heating up, the honey's main North Carolina source, the necessary nectar flow from tulip trees (*Linodendron*), more commonly known as tulip poplars, was drying up earlier and earlier, and there were fewer of the source trees within his bees' foraging distance due to the steady deforestation for business and housing developments. The resultant honey production now shut down in his apiary by the second or third week of May.

To add to the struggle, the parasitic *Varroa destructor* mites, invaders from Asia, were an incurable plague on his bees' health, sucking their vital tissues and infecting them with viruses lethal to bees.

On Friday night, he covered the garage floor with a well-used plastic sheet then set up the extractor, a four-foot-tall metal centrifuge that spun honey out of frames of filled honeycomb. Early this Saturday morning, before Jacob was to arrive, Phineas placed the necessities for stealing his bees' honey in the apiary and loaded a plastic bin, large enough to enclose two hive bodies worth of frames, on his garden cart. And finally, he readied the chemical scent and fabric fume board that Jacob and he would put on each hive, one by one, to drive bees down out of the honey super bodies on top and into the brood frames at the bottom of his hives. This morning, Jacob and he wouldn't use smoke to calm the robbed bees. Smoke makes bees consume the honey Phineas coveted.

Soon after Phineas took up beekeeping, he'd scheduled an annual honey extraction in the first weeks of June with a well-attended celebration that followed. By now, their neighbors had aged and resided in empty nests, and for them the wonder factor of harvesting honey had waned. As for his invited colleagues and medical trainees, fewer made the time to attend, preferring to stay home in air conditioning rather than venture out during their precious hours off work. So, turnout for the annual celebration was less than half of what it had once been— maybe not a bad thing—since it was just too hot to celebrate outside, and he had less honey to share. He and Iris guessed that a dozen might attend this year after the few affirmative responses they received to their email invitations, so he set out that number of honey jars to fill as favors.

As soon as Jacob arrived, Ruby bolted from his truck and inspected the perimeter of the backyard's fenced area with her nose, and at intervals, squatted and deposited her scent. His son donned his protective jacket and finished closing the three zippers that sealed it. "Seven AM and already 88 degrees. Should be over a hundred again this afternoon."

Phineas had already suited up and was ready to begin. "Thanks for coming over early—and happy birthday!"

"Thanks. After 38, it's a day like any other." He shrugged. "I was in bed by ten. Nothing going on for this newly single guy, and I didn't have to wait for Claire to get ready to come here this year." He pried off the top of the first hive while Phineas sprayed the fume board's fabric, filling the air with a pungent almond scent.

"I never understood why they hate this smell so much."

"Me neither." Jacob placed the board over the top super. "It can't be similar to the tree's blossoms." He took out his cell phone and set the timer for five minutes.

"Marie's inside the house changing." Iris hollered from the driveway. "She came dressed for the heat in shorts, tee shirt, and sandals." She paused for effect. "I told her that just wouldn't do and found her some baggy jeans and boots. And I gave her your extra jacket and some gloves. She'll join you directly."

Jacob pried off the freshly abandoned top box, swept a few straggling bees off with his glove, and sealed the super in the plastic bin. "Marie? You didn't say she was coming." His voice was more animated than it had been.

"Wasn't sure she'd show, especially for this part." Phineas studied the hive's second level of frames and lifted one. "Not much ripe honey on this next level. Let's do the next hive."

Marie approached in full protective beekeeping garb strutting stiff-legged, her arms out straight ahead of her. From behind the garb's face screen, her wide smile sparkled, reflecting the early sun's horizontal rays. "Take me to your leader, Earthmen. I've come to save your planet. I bear a gift, a book titled *How to Serve Humans*."

Jacob snorted. "Waddaya know? Another *Twilight Zone* fan! Haven't heard that one in a while." He turned to Phineas. "Did you know that *How to Serve Humans* was an alien cookbook?"

"I must have missed that episode, and I don't have that book on my kitchen cookbook shelf. I hope you aren't too late to save the planet, Marie." Phineas pried off the next hive's outer cover and replaced the inner cover with the odiferous fume board. "Let me take these honey supers to the garage, Jacob, and then you can give Marie an expert tour of the hive."

"That would be just ducky…You sure they can't get me in this getup?" She stepped closer to the action.

Phineas glanced at Jacob's cell phone timer. "You're safe—in that 'getup'—and in Jacob's capable hands." He cringed. Not the best choice of words.

～

Forty-six pounds total. Phineas' lowest yield yet. Not enough to fill one 5-gallon bucket. Gone were the one hundred plus pound honey harvests that used to leave him feeling wealthy with the liquid gold. He'd have to cut back on how he used it over the next year, especially after he sacrificed enough for each celebration attendee to take home a jar. Phineas was relieved that only four, so far, outside the family and Marie, were showing up, and they had all retreated into the house's 80-degree air conditioning.

Marie appeared ecstatic after her first beekeeping experience. "That was so cool!" She held her jar up to the bright sun penetrating the kitchen window. "And it's so beautiful." In yellow shorts and a U of W tee shirt, her face glowed in that beam of sunlight before Iris lowered the shade.

Jacob continued acting the part of her personal beekeeping docent. "One bee, over its lifetime, might fly hundreds of miles to produce a fifth of a teaspoon of honey."

Iris had been eavesdropping, keeping a mother's eye on the two, and winked at Phineas. Beekeeping nerd trivia. What a way to impress a young woman.

The door burst open, and a toddler under a mop of dark brown hair dashed in. Ruby intercepted the energetic lad and licked his face between protesting hands. Martha, a slim brunette in dressy campaigning clothes, set a bulky cloth bag on the floor and scooped her son up. "Sorry we're late. Mateo just took a long nap then dawdled over his lunch." Ruby poked her nose into the bag. "Felipe is tied up at the restaurant as usual and couldn't make it—and since when did you get a dog?"

"Hey, Sis. I'm dog sitting." Jacob pulled Ruby away by her collar. "This is Ruby—and her owner didn't warn me that she's kinduva bitch."

Mateo exclaimed, "Bitch!"

Martha frowned up at her brother and put her index finger on Mateo's mouth. "Mateo, that's a no-no word." She shook her head "no" for emphasis. "Thanks a lot, Jacob. He'll probably want to use that one on his daycare teachers." Her expression brightened. "By the way, happy birthday."

"Thanks. Funny card. Gave me a good laugh."

Martha scanned the room. "Where's Claire?"

"Moved on. Going on two months now." Jacob knelt and patted Ruby.

"Oh...Sorry to hear that. You okay?"

"It was time."

"Wayla!" The toddler wriggled out of his mother's arms and ran to grandmother Iris, whom he'd labeled Wayla, abuela in Spanish, with his early words.

"How's my favorite grandson?" Iris bent over to wrap her arms around her only grandson. "You're getting so big!" He accepted the hug for a moment, then pushed away to reestablish his freedom.

Marie lowered herself into a crouch and wiggled her fingers at him. "Hi, Mateo. I'm Marie. And your Mom's nicely dressed on a Saturday afternoon."

"I had a grass roots meeting for my candidacy before I picked Mateo up from my husband," Martha answered.

"Candidacy?"

"I'm running for congress."

Iris took two steps toward the kitchen. "I'm going to put out food. You all have to be hungry." She signaled to Phineas. "Burgers?"

"Hey everyone." He raised his arms over his head to get everyone's attention. "I'm taking orders for Impossible Burgers, with or without cheddar. And I baked honey wheat buns last night."

"Waylo!" Mateo had spotted his grandfather, his abuelo.

Ruby bolted ahead of them into the kitchen and sat in front of the refrigerator, her tail sweeping an arc on the floor behind her. Mateo followed and reached to pat her velvety head. She parried his effort by once again vigorously licking his hands and face and tasting him for traces of his lunch.

⁓

Later in the living room, Marie settled into a comfortable chair and carefully placed her full plate and glass of beer on the narrow end table next to it. The offerings in her condo's kitchen were at rock bottom, so the celebration's meal was a treat, maybe even the synthetic cheeseburger. She was sampling the bean salad when a trim and elegant elderly woman with long platinum hair and scarlet lipstick let herself in the front door. A Black Lives Matter tee shirt hugged her well-maintained figure, and her face looked vaguely familiar.

Phineas crossed from the dining area "Chelsea! So glad you could make it." He hugged her and announced, "Chelsea LaFever Bullock has arrived, everyone." Marie could now place the face, the younger version of which she'd seen in the numerous YouTube videos of 1998 UNC Bomber news clips.

Chelsea planted a peck on his cheek before scanning the room. "I don't see any eligible bachelors, Finman. I guess I'll just have to be satisfied with your cooking. Where's that gorgeous woman who somehow agreed to be your better half?"

"Pushing healthy food choices in the kitchen." He smiled broadly, suggesting how proud he was of his mate or of hearing a nickname that Marie suspected was now seldom used.

"I'll catch up with you after I've found some less healthy options." Chelsea glided past him on golden sandals, like she knew her way.

Marie took a cautious bite of Impossible Burger and chewed. Not bad, but vaguely less satisfying of some primitive need. Vague. That about sized it up. Tasty bun though. She swallowed and eyed the material left after her bite. The colors weren't a perfect match to real meat either. Good thing she was famished, or she might leave enough to embarrass.

Gold sandals stood in front of her. "So, what's the verdict on Phineas' latest culinary experiment?" Chelsea's voice was as eerily familiar as her appearance.

Marie looked up at just enough professionally applied make-up. "Just how hungry *are* you?"

"Hah! I figured when he left the real food world, his offerings would be chancy. I'm Chelsea Bullock. Mind if I join you?"

"Marie Porter. Please do."

"You're new." Chelsea set her plate and a goblet of red wine on the table and carried a folding chair over from the room's corner.

"I just moved here from the west coast. I'm working with Dr. Mann on a study."

"Well, you take good care of Finman. He's getting on, you know." Chelsea winked before she sipped her wine.

"I'll do my best. He seems pretty sharp to me. So, Finman's his nickname?"

"It's what his close friends call him. My husband called him nothing else. Said the name Phineas was too persnickety, and that he was already too persnickety."

SynMedical's doctor files mentioned that Phineas Mann was meticulous, bordering on compulsive. And Chelsea's husband? She came alone and wore no wedding ring. Marie put the burger back on her plate and lifted her glass of beer. "How long have you been coming to these events?"

"Let's see. Since 1998. That makes how many years? Well anyway…a long time. There used to be more than twice as many here." Her smile faded. "People die, move away, lose interest. My husband Ron was Finman's best friend. He passed from COVID. He was also a doctor taking care of those patients."

"I'm sorry."

"They wouldn't even let me see him when he was on life support—and then he was gone." Chelsea's voice trailed off, but her words brought back similar hospital scenes, painful scenes that Marie kept buried deep.

"I remember. It seemed the right thing to do at the time."

"I still blame the President. That second wave after the election, right before the vaccines—that's when Ron caught it." Chelsea dabbed at her eye with a paper napkin. "He was working night and day and got exposed—and being an older man, he got really sick fast...If we'd had a real leader, the second wave would never have happened, and I'd still have my Ron."

"Many of us taking care of those patients felt that the administration should have handled it better, that lives could have been saved."

"You a doctor too?" Chelsea's eyes narrowed ever so slightly.

"Just started working with SynMedical, my first time with the pharmaceutical industry. Before that, I was a hospital-based internist."

Chelsea lifted her synthetic cheeseburger in both hands and eyed it suspiciously. "Well, I still miss Ron. He was so much fun...but... but a girl's got to move on, right? So, tell me—" She scrunched her perfect face ever so slightly. "Are there any men at your workplace interested in dating a *mature* former news announcer?"

The doorbell rang, and Iris hustled to it from the kitchen. A middle-aged Black man stepped inside while balancing a sizable box on his shoulder. Marie could read "Gramma's Cookin'" in large red letters on the box's side, and Iris began laughing and chatting with the delivery man.

Chelsea eased her cheeseburger back onto her plate. "Now here comes some real Southern food. I put in an order before I left home, but don't tell Finman." She lowered her voice. "I've been a limited partner in their restaurant for years. So's Finman...We also lost their founder to COVID, Jericho James...He was a hero and a friend." She rose from her chair and threw her shoulders back. "Now, if you'll excuse me, I want to give Demetrius a hug—and get me one of those crispy, tender chicken breasts while it's still hot." Before Chelsea took a step away from Marie,

Demetrius had pivoted to hold the door open for someone trailing him.

"Yo, Demetrius! Thanks, my friend." The booming voice came from a withered and nearly bald White man who leaned over a red metallic walker with a satchel attached. He shuffled inside, and a better preserved full-figured elderly woman carrying a cake dish followed.

Demetrius gently patted the man on the shoulder. "Yo, Vinnie. Long time. Hey Theresa. How y'all doin'?"

Iris gently embraced the new arrivals and relieved Theresa of her burden. "Thank you for coming, Theresa, and thank you for baking."

"Well, I had to do *something* for Jacob's birthday. It's a carrot cake. I know you like to eat healthy."

Vinnie. Vincent DiCenzo was the detective in the 1998 bombing attempt. Marie recalled that he'd retired from the NYPD and just started with the Chapel Hill Police when Phineas brought down the UNC Bomber. He'd be elderly by now.

With a flourish, Vinnie extracted a long narrow bottle of a bright yellow liquid from his walker's satchel. *Limoncello.* Just like in Jacob's novel. Definitely the detective.

Marie hadn't known about Jacob's birthday. They weren't making that much of a fuss about it. Must be how he likes it. At least someone remembered. Now that her mother was gone, there was no one except SynMedical to remember Marie's, a day that slipped by two weeks ago, one that she acknowledged with a shrug and a "Hmph" when HR sent her a happy birthday email.

⌒

The Tesla's prompt and quiet air conditioning cooled the sweat that had coated Marie as she lingered outside to offer her thanks and goodbyes to the Manns. She settled her jar of honey in the cupholder between the front seats and said, "Siri, take me home." Her car deftly turned itself around in the driveway and eased into the street.

"Siri, tell me about Martha Mann." The car's computer announced that Marie would have to pull over before Siri would allow her to search the internet.

"Siri, park in the nearest parking lot." The car's computer screen imaged several locations before it took Marie to the first one with empty spaces. The sign over the one-story building screamed *Johnny's Guns* in three-foot red letters. Another sign in the large front window promised assault weapons and high-capacity magazines at the lowest prices anywhere. Maybe she should have checked other parking options.

Marie touched the screen over the newly familiar facial image as soon as it appeared. The display shifted to links under Martha Mann and Martha Mann-Hernandez. Recent information mostly centered on Martha's candidacy, nothing to explain why earlier Iris had taken Martha aside and earnestly whispered something about "the FBI."

When she heard those two words, a paranoid thought crept into Marie's brain. Had the FBI somehow traced her deceased fugitive mother to *her*?

But then, Marie's eavesdropping was interrupted by Jacob's attentions, and the situation with him began to suggest it could become sticky. What if he were to ask her out? Best to keep her half-brother at an appropriate distance. But then he mentioned he might move north to a new position at Cornell. Distance, for sure. Then his *Happy Birthday* song and candle blowing interrupted their conversation.

Barely a week ago, she'd started reading Jacob's novel while she was snug between 600 thread count sheets in her New Orleans hotel room. *Wow!* If parts of what he wrote were based on the true story, he must have been some kid. And it was hard to imagine her mother hooked up with anyone like the violent racist character who was the book's main villain. At least the news clips on YouTube and internet articles from that time she'd seen hadn't mentioned her mother. Phineas must have filled in the blanks for his son as he wrote his book.

Tonight, Vinnie had stepped out of the historical novel and into the Mann's household. Phineas had immediately escorted him to a place at the table, where the two sat next to each other and were immediately immersed in intense conversation. Were they also talking about "the FBI"? About her?

Marie had chatted briefly with Theresa after accepting a piece of her delicious cake, while Vinnie planted himself at the table and sipped limoncello. Marie finished her piece of cake before she edged closer behind Vinnie and Phineas, hoping to hear snatches of their conversation, but Vinnie spotted her and stopped her with, "You're new."

So I'm told. "Hi. I'm Marie. Your wife makes a great cake."

Phineas sat back upright. "Marie's working with me on a study, Vinnie."

Vinnie lifted his luminescent bottle. "Care for some limoncello? Made it myself." Then Gabby arrived as Marie began sipping the fiery liquid, and nothing else was said within her earshot about "the FBI".

She looked up from the computer screen as a man exited Johnny's Guns carrying a long box. He tossed it into a dark grey Jeep and drove away.

"Siri, search Vincent DiCenzo." She scanned the first two entries and learned how he'd made the headlines after he solved a famous cold case when DNA technology was in its infancy. *DNA identification. Hmm.* Would his knowledge on the subject prove useful again?

She tightened her grip on the steering wheel. *How would the Manns react if they learned the truth of my heritage?* There was more to sort out. Marie commanded, "Siri, search Chelsea LaFever Bullock."

Younger images of a brassy blond Chelsea appeared in a row above a *Wikipedia* link. Marie touched the link and scrolled to the *Personal* heading. She read about Chelsea's marriage to Ron Bullock in 1998, and that she'd been widowed in 2020. There was no mention of children. The *Professional* paragraphs revealed that she'd won coveted journalism prizes for her coverage of the UNC Bomber, and that several national news programs had courted her. She'd turned them down to stay in North Carolina, sacrificing fame for love.

Marie sighed. It'd be amazing to have that choice.

Then the very "mature" Chelsea had won a Pulitzer for a special news program she produced and narrated during the second wave of the COVID pandemic at the end of 2020. The final segment was an intimate, heart wrenching report of her husband's rapid downhill course and lonely death. She concluded the show by laying the blame for hundreds of thousands of deaths at the President's feet, claiming they shouldn't have happened, that her husband's death shouldn't have happened, and that the nation's administration was incompetent. In her final lines, she instructed her viewing audience to be extremely wary during the President's second four years.

Despite the Pulitzer, political fallout caused the station to suggest that Chelsea should retire. It had to be the way she wanted to go out.

That was enough of COVID and politics and pain for one day. "Siri, let's go home." Goodbye, Johnny's Guns. She forced her thoughts in a brighter direction. *At least it's nice to have a family, even if they don't know it.*

⌒

This year's after party cleanup went easier than it had with former years' larger crowds. Iris fit most of the dishes into one load of the dishwasher, while Phineas sealed leftovers into Tupperware containers. He was spent after the very long day.

"My Incredible Burgers weren't much of a hit, even with the home-baked buns."

"Burgers are a guy thing, but the buns were really good. Veggies and carrot cake did well—and Gramma's Cookin'—well, there wasn't any chicken left over."

He chuckled. "That sneaky Chelsea—but I was glad she ordered it, and it's always good to see her—and Demetrius, Vinnie, and Theresa."

Iris closed the appliance's stainless-steel door, pushed START, then turned to him. "Phineas...I've made a decision..." Her somber demeanor was unsettling.

"About what?" He froze. Drumroll?

"I'm going to retire." Cymbal sound.

Her news startled him at first. "Why not? You've fought the good fight, and we've tip-toed past seventy." He studied her face. Really studied it. Her trying recent years under the President's cutbacks had added fine lines radiating from the corners of her eyes. Before now, he hadn't fully appreciated the delicate creases that angled outward from each side of her nose and skirted her upper lip to extend, more subtly, inward toward her chin. He loved how they framed her pretty mouth. He loved that her striking beauty found its way out from deep inside.

"I've been considering it for a while." Her voice was soft but its delivery firm. How elegant she remained after all their years together.

"You're not alone." He couldn't imagine being alone, being without her. "I think about it too—usually at the end of a tough day."

"It could be years before NIH grant support comes back. I can pass on my teaching load to young faculty. They could use the visibility and extra financial support at this stage of their careers."

"If you'd told me a day earlier, this could have been a retirement party too."

"I haven't informed my chairman. I need to do that before we tell anyone else."

"Of course." He knew that. Standard university protocol.

A twinge in his lower back and stiffness between his shoulder blades had settled in for the night. At his age, hoisting heavy honey supers and cranking the extractor left their reminders. He passed her the first of the plastic food containers destined for her exact system of storage, and his left hand decided to feature an unfamiliar fine tremor. Was this one more sign of fatigue in an elderly beekeeper? In a doctor approaching his time to hang up his stethoscope? "Got plans for after you clear your office?"

"Just think for a while. Take a trip somewhere. And help Martha."

"From what we saw today, she could use help with Mateo." He knew Iris longed to be with her grandson. Mateo would ease her transition, and if Martha somehow pulled off an unexpected win in November, she'd need all the help they could provide with childcare, an issue not yet broached.

"And with her campaign." She began stacking leftovers in the refrigerator. "And the Democratic party could use help—if we're to have a 2024 election." She was back to business.

"That's a big if."

"Can you believe he's dropping hints about putting elections on hold if he declares another national emergency? He wants to be king—or dictator for life."

"The mayor of New York City did it in 2008, citing the financial crisis."

"The biggest crises have been created by him, our so-called Commander-in-Chief. The cyber war with Russia, China, and even Iran. He let *that* happen with his 'nothing to see here' tweets and his handcuffing of U.S. intelligence. Think Russia's meddling helped him get elected, then re-elected? Hell yeah!" The volume of her voice steadily escalated.

"I'm worried he's become so erratic; he could take us into actual military combat," Phineas mumbled.

"He could. And he might—just so the evil bastard can claim he needs to stay in office—and out of jail." She was almost shouting now.

"So, tell me how you feel about him." Phineas forced a wry grin.

His kidding defused her anger. She sauntered back across the kitchen and stood close, placed her hands on the small of his back, and pulled him to her. He planted a lingering kiss on her lips.

"So, Iris, I have an idea for the trip you mentioned."

"Oh?"

"Italy. Start using our new passports—get some EU stamps in them." She nodded enthusiastically. "Okay. I'm in. What part?"

"North, where it's still cool in the summer. Leave the brutal dog days of August in North Carolina behind."

"Since you've obviously been thinking about it, what is it you want to do there?"

He needed to sell the idea he'd been exploring. "Well...now that you ask... there *is* a beekeeping workshop in the Alps—it's just for a few days. It includes sessions on honey tasting. The first step to becoming a honey sommelier."

"Hah! I *figured* you had something in mind." She took on a serious expression. She wanted him to feel a moment of suspense before she countered. "I'm sure I can keep busy, while you hang out with the bee nerds." Now the crooked grin she always flashed before teasing. "There are probably spas—and there'll be shopping—after I sleep in then drink espresso on the balcony, of course."

"Sounds like it could get expensive." He kissed her again. "Can we take this discussion to the bedroom, where we can begin to flesh out some details?"

⁓

Before 6 AM the temperature in the backyard hadn't yet risen above the day's nadir of 88 degrees. Phineas sipped hot coffee and ambled among his raised vegetable beds, fruit trees, and beehives, inspecting for new growth and signs of destructive pests. His thoughts were consumed with Iris' retirement announcement. She probably would have done it earlier, had the President not pushed Medicare eligibility past seventy years of age. She needed to work to keep health insurance. Her life, and so many others, had been forced down rocky detours after the right-wing president's unexpected re-election. How did it all happen?

The President had cited ballooning deficits as the reason to delay Medicare, deficits from a combination of his tax reduction legislation—an act that made his rich friends richer—and the addition of the lavish COVID-19 cash infusion. During that 2020-2022 pandemic, the U. S. government, and the rest of the world, had been forced to print trillions of dollars to prevent economic collapse, and the hyperinflation that followed this massive infusion had skyrocketed valuations of real estate and shrunken pre-existing debt burdens, a combination that allowed the President to claim his net worth had increased by multiples. The rich had gotten way richer.

Delaying Phineas' and Iris' Medicare eligibility had been one of the incumbent president's first acts after his tragic 2020 re-election, the election he would surely have lost, if his inner circle hadn't plotted a devious path to a stolen victory. From the coronavirus' beginning, they'd allowed it to rage mercilessly through the country, peaking as the election loomed. In hindsight, that was part of their strategy to win before a vaccine could offer protection.

Democratic voters, believers in science, had feared going in person to crowded polls, anticipating concentrated clusters of viral exposure from reckless, maskless Republicans. Democrats had expected safer voting by mail, but the administration's last-minute sabotage of USPS had caused countless ballots to vanish or arrive late, miss deadlines, and be declared invalid. The soulless Attorney General's smoke and mirrors investigation of voting snafus and debacles miraculously found no foul play.

Voter intimidation reigned. Armed right-wing militia members formed crowds outside polling sites where they threatened lines of voters and their approaching vehicles from Election Day's opening minutes. News coverage so frightened Democrats that only a fraction bravely showed up, and fewer endured the threats to make it inside to finish marking their ballots. Voters who wore red hats were welcomed by their right-wing guardians.

Those militias were later rewarded with membership in the new government gestapo tasked with keeping demonstrations from happening. The manageable members of Proud Boys, Wolverine Watchmen, and other vile groups were hired and formed the nucleus of this presidential force. The less bright and less photogenic remnants of these domestic terrorist groups were left to scratch out existences like the ragtag Proud Boy remnants of Alamance County—those big-mouthed gun-toters who'd hassled them at Apple Chill.

As the pre-election polls had suggested, the Democratic candidate again handily won the popular vote, but his electoral college margin was razor thin. (Martha had commented how once again, blue state voters got less than a vote, and red state voters got more than a vote. One person, one vote remained a lofty ideal only.) This margin was narrow enough that the incumbent challenged the results of two swing states with vote margins less than a few thousand and demanded recounts. These states somehow reversed the winner. Democrats screamed foul, and the decision made it to the Supreme Court, as it did in 2000 when there were hanging chads to adjudicate. The 2020 Supreme Court, packed with fresh conservatives beholden to the President, completed the tortuous path to his tragic re-election.

His base celebrated with countless clips of ammunition discharged into the atmosphere. The rain of bullets that followed took numerous innocent American lives. A seven-year-old girl in Pennsylvania was instantly paralyzed, her spinal cord severed as she floated in a kiddie pool—until all its water, along with her hopes and dreams, drained out through the bullet hole. The right's precious right to bear their arms was preserved, not the simple muskets familiar to the founding fathers, but modern military grade assault weapons possessed for imagined threats and manly posturing.

In early 2020, Iris had hoped that the pandemic would finally lead to an increase in NIH grant funding, especially in health delivery to the underserved, her specialty. That never happened. The underserved succumbed in higher numbers during the first wave of the pandemic, especially the newly created uninsured high-risk baby boomer cohort aged 65 to 70, who lost the safety net of their Medicare coverage. Following the deaths of over a million U.S. citizens, the annual national deficit began shrinking from a historical peak, and the administration pointed at this number to declare success for their economic policies.

Phineas shuddered with the memory of the many months he'd spent in and out of hazmat personal protective equipment caring for COVID-19 patients in the ICU and on the wards, and the intense sadness he still felt after the death of his close friend, infectious disease specialist Ron Bullock. In the 1980s, Ron and he'd faced caring for AIDS patients during the early days of that mysterious and frightening epidemic, before the discovery of the human immunodeficiency virus that was behind the syndrome. And Ron had survived his Ebola virus work in Africa while its vaccination was being developed. When COVID-19 arrived, the elderly had been warned that they were high risk for life-threatening complications from it, and neither Ron nor Phineas admitted the obvious, that they fell into the category of 'elderly' in 2020.

They'd both signed the letter to POTUS, the one with tens of thousands of physician signatures, urging him to not open up the country until COVID-19 was better contained. But the so-called leader of the once free world had chosen to sacrifice lives, declaring the economy was on life support. The businessman had chosen business over lives in the pandemic war...and Phineas' closest friend had died on the front lines.

Phineas' family and friends celebrated when a vaccine finally became available in 2021, but red states and the FOX News faithful believed wild conspiracy theories over science and failed to immunize. When a more transmissible viral variant, labeled delta, created a second wave, millions of the suddenly sick unvaccinated overwhelmed the healthcare system. He'd had to make rounds on those critically ill patients in parking lots waiting for oxygen and precious hospital beds.

Almost a million conservative voters were culled from the electorate, but it was too late. Their man was president for four more years, and it took two of these for the pandemic to abate from a raging wildfire to smoldering and recurrent endemic outbreaks—like a whack-a-mole carnival game hammering anti-vaccine science deniers. A universal coronavirus vaccine became available in 2023 and gave additional protection to believers.

2024 posed fresh nonbiological threats that regularly affected Iris and him, threats that could have been minimized under competent leaders. Computer viruses from rogue nations regularly attacked the inadequately defended US infrastructure, especially the power grid. Hackers probed porous firewalls and manipulated social media and financial systems. The archaic administration, full of appointed incompetent elderly donors and bootlickers, haplessly tilted at playing catchup after years of pouring trillions into conventional military hardware and comparative pittances into cyber security. Threats of economic sanctions against bad actor regimes became toothless. The President hinted at military action against China,

North Korea, and Iran, and he continued to drop repeated suggestions on Twitter that the world was too unstable for a 2024 presidential election, that it should be delayed until things were "better," that he should continue to lead the United States of America in uncertain times.

Such was the world that Mateo had been born into, a world of created global instability disintegrating with accelerating climate degradation. Phineas and Iris had celebrated Mateo's birth in public but worried about his future in private. Martha wanted to change Washington for her son and had plunged herself into the uphill task of getting elected to the House. She was a shy child once long ago but had undergone a metamorphosis, emerging from her cocoon after being plunged into the terrifying events of May 1998. She would need Iris' and his help now, and Iris had declared she was all in.

Phineas swallowed the last of his coffee, now too a disappointing 88 degrees, and trudged back toward the house and another day's work, facing into the sunrise's flame red haze-piercing rays.

⌐⌐

CEO Eugene Schmidt, in his New Balance running shoes, struggled up ahead. Marie had watched him begin the company's charity 5K almost at a sprint. Despite the intense heat, he'd fought to get ahead of constricting packs in the crowd of runners, packs that instantly parted when they recognized the boss and his mustache.

She'd decided before the race to relax and jog the route at an easy pace, one that kept her from looking spent when she hit the finish line. She didn't want a medal. After being drafted into attending, today's event would be reconnaissance, getting to understand better those who'd determine her work experience. With a half mile to go, the gap was closing between Schmidt and her. She could hear each of his labored breaths.

She pulled up shoulder to shoulder. "Almost there, Sir." Her breathing was still easy. Should she pant some for effect?

He said nothing. His focus appeared to be on the asphalt six feet in front of him. Sweat poured down his shiny scalp. If she were racing, she'd kick it into high gear and leave him in her wake, but he looked like he might collapse at any moment. She stayed at his side. He might need CPR.

The colorful finish line arch was now just fifty yards ahead. Tables beyond offered iced bottles of water. She could read each word of the corporate motto on the arch's cobalt blue fabric. *Taking Care of All Your Medication Needs.* Boring boardroom speak and just begging for Marketing to revise.

Schmidt glanced up at her. His face was stretched over his skull, his jaw hanging. He turned it back to his path and somehow found a last ounce of acceleration, pulled ahead, and crossed the line a split second ahead of her. He staggered two steps and bent forward clutching his shorts with both hands, his chest heaving. She scooped up two bottles of water from a tub, a shocking ice cold in the morning heat.

"Here you go, Sir. You've earned this. Nice race."

He snatched the offered bottle and poured half over his head. His Adam's apple bobbed when he greedily chugged the rest. The caterpillar was coming back to life, twitching. His focus shifted up from the ground to her ankles, her legs, her chest, and finally, her face.

"Bet you...thought you...had me...You didn't know...I had more gas... in the tank." He sounded almost giddy, adolescent.

"Impressive finish, Sir." She unscrewed her bottle's cap and sipped. If this had been a high school practice, her coach would have told her to run extra laps for dogging it.

A man his age might be thinking he'd pulled off a classic Muhammed Ali 'rope a dope', lulling her into thinking she had the win, while he'd rally to beat her. Let him. She'd done what she planned, had a morning run *and* allowed her boss a feel-good moment that might just benefit her career.

A rush of finishers from behind herded her away from Schmidt and toward the sidelines. Standing on the periphery of the crowd, she observed that those runners all wanted to be seen by and with Schmidt as the company photographer snapped away. She hoped she didn't appear too rested; in the event her image was captured in a publishable photo.

Marie heard voices she recognized from the office coming from flushed and sweaty faces she might not have identified in this new context. The voices were coming to a consensus on a brewpub for celebrating the day. O'Malley's. She had no idea where it was. There seemed to be enough boisterous employees that she wouldn't be missed when she didn't show up. Hanging out and drinking with the same people she spent workdays with was not her idea of a weekend off. And an endorphin and beer stoked coworker might make an unwelcome pass at her.

She knew the drill. She'd stay at the 5K only long enough to not be noticeably absent when Schmidt presented awards. She had to be visible then, since she'd escorted him safely across. He might not take it kindly if she were to abandon him and his company in his proud moment. After, she could slip away.

Marie refilled her empty plastic bottle from the barrel-sized orange cooler before smiling and nodding her way into the shade under one of the corporate tents. At least she'd slathered on sunscreen *this* time. She watched the last of the dripping participants, some walking, cross the finish line. Damn! It was hot in North Carolina. She hadn't noticed anything like this heat as a sixth grader twenty-six years ago.

Schmidt, looking resurrected, hoisted a microphone. His voice boomed from a loudspeaker. "Time for shiny medals! But first, thank you, everyone, for helping raise money for lung disease research. SynMedical Biopharma will proudly match every dollar contributed today." He rattled on in lofty corporate-speak before finally getting to the awards. He started with the older groups and worked his way down a clipboard while he handed out medals and delivered stale attempts at humor. "What's this? Third place in the men's fifty plus is...wait for it...Eugene Schmidt!" He took a bow and draped a medal around his own glistening neck. Marie clapped for him and the next few recipients. Maybe she could escape soon.

"And in fourth place in the women's thirties, we have...our own Marie Porter!" He displayed her medal to the crowd and gestured for her to approach. "To those who haven't had the pleasure of meeting her, you should introduce yourselves at O'Malley's Pub this afternoon. She's going to do some exciting work for us at SynMedical."

Damn! Now I'll have to go hang out with them. Well, at least today was good for job security—and the goal of continuing to work with Phineas Mann.

Marie accepted the medal and shook his hand, deftly ignoring his overture to get her to bend low, so he could personally drape it on her while inspecting her chest. She sensed multiple pairs of male eyes, and a few female pairs, surveying her. She felt like a slab of meat and longed for that long-gone brief respite following the 'Me Too' movement. Its demise lay at the feet of the emboldened president after his re-election, resulting in a palpable uptick of leering men.

She'd go home, clean up, cover up, and make the required appearance. It wouldn't be for long enough for anyone, married or single, to get drunk enough to hit on her. Life needed to stay simple.

JUNE

"There's one issue that will define the contours of this century more dramatically than any other, and that is the urgent threat of a changing climate"

"Climate change is no longer some far-off problem; it is happening here; it is happening now."

BARACK OBAMA 44TH PRESIDENT OF THE USA

Iris' attention was locked onto her cell phone, as she paced circles around the kitchen. "Can you believe that sonofabitch president just trolled our daughter?"

"Where are you seeing that?" Phineas glanced up from his iPad.

"On Twitter—where he lives."

"Thought you got rid of Twitter after the FBI visited."

"I did, but Martha said I had to have it—and that damnable Facebook, if I was going to help her campaign." She stopped pacing.

He figured Iris would have to choose Martha over sanity. "What'd he tweet?"

"That her husband is an immigrant." A crease in the middle of Iris' forehead formed a 'V' that pointed toward the bridge of her slender nose. "That we need people with All-American values in office, people without loyalties to other countries, people with 'American' names." She grimaced. "Then he endorsed her Republican opponent, of course, who happens to have a German name. POTUS put out a bold-faced lie about our son-in-law, who was born in and has always lived in this country."

"Wasn't the President's grandfather a German immigrant?"

"Yup. Came as a child."

"Guess you can't do anything with that?" Phineas searched his memory to find anything more useful to contribute.

"Been tried without success. Too long ago."

"So, it was the ICE raid on Felipe's restaurant and his arrest that planted a bullseye on Martha's back." He scrolled local news articles searching for anything on Martha.

"You mean his false arrest—even though he's a US citizen. They had to be planning it so POTUS could tweet about it. Actually, it was Martha's gaining on her Republican opponent that put the bullseye on *Felipe's* back." Iris brought her arm back like she was about to throw her cell phone at the wall, before she adjusted her reading glasses and began studying it again.

Two days earlier, Phineas and Iris had to rush to Martha's house to babysit for Mateo, so Martha could deliver Felipe's birth certificate and passport to the city jail. ICE agents had descended en masse on Felipe's French themed restaurant and waved falsified papers that claimed one of his kitchen staff was undocumented. ICE's target had prudently called in sick, so the frustrated agents rounded up everyone who didn't look lily white.

Iris balled her free hand into a fist and began pacing again. "It doesn't matter that Felipe was released without charge. Our sonofabitch president won't undo the damage he creates. He just repeats lies that justify his actions, until he and his base believe the crap he's spouting.'"

"That's the second time I've heard you call him that." Phineas held up both hands like he was trying to stop traffic. "Better be careful attaching that tag to the President, our so-called Commander-in-Chief. You might slip and say it when you shouldn't during Martha's campaign. Remember Joseph and his dissertation?"

Iris let out a single chuckle, undoubtably recalling how their long-ago neighbor had suffered such a slip. Saintly Joseph was working on his PhD in religion and, in uncharacteristic frustration, repeatedly referred to his challenging final treatise as his "fucking dissertation." Then he absent-mindedly slipped and linked the words in the presence of a horrified theological advisor.

"Okay, Phineas. Point taken. But it's ironic that our hard-working son-in-law, a master of *French* cuisine, trained at the Culinary Institute of America—otherwise known as the CIA—Hah! —is one more innocent bystander in the President's war on immigrants." Her eyes glistened before she took off her glasses and dabbed the heel of her hand against the rims of her eye sockets. "It'll probably be months before his restaurant's business is back to where it was." She brought her phone close to her face and squinted. Iris was, without a doubt, still capable of exploding, if jostled.

"That does it!" The volume of her declaration suggested detonation was imminent. "He just tweeted about her again. He says he saw a picture of her in her college soccer uniform and posted 'Whoa! For a loser, she's HOT'. He's telling his followers that he's nicknaming her 'Whoa-Mann'. What a pig!"

Phineas clenched his jaw and opened his seldom-used Twitter app. *That misogynist sonofabitch is ogling MY DAUGHTER?*

⌒

The Wednesday clinic schedule indicated that Phineas' last patient had been added on only yesterday. The address in the computer suggested that Dolly Jones had traveled all the way from the mountains west of

Knoxville, Tennessee, at least a six-hour drive. Add in parking and the lengthy process of registering as a new patient in the UNC system, and she was finally ready for him almost thirty minutes after her scheduled appointment time. She was bound to be tired and hungry, even more so than he at the end of his long day. And where were her medical notes? Nothing on her existed in the electronic record.

He tucked his trusty notepad under his arm and tentatively pushed the exam room door open, barely missing a tow-headed three or four-year-old on the floor. Phineas had learned over the years that many families didn't appreciate the threat of a heavy swinging door. The child pushed a rusty toy fire engine missing its front wheels and shrieked like a siren. Ketchup streaked the smiley face on the boy's tee shirt.

The odor of stale tobacco smoke filled the room, probably emanating from the wiry young man in coveralls, with Darrell stitched on the chest. He sat next to a moon-faced woman in a sweat suit, flip flops, and sweat-stained red MAGA ballcap, her half-bleached hair escaping from its back.

Phineas reached for the hand sanitizer dispenser on the wall and levered a jet of the cool gel onto his palm. He massaged it onto both hands before offering his right to the couple. "Hi. I'm Dr. Mann. You must be tired after a long drive."

Darrell tucked stringy hair behind his ears and cautiously accepted the offered handshake, peering up at Phineas from under thick, black eyebrows that came together over a long, narrow nose. "Darrell. Darrell Jones. And this here's Dolly. She needs your help." The husband's right index and middle fingers were stained amber between the first and second joints. The rest of the skin creases on his digits were highlighted with indelible black.

"Hello, Dolly." Phineas' eyelid involuntarily twitched at his word choice, but at his age he was finally comfortable calling most patients by their first names. "The computer says you're here for asthma."

She glanced at Darrell and murmured, "Least he didn't start singing it." She began rummaging through a bulky silver handbag with a 'Gutzi' label. "Got a CD for you to look at. My lung doctor back home says you have a new miracle azma drug I might be able to get. He says I might even get paid to take it."

Talk about managing expectations.

Phineas inserted the CD into the side of the computer monitor that hung from the ceiling and waited for the images to load. He clicked on the first of a long list of hospital discharge summaries and recognized the name of the referring doctor. A good guy, young and isolated as the only pulmonologist in an economically deprived area, a place he'd undoubtably settled in as part of a medical school debt-forgiveness deal, and an outpost the noble doctor couldn't feel right about abandoning after his obligatory stint.

His notes revealed that Dolly was cursed with asthma that defied control on the conventional medications and, at least three times in the last four years, she'd landed on ICU respirators after she almost died. She'd tried the two newer injectable biological medications that her local hospital pharmacy could access under a combination of her disability's Medicare coverage and the pharmaceutical companies' patient assistance programs. Neither had calmed her disease.

The notes also suggested that she often couldn't fill prescriptions for her lifesaving daily maintenance inhalers, since her husband's job as a truck mechanic paid just enough that she didn't qualify for Medicaid. This had forced her to repeatedly call her local pulmonologist and beg for precious, teasing drug samples and higher levels of prednisone on top of her everyday doses. The young family's medical debts had to be crippling, and the strain on their marriage and the fearful toll on a young son...Phineas struggled to imagine. He admired Darrell's loyalty. The young husband and father could have abandoned Dolly's chaos and moved on to an easier existence. Phineas had seen other severe asthma patients lose all support and give up hope. Despite Dolly's prior near-death scares, her upright posture and upturned face today radiated cautious hope. Could SYMBI-62022 offer it?

Phineas reminded himself that he should praise the referring doctor's care and documentation in the note he'd send to him after Dolly's visit. On paper, she seemed appropriate for the Phase 3 trial. Would she be able to make the required visits to Chapel Hill on the strict protocol's schedule?

When he looked up from the screen, she was staring at his face with wide open doe eyes. "Doc, you gonna be able to help me?"

Those dark brown eyes melted his weary heart. "Dolly, I'd like to hear more about your asthma. How old were you when it started?"

"I was just a youngin. My folks was always rushin' me to the GP for adrenaline and cortisone shots. Then I mostly outgrew it for a while after my monthly got goin'. Those was good years." She cast a wistful glance at the ceiling. "But it came back with a vengeance when Darrell Junior here was inside me. That was my first time on a respirator. Never left after." She studied her feet and spread her puffy toes. The edema extended from there up and under her sweatpants.

Her husband blocked a pair of wet coughs with the back of his hand and added, "It's gettin' worse, 'specially in the heat and on the code red an' orange days we been havin' 'bout every day. Our bedroom window's A/C unit's runnin' all the time."

"I've been hearing that more and more from my patients, Mr. Jones." Phineas nodded sympathetically. "With climate change, pollen and dust mite levels have increased substantially—and allergic conditions like asthma with them." He made a mental note to coach Darrell Sr. on how to keep a window air conditioner as free of mold as possible.

Despite Darrell Junior's frequent protests and attempts to open drawers and inspect equipment, Phineas worked through the rest of Dolly's history in his habitual compulsive fashion before he stood to examine her. "The doctors say her lungs only sound clear when she's had big doses of prednisone," Darrell Sr. murmured. Phineas heard an abundance of soft wheezes of varying pitches, like a distant woodwind symphony.

Phineas excused himself to gather the forms for the Phase 3 trial. As it was close to quitting time for staff, he didn't have the heart to ask anyone else in the clinic to assist Dolly in filling out the lengthy forms. He held them up as he re-entered the room.

"We need to fill these out and, after you sign them, I'll submit them. Also, before you go, we need a simple breathing test." He was grateful that his respiratory therapist always made sure she wasn't needed before she left for the day. "I believe you have a good chance of qualifying for the drug study. You'll need to come to this clinic at least once a month. Will you be able to do that?" He'd had two patients decline upon hearing that condition, so far. "If you do, the company will provide a stipend for your time and travel."

She sat up straight and reached for her husband's knee, a wide smile on her round face. "I'll be here when you say so. Thank you, Doc."

"This explains that two out three patients in the study receive the drug." Phineas pointed to a paragraph on the last page of the form. "One out of three will receive a placebo infusion. Neither you nor I will know which you're getting."

The corner of Darrell Sr.'s mouth twitched. "A *what* infusion?"

"A placebo. A solution in your wife's vein without any drug, so we can tell if the drug helps or if any improvement she might have is just from coming to this clinic."

"Tell me how driving six hours to get no drug's goin' to help her?" Darrell Sr. leaned forward, hands on his knees, like he was about to escape the cramped room.

"Sometimes suggestions we make for the rest of the asthma treatment help." Phineas prepared himself for their refusal.

Dolly's smile disappeared into a pout. "Guess that's the way it'll have to be." She looked at her husband. "Them odds ain't *too* bad, Darrell. Doncha think? Better than what I been dealt so far."

Marie balanced a tray of antipasti on one hand and carried a white cardboard box of oatmeal cookies in the other, offerings that SynMedical's files indicated would make her a welcome visitor more than a late day bother. She used her buttocks to push open the glass entrance door and wove her way past the vacant nursing command center toward the doctors' workroom she'd been told was tucked in the back. Phineas Mann's file reported that, after 6:00 PM on a Wednesday, he'd be hungry and at his clinic computer typing notes from his afternoon patient encounters. As predicted, his was the lone figure hunched over a keyboard with a notepad propped against the monitor. She noted his laborious typing, typical for men of his generation, who'd never been forced to take Typing I in middle school. By the time she'd taken it, the name had been changed to Keyboarding.

The instructions to bring even a modest bribe for an audience with him made her feel shabby, a sensation she wasn't accustomed to as a doctor. She cleared her throat softly. "Thought you might have worked up an appetite by now."

He spun around in his chair. "Oh, hi. Wasn't expecting anyone." He'd neatened his trimmed beard with freshly shaved cheeks and neck. She suspected this was his midweek pre-clinic routine. His long white coat was draped over the seat back, and his tie, gray with white polka dots, was loosened.

"Brought you something to whet your appetite before supper, and a dessert you can bring home." She lay the tray on the desk beside him and set the box next to it.

"Nice of you. Thank you. Now that you mention it, I was beginning to feel a bit peckish." He surveyed the tray's contents through its clear plastic lid. "Do I see prosciutto?"

"And a couple of Italian cheeses, some sliced crusty bread, olives, dates and—"

"Just what *I'd* have ordered." He looked elated.

She lifted the lid and offered it to him. He plucked an olive and popped it into his mouth then assembled a meat and cheese finger sandwich.

While he was busy chewing, she reached into her briefcase and removed her laptop. "I need to document my meeting with you."

"And the food expense?"

She shrugged. "Necessary detail. So, how is enrollment going for our Phase 3 study?"

"It's picking up. Three more today, referred from pulmonologists hours away. They'd been at ATS when I gave my talk. I'm getting optimistic we'll more than make goals." He continued to survey the platter.

"That's great. All I need to know. Any questions for me?"

"Not yet. SynMedical's trial manual is very thorough."

"Well, that makes this a business meeting. How's life? And how's Iris?" She typed, focusing on him and not at her laptop's screen.

"Wish I could type like that. I'd get home earlier." He picked up a pitted date. "Well, nothing's new for me, but Iris has decided to retire."

"Wow! Big step. How long has she worked at UNC?" She closed her computer.

"Let's see. We came back to Chapel Hill in '86, and she started grad school in '87. Finished her PhD in '92 and joined the faculty then. So, that makes 32 years for her."

Marie released a long, slow sigh. "I'd call that a career. What's she planning to do?"

"She says 'Think for a while' first, but she's already full speed ahead in helping with Martha's campaign."

"That's got to be exciting. Something new to fill her days."

"Already plunging into the nastiness of politics and social media. The President doesn't want her incumbent opponent to lose his House seat."

"Please remind her that I'm up for helping Martha. I'm still learning my way around here and hardly know anyone outside work. It'd be fun for me, and I've got the time." She opened the dessert box and offered it to him. "Oatmeal cookie?"

"I'm curious." He tilted his head forward like he was pondering a puzzle. "Does your company always offer doctors oatmeal cookies, or is it only for me?"

"It's what's in your file. Says they're your favorite."

"My file?" His eyes narrowed.

"Oh, the reps maintain files on all the docs." *He didn't know about his file.* "Yours is pretty long after all your years here."

"Seriously?" His head jerked back. "I had no idea. What *else* does mine say?"

"Let's see. I studied it when I first started. As I recall, you tend to gravitate to more adventurous cuisine." She lowered her voice. "And short skirts plus a glimpse of cleavage don't get reps extra face time with you. You'd be surprised how many male docs have those boxes checked." She was glad his weren't. Her sudden blush that followed that revelation piled on to her embarrassment.

"Okay. I don't think I want to know any more." He covered his face with both hands. "I'll have a cookie, but why don't you take the rest of this home. It'll save you making supper."

"You talked me into the antipasti, but you keep the cookies. I'm not interested in shopping for a new wardrobe. You can freeze what you and Iris don't eat tonight...And take her some olives and dates, at least." She scraped several into the box and handed it to him.

He set it next to the computer screen and turned his attention to his notepad. "I'm close to done here. Thanks for stopping by, and for the well-orchestrated treat."

"Don't mention it. Hope to see you again soon." *He wants to finish up and get out of here.* She backed her way to the workroom door.

His fingers settled on the keyboard before he glanced back at her. "And Marie, you don't have to bring food to meet with me. You're a doctor and a colleague on this study, not a drug rep."

"Thank you for saying that." *I needed it.*

Finally at home, Phineas set the box on their dining room table next to Iris and her laptop. "Marie dropped these at clinic for us. And she said I should tell you that she still wants to help with Martha's campaign."

"What's this?"

"Oatmeal cookies—and some olives and dates, if you'd like a snack before dinner."

"Huh! Oatmeal cookies. Your favorite. Interesting." She stared up at him.

"What I said. Turns out the drug reps have been keeping a file on me for years."

"Oh, Phineas. For someone medically sophisticated, you can be so naïve." She smirked and shook her head.

"Think they might have shared my file with the FBI?"

"Now that's a disturbing thought, but I can't think of why they would. SynMedical and the FBI? Hmmm...Well...except the FBI didn't bring oatmeal cookies."

⌒

Marie combined the remnants of prosciutto and cheese with slices of carrots and zucchini from her refrigerator, together almost enough for her dinner. One of these days, she'd figure out when to fit shopping for groceries into her routine. Provisioning food was not her strong suit.

She propped herself up on her sofa with her iPad and ran the CNN headlines. More disturbing news. Massive fires still devoured her beloved Washington, Oregon, and California, and the administration let those blue states beg for federal assistance. Another environmental protection of lakes and streams rescinded. The more she scanned, the more her appetite dwindled. Expanded drilling for oil in the Arctic and in National Forests. More fracking sites. More wealth to fewer citizens. An attack with assault weapons on peaceful protesters by right-wing counter protesters. Four murdered. No one charged. Queasy replaced what remained of her hunger.

She switched to FOX News for the cringeworthy opposing views. Economy booming. Miracle breakthroughs in American medicine. The President's border wall working to protect America from drug dealers and rapists. Great white shark attacks health-obsessed triathlete in San Francisco Bay.

Ugh!

She closed the news and opened her Kindle app to Jacob's novel then reread the attempted kidnapping scene, the one where she found herself in the backseat of Iris' SUV with the seven-year-old daughter's feet sticking out the passenger door. The thirteen-year-old son had just hurled stones with his strong right arm and vanquished the violent racist.

She shifted to the 'About the Author' paragraphs on the last page. It said he'd written chapters of the novel for his creative writing classes at Cornell University as an undergraduate. Teachers had encouraged him to expand his work into the novel he self-published at the end of his PhD stint in entomology there. Beekeepers had picked it up on Amazon at first, before an agent spotted it and sold it to a major publisher. Books featuring racism were becoming hot. Then the *Times* best sellers list for twenty weeks and Oprah's book club. Then the movie.

His bio must have been updated since the publisher's first printing, since it mentioned Jacob's current position at NC State. It also mentioned that he was working on a prequel. She let her head sink into the pillow and closed her eyes. How would her mother appear in *that* story? Would it feature her at her most deranged? Yes, because it would have to end with her crazed *60 Minutes* meltdown. One loss of control had ruined her mother's life. How might it nip at her daughter's?

She spoke with her half-brother at the honey extraction almost a month ago. He mentioned he was considering at a faculty position back at Cornell, located in the middle of nowhere. Then he explained that it had become a more reliable location for his honey bee research, since North Carolina's heat and the invasion of deadly pests and Africanized bees increasingly sabotaged his experiments.

She checked out how to get there—just out of curiosity, she told herself—and learned it was not a quick trip from North Carolina. Her search turned up pictures of the gorgeous campus and surrounding region and the revelation that Ithaca was warmer with climate change than its cold, wet past and was now often more pleasant than most parts of the US.

Climate change was transforming Ithaca into a respite travel destination. No wonder Jacob was drawn north.

She hardly knew him. So why did her gut tell her that she'd miss him if he left? Must be what it feels like with siblings.

～

Phineas finished strapping down the three beehives onto their heavy landscape timber stands and went inside to check the pantry. Its shelves of batteries and candles appeared well-stocked. He counted the repurposed plastic orange juice bottles Iris had filled with their well water: thirty-six half gallons, enough for a couple of weeks. Same with canned and dried provisions. Two coolers of potable ice sat in the garage with extra in the freezer, left over from ten days ago, the last power grid failure threat—that time from North Korean hackers, or so the rumor went. In the tool shed, he had a spare tank of propane for the grill, and the koi pond could provide a source of non-potable water for toilet flushing and garden watering, when the well pump lost electricity. Iris' Prius was tucked safely in the garage, and his pickup secured away from any tall trees that might fall in high winds.

Mise en place.

Despite the trauma inflicted on him by Hurricane Jezebel so many years ago, he remained spellbound by his morbid attraction to want to experience as much of a storm's violent energy as he could safely tolerate, like the painful pleasure of wiggling a sore tooth or pressing on a deep bruise.

In the last hour, the temperature had fallen more than ten degrees, quick relief from the earlier oppressive heat. Dusk accelerated under soot-colored clouds, and the gusts of wind that encircled their house began to sway the mature trees and to bend saplings like disciples at prayer. Nickel-sized drops dotted the deck planks around him. One struck his forehead and dribbled along both sides of his nose. He caught the cool liquid that filtered through his mustache on his tongue. In the southeast, a lightning bolt ripped the sky's grey fabric. One. Two. Three. A deep rumble shook his guts. *Close.*

The porch door cracked open, and Iris' voice escaped it. "Better come inside."

"In a moment." Another jagged bolt lit up the tree canopy. One...

CRAAACK! The exhilarating whiff of ozone.

"Your UNC life insurance paid up?" She yelled this time, the howling wind competing with her words.

"Last I checked." He followed her inside and took up an observation post behind the glass door.

"They're now saying Chastity's eye will pass just east of Raleigh around 2 AM, and we can expect winds over 115 miles per hour. They also said a bomb cyclone hit east of Fayetteville."

"*What* is a bomb cyclone?" Rain pounded the deck like a protracted drum solo.

"I saw an article about bomb cyclones in the *Times*. The barometric pressure falls really fast causing high winds and sudden heavy precipitation. The one in Fayetteville had hail the size of baseballs. There were two deaths and multiple injuries." She watched him for his reaction. "They're happening more often—and sometimes they form suddenly, even when there's no tracked storm."

Phineas felt less shocked by her tragic news than he once would have been, having heard so many reports of devastation in recent years. "Why do disasters always have to peak when it's dark?" He wanted to watch it all.

"Why are we having our third hurricane in June?" Iris extended her hands out in front of her as if she was pleading to a divine power.

The swath of North Carolina up the Cape Fear River had long ago been named Hurricane Alley. In the last several years it was a hurricane superhighway.

An earsplitting boom matched a blinding flash.

In the kitchen and dining area, the overhead lights flickered and went dark. The hum of the air conditioner ground down to a moment of eerie silence followed by the shrieks of the gale outside their suddenly vulnerable wood and brick shelter.

He felt Iris' hands on his hips. "Leftovers are on the table. I'll light candles."

~

By midnight the rains were a torrent. Phineas returned to his sentry post, though now he positioned himself several feet back from the windows and aimed his 500,000-candlepower spotlight at the backyard orchard and apiary every time a loud crack suggested a broken limb or snapped tree.

A brilliant flash lit up every glass pane, and the simultaneous linked thunder was immediately followed by a resonating crash that came from— oh no!—from the direction of his apiary. He swung his bright beam of light across the expanse.

Shit!

A mature poplar, sixty plus feet tall, had crushed one of his three hives, and now, 50,000 disturbed honey bees, mixed with the downpour and illuminated by his bright light, formed a dynamic sparkling cloud over their flattened dwelling. He felt a hand pat his shoulder.

"Where was that one? It woke me up." Iris spoke close to his ear.

"You don't want to know." He wished he didn't.

"Try me." She stifled a yawn with her fist.

"A tree just smashed one of our hives." And there was nothing he could do about it tonight.

"Oh no! What can you do?" She stared at the unique and disturbing image his beam spotlighted.

"Obviously nothing now. In the morning, I'll try to find the queen. Her workers'll probably be around her. If she hasn't drowned, I'll put her in an empty hive and hope enough survivors come to her."

"I'm guessing they won't be happy bees." She pressed against him.

"*That's* an understatement. Their beekeeper isn't happy either." His guts were twisting.

"Come back to bed. With no electricity and all this destruction outside, I need you next to me." She kissed him on his lips, a lingering kiss with her hand firmly on the back of his neck. On any other night, he'd be instantly aroused by such attention.

⌒

At the first pre-dawn light, Phineas left the warmth of his wife, donned his protective bee jacket and gloves, and slipped a protective queen cage in his pocket. Then he packed the smoker with as much pine straw as it would hold, lit it, and pumped clouds of nature's incense. The rains had dwindled to intermittent sprinkles, and gusts from the west only flipped leaves on their stems. The back yard was awash in disturbed bees generating enough of a buzz to be heard over the swooshes of the waning winds.

The poplar was at least eighteen inches in diameter where it had torn through the deer fencing and splintered the hive. Collections of worker bees formed loose mats on the hive's remnants. At least a dozen of them bumped him and explored his jacket and pants for openings. He used his index finger to part clumps on the ground, hoping to spot the bee with a stout and elongated abdomen, while dozens of workers, furious and defensive, pointed their stingers at him and his disruptive finger. No luck on that first hasty inspection.

The second time Phineas resolved to be more systematic. There. On the ground partially hidden by the poplar's trunk was a trembling pile of at least a hundred bees. He blew on the center, coaxing the top layer to part and expose her highness. He pushed most of her retinue aside and slid the cage in front of her. A gentle push and his most essential bee was inside. He snapped the lid in place. *Whew!*

For the next half hour, he hurried to assemble a new home for this displaced colony before hordes of robber bees from hives elsewhere discovered the exposed fragrant, golden honey treasure. The hive equipment leftover from his trash bag smothering, his painful but essential genocide, of the Africanized colony weeks earlier would form the external structure. The intact frames packed with fresh honey from the crushed hive went in the planned top level, which he set aside with protective covers. Next, he inserted the frames of brood the storm had spared side by side in the center of the lower hive body. Finally, he settled the top level in place and released his queen into her new castle to enthusiastic greetings from her subjects. Hundreds of loose bees from all around him clamored up the landing platform and into the entrance of their new home. Mission accomplished, and he'd only had to tolerate two stings through his loose jeans.

Trees, flattened in the direction of, but out of reach of his house, littered what had been a stand of poplars behind the apiary. Masses of green foliage blanketed previously open ground. Yesterday everything under six feet high outside his protective fence was an umber hue, scorched earth under relentless pressure from hungry deer, whose habitat was steadily shrinking.

Three does, like soft statues, watched from a tiny cluster of still vertical pine saplings, the deer's round brown eyes alternating their focus between the rent in the fence and the lush, raised vegetable beds inside. A months old fawn pressed against one of their legs. Her attention was on the raucous bees.

Better patch the hole before they invade the compound.

Phineas loaded the pieces of the destroyed hive that weren't pinned down by the poplar into his garden cart and moved it to the far corner of the yard for forager bees to clean out. He dipped his honey sticky gloves in a puddle and wiped them through a thick patch of clover. Then he fueled his chainsaw and gathered plastic cinch ties from his tool shed for the fence repair.

Iris leaned out the window. "What are you planning to do now?"

"Saw the tree enough to patch the fence, before we have a herd of deer in our yard. They're just outside, salivating and taking inventory of your ornamentals and my vegetables."

"Be careful. I don't want to have to take you to the emergency room after you've cut off a toe—or worse. The roads may not be passable." Her first smile of the day emerged. "And you know I just get all *swimmy-headed* at the sight of your blood." Her voice acquired the lilt of a Southern Belle's, as she fanned her face with her hand.

Her concern and humor lifted his dour mood. "I'm coming up for my steel-toed boots."

"What about your helmet and face shield?" Her smile vanished.

"Won't fit under my bee jacket's screen, and I still need that. The bees are really pissed off."

"Suit yourself." She held up a mug. "Want coffee first? I boiled water on the grill burner."

"Soon as I seal the fence. Thanks."

⌒

Phineas shut off the chain saw and lowered himself into the weathered cedar chair next to the hives, a place that he previously enjoyed as a respite place, a haven where he could recharge his spirit's batteries and observe his bees' comings and goings. His beekeeping jacket now clung to his sweaty arms and back, and a few unsettled guard bees persisted in probing his protective covering for vulnerable spots to deliver venom.

A vehicle's door slammed.

"Hey Dad, you look like you could use someone to spell you." Jacob's deep voice preceded his arrival. He had a bee jacket in hand, and work gloves dangled from his jeans' back pocket. Phineas could just make out those details as the day's early rays seeped through departing clouds and silhouetted his son. The beagle, Ruby, paused beside the raised garden beds to squat.

"I won't turn down help. How'd you know I could use it?" Phineas squinted at Jacob.

"Mom called."

"Ah! Of course." Iris's cellphone tree in operation.

"So, what should I do next?" Jacob zipped into his jacket and hood.

"I was just able to zip tie a patch in the fence, so I've managed to keep a herd of hungry deer at bay. You had coffee? I was about to get some."

"A cup on the way here." Jacob began tossing small limbs over the fence. "You go ahead and grab yourself some. I'll tidy up some of this mess, and then we can finish up sawing and moving the heavy trunk pieces." He heaved a larger branch and paused. "Heard some really bad news from California last night."

"Oh, what's that? We lost internet."

"Me too, but I texted with someone I know at UC Davis. Those fires that were near the biggest almond orchards suddenly shifted and advanced into the trees too fast for the firefighters to hold them off. Almond crops for decades to come will be a miniscule fraction of this year's—and that's not the worst of it—most of the commercial beekeepers in that region lost their hives."

Phineas cringed at the image of burning hives. The bees would be hunkered down inside pumping their wings in a futile effort to ventilate the rising heat out the hive entrances. Then the hive would catch on fire, and the bees' wax comb would explode into an inferno that within seconds would march from one colony to the next, incinerating everything.

The downstream effects would be far reaching. Without almond orchards and the pollination fees that were many of the nation's commercial beekeepers' main support, they would become insolvent.

"Are your colleagues at UC Davis okay?"

Jacob nodded inside his hood. "Yeah. Physically, but their research apiaries are gone. Years of work up in smoke. Yesterday was a tragic, career changing event for their whole department—and for the whole beekeeping world." He pointed at the pile of Phineas' smashed hive parts. "I ran by the NC State apiary on my way here. Lots of standing water, but nothing like that."

"I guess there are worse things during the climate crisis than a Category 3 east coast hurricane." At least he still had his house, his job, and his bees—and Jacob still had *his* research—for now.

Phineas was glad to finally peel off his soggy jacket as he trudged toward the house and coffee. Two more car doors slammed. When he rounded the corner, Marie and Chelsea were standing next to Marie's Tesla. The sun's rays broke through the departing storm clouds and shone upon them. Chelsea waved with both hands. "Thought you and Iris might need cheering up." Her tee shirt read "Climate Change is Real".

Marie hugged a shopping bag to her chest. She wore a purple and gold U of W ballcap, and her hair was tied back. "Good morning. I hear you've been busy already."

"That's an understatement. I'm a little surprised to see you two here— but glad to have you stop by."

"Iris texted us. She said Martha's coming over, and we're going to work on campaign items—and she said you have lots of ice, so I brought my humble stores to share what might otherwise spoil." Marie patted her jeans with her free hand. "I wore work clothes, so I can help with cleanup. She said you had a mess in the yard."

"I foresee a busy afternoon of grilling. Jacob's out back doing cleanup. Want coffee?"

"I'm good. I'll drop these groceries off with Iris and go help him."

Chelsea stepped toward Phineas for a hug then backed away. "Eww, Finman! You're all wet...I think I'll go get started on the campaign with Iris. I'm more of an *inside* girl."

Standing at his study window, Phineas munched on a peanut butter sandwich and sipped strong coffee while he surveyed the yard's cleanup tasks ahead. The rise in the house's temperature and humidity still lagged behind that in the yard. Without air conditioning, they'd soon be approaching an uncomfortable equilibrium. He felt a familiar hand on the small of his back and said, "Could be worse, Iris. At least nothing hit the house."

"We'll see. Depends on how long the power company takes to fix the grid." She pointed at Jacob and Marie. "Those two remind me of years ago, when school was canceled for bad weather."

Jacob stepped away from the hives, removed his bee jacket hood, and guffawed at something Marie said. She plucked a couple of Phineas' ripe cherry tomatoes and plopped them in her mouth then bent to gather fallen branches and leaves from the garden's raised beds. When she found a fractured baseball-sized green tomato, she chucked it at Jacob. He dodged it and sent it underhand back at her.

While watching their play, Phineas felt his mood lift. "I'm sure we're luckier than most. Nothing that can't be cleaned up or repaired *this* time."

"And those two don't seem to mind."

A car door sound, then another. Mateo sprinted into the backyard and zeroed in on the hives before Martha grabbed a handful of his shirt and hoisted him into a two-armed protective hug. Marie waved at Mateo then engaged him in a game of peek-a-boo behind her work gloves. She and Martha marched back toward the driveway. The sounds of Mateo's tiny feet racing through the house soon followed.

"Wayla! Waylo!" He'd found them. His arms stretched up toward Iris. "Big trees fall down!" She lifted him and balanced him on her hip, so he could see out the window. He pointed at the splintered hive remnants in the corner of the yard. "Bee house broken." A quieter, sad voice.

Martha was close behind, lugging the obligatory diaper bag, a separate sack of books and toys, and her nylon briefcase. "Glad you texted, Mom. Sitting home with no power was quickly getting pretty darned dull, except for this one's excitement. He seems to enjoy storms."

"Like his grandfather." Iris poked Phineas' ribs with her free hand. She led them to the dining room. "Where's Felipe?"

"At the restaurant. Since they have gas ranges, they're cooking the food in the walk-in coolers for employees' families, police, and firemen until it's all gone." Mateo accepted a fuzzy polar bear from his mother. "We'll make an appearance later. Felipe said he'd call when it was a good time for us to come." Martha opened her briefcase and extracted a laptop.

"Aw...We'd hoped your chef husband would be here to help us when we grill our stuff," Iris pouted. "Well, make sure you have someone take lots of pictures of you, Mateo, and Felipe with our public servants. We can post those images online and get them into the news—when the power's back and we have news again."

Phineas reached for Mateo and secured him in his embrace. "I'll take this guy, so you three can strategize without him. It's been long enough that those crazy bees should be settled down by now. Mateo, come on. Let's go check on your Uncle Jacob."

Marie held up her work gloves. "Why don't I help out back a while longer and let you political pros get organized. Later, you can tell me how I can help. Sound good?"

Iris cleared the dining room table for what would soon be piles of campaign material. "We'll call you in before it gets too hot outside. Shouldn't be long."

⌐∿

Marie helped Jacob tidy up the yard for another half hour in the heat and humidity before a window opened and Iris waved Marie back inside for their strategy session. When she glanced down and realized perspiration had not only soaked her cotton tee shirt but wicked down, darkening the inner thighs of her jeans, she was mortified. Good thing she had the foresight to bring a change of clothes—and thankfully, at the last minute, included underwear.

"Sorry to abandon you, Jacob."

"No problem. I'd rather pick up brush than do politics, so have at it." His thick hair and beard were plastered to his face and his neck, and his wet shirt adhered to his long and lean torso.

Marie made a conscious effort to return her focus to his face and reminded herself that he was her half-brother. "I'm not sure what I can add to their planning, but I guess I can learn from Martha, and I'll follow orders." Orders from her younger half-sister.

"There's not *that* much more to do out here. Then I'll start helping Dad with Mateo and the cooking."

"Glad you men cook. I'm good with washing dishes."

"It's mostly Dad who cooks, but I've learned a fair bit from him." He abruptly studied the ground then looked up at her face. "It's really nice of you to come over and pitch in."

Marie caught that he'd stolen a glance at her figure, so she lifted the sticky shirt fabric enough off her skin to have less of her body on display. "I was glad when your Mom texted. This is way better than hanging out in my condo with everything dark and shut down." She began trudging toward the house and hollered back over her shoulder. "I'd better go in before your mother wonders if I abandoned them."

Jacob watched her as he wiped his hands on his jeans and pulled his gloves back on. "I'll be up before long. See ya' there."

With her change of clothes in hand, Marie begged a towel from Iris and began the task of freshening up. Her glowing cheeks in the bathroom mirror confirmed that she'd had more than enough sun for the day.

In her early morning post-hurricane excitement, she'd again forgotten how hot and humid North Carolina could get in summer, the misery that had clearly worsened as the Earth baked under a clear lid of carbon-based gases. And the new home she'd chosen had plenty of sudden, violent storms—and *lots* of hurricanes. At least North Carolina hadn't yet fought the massive forest fires that regularly incinerated and suffocated the swaths of the West she abandoned.

She rinsed her face in water from a plastic bottle left on the dry sink's counter. After considerable effort, she emerged looking better than presentable and grateful for dry underwear. A day with new friends and her new family demanded nothing less.

She slipped into a chair across from Martha and surveyed a table covered with neat piles of handouts, posters and documents. One of the piles consisted of sheets that listed Martha's positions in columns on its left side and contrasted them with her opponent's on its right. It highlighted Martha's views on climate, healthcare, women's rights, gun control, and other planks in her Democratic platform. Her opponent's columns listed opposite views and was topped by an image of him holding an AR-15 assault rifle and kneeling behind a dead black bear. Marie shuddered at the image, then, in a more controlled motion, raised her hand to her forehead in salute. "Ready to follow orders, General."

Martha handed Marie a laminated card and a schedule. "Here's your campaign pass and my upcoming events. When you're available, I'd love for you to come and help with handing out information and swag. I've got lawn signs in my car you can install—and please, call me Martha."

Chelsea patted Martha's arm. "You *can* sound like you're planning a military operation, Honey...That's a good thing, considering."

"Funny you would say that. When I told Dad I was going to run, he gave me a copy of *The Art of War*."

Marie picked up the sheet outlining Martha's and her opponent's positions. "Your opponent looks like he's studied it."

"Maybe if it was in comic book form." Martha snickered. "He's not that deep—and he never served in the military—just like his Commander-in-Chief. Also, something to do with his feet."

"Don't underestimate the man. 'Know thy enemy.'" Iris shook her head in warning. "And remember, he has the President in his corner, and that sonofabitch has shown his willingness to personally attack you."

Marie must have looked puzzled at the comment.

"He sent ICE into my husband's restaurant, and they wouldn't let him out of jail until we showed legal proof that he's an American citizen," Martha explained.

"Shit. Really?—Oops, sorry."

"Don't apologize. It is shit, total bullshit." Iris pounded the table with her fist. "Abuse of power. That man needs to go."

Iris' sudden temper was startling...and more startling still was the question of how much risk Martha's team might actually be facing? Marie asked, "Have there been any actual threats?" and more specifically, wondered whether Martha's opponent would try to figure out a certain new and dedicated supporter's background too—once his team saw her around?

"Social media trolls. His base." Iris massaged her temples with the heels of her hands. "Nothing yet that qualifies as breaking the law. Still first amendment allowable." The women exchanged looks and fell silent.

Marie cleared her throat to break the tension. "So, what can I do between events?"

"Hand out these position papers and flyers and tack up these posters wherever you can." Martha passed her a portion of three of the piles. "And don't worry about running out. We still have enough in our war chest to print more."

"Is your war chest going to last till voting?" Marie asked.

Martha's eyebrows scrunched together as she shook her head. "We'll need more soon, which means fundraising, one of my least favorite parts of this." The dirty reality of financing the effort.

"We're spending everything we raise, and everything the Democratic party gives us, but it's less than Martha's opponent gets from the gun lobby and other Republican sources." Chelsea leaned closer to Marie. "We could use extra for more TV spots—Martha's messages and the ones I'm going to make endorsing her."

"Perhaps I can help a little with that part. How does one contribute?"

"Thanks, Marie." Martha pointed at a line on a flyer that indicated checks, credit cards, PayPal, Venmo, and Bitcoin were gratefully accepted. "We're ready to take anything our supporters offer."

Mateo galloped around the corner and climbed into Martha's lap. "Now, is my little man going to help us?"

In a single decisive motion, he swept the neat piles over the edge of the table and onto the floor and exclaimed, "All done!"

"Mateo!" Phineas trailed close behind his grandson. "Sorry. Want me to take him again?"

"No. He's right. Time for a break." Martha nuzzled her spirited boy.

Phineas took a step back. "From what I heard, it sounded like it *was* starting to get kind of hot in here."

"And it's going to get hotter." Iris wrinkled her nose at him then stood and pushed her chair against the table. "Phineas, why don't you get the grill ready, and I'll make a food inventory? Mateo, you can take your mother and Marie and venture out to see how many of our neighbors want to come join us?"

Chelsea still looked the freshest of all. "I'll assist in the kitchen. I know my way around in there."

⌐

As Marie helped round up the grateful neighbors, she saw how they and the Mann family were clearly practiced in the art of managing after hurricanes crippled the power grid. They silenced their chain saws for the afternoon, and the relaxed, spontaneous potluck that followed confirmed friendships and support. As dusk approached, the coolers of iced beverages softened the misery of no air conditioning in the North Carolina summer swelter that now penetrated all the way inside to Marie's seat at the dining room table.

During her previous life in the Northwest, she'd gone through a limited number of crisis events, but the trauma of her hospital work during the 2020-2022 COVID-19 pandemic left scars that she tried to quickly submerge each time they surfaced—especially the patients she couldn't keep alive and had no time to get to know. They'd died alone, without family nearby. Family. Her sadness and exhaustion had been camouflaged in the anonymous cocoon of personal protective equipment. And then finally the wracking muscle pains and blistering fevers she suffered alone in her apartment eating the meager dry goods she'd stored. She was barely recovering from the virus when she pitched back in during the pandemic's prolonged and messy tail. It took more than six months for her to gain back the lost weight and stamina, and each morning her gaunt face in the mirror had reminded her of a skull, of death.

"Up!" Mateo rescued Marie from her somber reverie by patting her leg with both hands then raising his arms over his head. "Up!"

She lifted him onto her lap. "And what can I do for you, Sir?"

"Read book." He scanned the surface of the table.

Martha trailed him at a respectful distance then found a frayed volume in her bulky cloth sack. "He likes this one, Marie." She wiped catsup from her son's face with a ready tissue. "Then he and I need to head to Felipe's restaurant. He just called."

"Can I help you there? I can at least sit with Mateo while you make speeches, press the flesh, or whatever it is you do at those things."

"That would be great. Felipe will be super busy." Martha sounded truly grateful.

Mateo's head swiveled to stare up at Marie's face. He cupped her chin in his pudgy hand. "Read."

Marie read the cover. "The Lorax by Dr. Seuss." She cracked it open and read about the mythical creature who spoke for the trees.

As she passed the book's halfway point, she realized that Jacob was propped against the door jamb watching. He whispered, "Your audience's eyes are drooping. He should be ready for a nap in a page or two."

Marie read the part about caring a whole awful lot.

Jacob bent to hoist Mateo into his arms and cradled him against his chest, taking care to not tickle him with his beard. "I'll carry him to his car seat, if you'll help Martha with all her stuff."

"Sounds like a plan. By the way, you look like a natural at that." It couldn't be right to feel such a stirring over one's half-brother.

"He's my only nephew. Also, my godson." He rocked Mateo side to side ever so slowly. "Mind if I tag along? Haven't seen Felipe in a while." He peered into her eyes, probing her soul. Ruby whined and stared up at him, begging for his attention.

Marie felt her cheeks flush, so she quickly bowed her head to gaze down at Mateo. What if Jacob wasn't her half-brother, and it was perfectly fine to be attracted to him? But her mother had been so convincing...it couldn't be okay. He'd offered to carry Mateo and then join them at Felipe's restaurant. Sure. Why not? "Yeah...I'd like that...He looks so peaceful now."

"You young folks run along." Chelsea appeared behind her. "It's getting dark, so I'll just crash here."

⌒

Traffic lights were all out, and one of the intersections split their three-vehicle caravan. Third in line, Marie had been following Jacob's truck. A sweaty, red-faced cop let Jacob through then blew his whistle and held up his hand with his palm aimed at Marie when she tried to follow. He bowed deeply and smiled at her before he let the whole line of cars that traveled across her path pass through. His antics would have been irritating, if her car's lights didn't make him look so pitiful, like he was melting in the heat under the weight of his bulletproof vest and weaponry.

She'd considered trying to hug Jacob's bumper to slip by, but the long, hot day had tempted her into a second IPA. Marie guessed there'd been adequate time to metabolize enough alcohol to comfortably pass a Breathalyzer, but there was no reason to take unnecessary chances. She'd eventually catch up with Jacob's red pickup. She rewarded the traffic cop with a smile when he finally waved her through.

Images of sparse traffic were illuminated on Marie's Tesla's computer screen over the twisty segments of suburban roads Martha had chosen. The Waze app indicated a vehicle stopped around the next corner. Marie slowed as she came around it and recognized Jacob's truck parked on the soft shoulder with warning lights flashing. Ruby's nose protruded from a mostly closed window while her master crouched over an object the size of half a cantaloupe straddling the road's yellow center line.

She switched on her caution indicators, pulled over, and lowered her window. "You lose something? Maybe a Truffula fruit?"

Jacob approached her, displaying his find. The turtle in his sizable grip promptly pulled its head and legs into the shell. "It's a yellowbelly slider. Genus Trachemys. They're on the move this time of year. Bad for it and any car not paying attention." In several long strides, he covered the distance to the high weeds well off the road and gently deposited the reptile.

She clapped three times on his return. "Very noble of you. I'm impressed. Okay, shiny knight, how much farther?"

He returned her smile but tucked his beard, looking almost bashful. "Almost there. Then you get to meet Felipe." He was standing next to her window, out of potential traffic. "And his French cooking."

My brand-new family just keeps getting better. She sure as hell wasn't going to ruin it now by demanding they acknowledge her as an official member.

He squatted to bring his face to her level. "Marie?"

"Jacob?" He looked like he was gathering courage. Her instincts told her to be ready to defend.

"A confession. The day I met you, you left your card on Dad's desk. I entered your contact info in my phone...Would...would it be okay if I called you for a date?"

"Wish we could." She'd thought this one out. "Our employee handbook forbids anything beyond business or casual meetings with our investigators or their family...Sorry. I'm too new there to break rules." The inside of her car provided a safe bunker for her.

An eighteen-wheeler came around the corner behind them, its headlights spotlighting Jacob's disappointed expression. He bolted to the front of her car, further from the massive truck's approach and SynMedical's rules.

After it passed, she offered him a spark of hope in place of the real reason. "Maybe when your father's study ends?"

"When's that?" He sounded hopeful.

"One, maybe two years?" Her words filled the perfect silence surrounding them. Where had all the cricket sounds gone?

"Seems like a long time for someone my age." He kept his distance.

And mine. Can't argue with him there. "Why don't you send me your contact info, and we can communicate—as friends." *Or siblings.* She needed to end this conversation or take it in a new direction. "By the way, I read your novel." She couldn't stop herself.

"How did you know?" He stepped closer.

"It's a little embarrassing to admit, but SynMedical has an extensive file on your father." Not yet a lie. "I saw it in there." His head snapped back at the mention of the file. Time for her to pivot again. "How did you come to write it?"

He stared at her from under a creased brow. "You talk to the FBI or something?"

FBI again? "You'd be surprised what info drug companies keep on their doctors. *I* sure was."

He came back to her window. "Since you asked, I wrote a short story in my Creative Writing class in college. The TA liked it, so I kept adding chapters with each assignment. I'd call Dad when I needed details. At the end of the semester, the professor over all the TA sections suggested I put it all together and offered to help me. Still took years to get it published."

The darkness and desolation of their location momentarily emboldened her. "You did quite a job on the characters—especially the villains."

"They were so bizarre, they wrote themselves."

My Mom. If you only knew what came before and after. And Marie wanted to read the prequel that his novel's cover promised. "So, when's your next novel?"

"Research and teaching are keeping me too busy. Haven't yet gotten traction on writing it." A smile finally emerged. "Want to stream the movie with me sometime?"

He doesn't give up easily! "Sometime. I'll let you know. We should get to Felipe's before Mateo gets too rambunctious." She pressed the Tesla's power button, and its headlights shot beams into endless black.

⌒

In his cell's contacts, Phineas touched Vinnie's number for the third time. No answer. The battery level was down to 30% as he shut it off. "Still not answering." Iris and he were hoping for reassurance that Vinnie and Theresa still thrived despite having no electricity.

"It's gotta be hard to navigate in the dark with a walker. He could have fallen and broken his hip." She worried more about everything recently since the FBI, Martha's campaign, and all the troubling national news.

"Theresa would have called us, if that happened. He probably just turned it off to save battery." Had Phineas become too desensitized to worry from all his years of critical care, preferring to react to instead of anticipate trouble?

"She could be hurt too, or they could both be *sick*." She was easily wearing him down. "I'd feel better if we check on them."

"You want to go there now or later?"

"Now." She released him from her stare. "After I pee and freshen up."

He collected his keys and wallet and waited next to the front door. A quick sniff of his tee shirt armpit made it clear that he should "freshen up" a bit too. When he returned, she was tapping her foot and wearing an impatient expression. "Which vehicle?" she asked.

"Let's take the truck. Save your Prius for longer trips."

He climbed into the stifling, stale cab and cranked the ignition. She started to buckle her seat belt, then stopped and glanced at him. "Wait. We should bring them some produce."

He shut off the engine. As she jumped out, she said, "I'll get some from the kitchen. Why don't you go out back and harvest some more?"

With two bags of vegetables wedged behind Iris' seat, they motored down the nearly empty back roads and into town. Fallen trees and piles of branches covered with wilting leaves lined the streets. Some had been sawed to allow traffic to pass. Once the truck's cab approached a tolerable temperature, Iris adjusted the aged air conditioner to a less deafening level.

Phineas eased his pickup past a clump of children kicking a ragged soccer ball in the cul-de-sac and parked in the driveway behind Vinnie's ten-year-old Lincoln, its wax job gleaming in the late afternoon sun. Iris whispered, "Seems awfully quiet" before handing her husband one of the bags of produce. She marched up the handicap ramp in front and opened the screen door. Her finger was on the doorbell, when the heavy bright red wooden door flew open, and its suction tried to pull her in.

Vinnie, in pressed button-down shirt and slacks, leaned one forearm on his walker. "Hey Iris, Doc, sure glad to see you. You guys okay?"

Iris gave Vinnie a quick hug. She showed him her bag of produce. "Thought you might like some fresh veggies."

"Jeesh, that's awful nice of you to think of us. Theresa makes sure we've got plenty of everything when these storms are coming. *You* need anything? Got enough water at your place? We're on city water here, so that's good."

Wearing black slacks, a loose silk blouse, and makeup, Theresa glided around the corner from the hallway like she'd stepped out of a photoshoot. "Vinnie, your manners! Invite them inside." She reached up to hug Iris then Phineas. "Before we lost power, I made a bunch of brownies. You'll have to take some home."

She led them into their immaculate kitchen. A plate on the center island displayed olives and slices of meats and cheeses. "We were just having a little antipasto from one of Vinnie's regular orders from New York. Have some. We've got some coppa and Toscano salami that we cut up before we lost power. You'll have to take some of it home too." On a side countertop, a formidable meat slicer rested, unplugged.

Vinnie used a battery-operated device to uncork a wine bottle. "This Brunello's good with it." Theresa produced four stemmed glasses, and her husband poured. He gesticulated at the food plate. "*Mangiate. Mangiate...* Eat already!"

Iris emptied her bag on the counter, relieved Phineas of his, and arranged the contents on the island. Phineas pointed at each item. "Brought some zucchini, green beans, potatoes, tomatoes...a little of this and that." He accepted a glass, sipped, and nodded his approval.

"Your garden must be doing well. Thanks." Vinnie smiled. "So, your place come through the storm okay?"

"Could have been worse. One hive smashed by a tree, but I saved most of the bees." The rest of the mess was routine in recent years.

The elderly detective winced at the bee news. "At least *we're* all safe." His eyebrows pinched forward. "Doc, I finally heard something from the guy I know at the Bureau." He looked from Phineas to Iris.

Iris was about to pop an olive into her mouth but paused with it inches from her lips. "Bureau. You mean FBI?"

"Yeah. The only guy I still know there. He told me at first that he couldn't help us with your agents Meyers and Richter." His forehead relaxed. "Then I reminded him of how you took down the UNC Hospital bomber. Told him you'd once been threatened by the KKK, that your daughter was running for Congress, and that we're worried something else is going on. He remembered you. Said he'd see what he could do."

"And?" Phineas' neck and jaw muscles tightened.

"So, Richter is ex-Marine. Been with the Bureau about ten years. Tough guy reputation and has worked some pretty rugged assignments. Meyers has been around a lot longer. Gets assignments that require a more... *delicate* touch. Kind of an intellectual by comparison, but willing to be rough, if necessary."

"So why on Earth are they interested in Iris and me?" None of the new information helped.

"My guy says they were both pulled from what they were doing a few months ago, and he doesn't know what for. Something confidential at the highest levels. Something above my guy's clearance level and paygrade."

High-level FBI agents on a high-level secret assignment to watch the Mann family? What was their purpose? When would Iris and he find that out? Phineas sipped wine to moisten his suddenly parched throat. Iris stared at him with a puzzled and worried expression that mirrored his feelings.

Theresa held up a plate between them. "You two look like you need brownies."

～

12:00 on the bedroom's digital clock flashed through the darkness. The hum of the Mann's air conditioner followed. Phineas rolled out of bed and into his sandals. Flat on her back, Iris snored softly. He pressed the button on his digital watch. 3:30 AM. As he stepped into the bathroom and flipped the wall switch, the overhead light made him cover his eyes. Before he could shut the door, a sliver of the bright light scanned across Iris' face.

Her snoring stopped and she groaned. "What time is it?"

"3:30. Power's back on."

She sat up and stretched her arms over her head. "I'll refill the water jugs. Why don't you put the remaining ice in the freezer? Who knows how long it'll last this time?"

Phineas emptied his bladder and flushed his and Iris' collection of urine, accumulated to save on trips to the koi pond. The rush of the toilet tank refilling was comforting—one more hopeful sign of returning necessities. He didn't want to argue with Iris about the refrigerator, but after five days without power, it'd be warm inside. Still, he couldn't stop himself from cracking the door open to confirm that they'd have to wait hours before he should install their remaining ice and perishables. There wasn't that much ice remaining anyway, maybe a half cooler's worth. He proceeded from room to room resetting clocks and turning off lights that were still on when they lost power.

Iris stood over the kitchen sink filling jug after of jug with water. "Well pump's back to full power. We should hit the grocery early, if the grid is still working then." Neither of them counted on the electricity lasting long.

"You go back to sleep. I'll take over here." Phineas rested his hand lightly on her shoulder.

She spun around and kissed his cheek. "Thanks, Honey. Extra points. See you in the morning."

⁓

On the way to Harris Teeter, Iris' Prius crept by the gas station. Lines beside the pumps snaked back into the right lane of the road and slowed traffic to a crawl. Phineas pushed the passenger seat lever to bring his tired self from reclining to fully upright. "Glad you filled up before the storm." Usually after outages, the fuel pumps ran dry by mid-morning.

Even in the first minutes of its opening, the grocery parking lot neared capacity. Iris eased them into one of a few open slots on its periphery. "Got the list ready?"

"We'll see if they have any of it. So, the plan is you'll hit the staples sections and I'll start in produce and work my way into canned and dry goods." Phineas was not hopeful. Inventory was likely depleted before the storm, and he could only guess whether deliveries would have resumed. Stores usually closed when the grid was out, but he'd learned that backup generators saved some of the store's perishables. For local outages, grocers sometimes sold ice brought in from surrounding states, but Hurricane Chastity had knocked out most of the Southeast.

Iris and he joined the queue at the entrance and waited for it to inch inside. They each carried three reusable cloth bags. As expected, carts were all in use. When they finally gained entrance, the produce shelves were mostly empty. He was reaching for the last bag of Fuji apples when an elderly lady snatched it away. *She needs it more than we do.* He managed two lemons and four sweet potatoes. What remained was on its last legs or had been pillaged. A store clerk trundled by, wheeling cases of peanut butter on a hand truck. Phineas grabbed a jumbo jar. *Score!*

As he reached far back onto the pasta shelf for a lonely box of off-brand fusilli, he felt a tap on his shoulder. Iris showed him one bag with a bulge. "Got two bars of soap and a box of crackers. Flour, sugar, and the rest of the baking ingredient shelves are empty. Batteries and toilet paper are gone. Glad you installed our bidet." Phineas had located one online during the first wave of COVID in 2020, when hoarders cornered the bath tissues and sanitizer markets. Iris flashed a sheepish grin. "But I found chocolate. Three bars. 85% cacao."

Phineas added two cans of tomato paste, and they headed to Meat and Dairy. The remaining cartons of eggs each contained at least two cracked ones. He gingerly placed one carton in a bag. A half-gallon of high-end organic whole milk was still within date. The few remaining meat packages were brown. "I think we're done."

In the back of the lines at checkout, Iris caught his eye and wrinkled her nose for an instant at the cloud of body odor. She and Phineas had taken welcome two-minute showers before heading out. A young man looked like he was going to cut into the queue before he noticed two burly armed security guards leaning against the far wall, scanning the crowd.

Iris whispered in his ear, "Awfully glad you have your garden. Disappointing trip."

"At least we got out for a bit."

Darkness. The only illumination entered through the glass front door. A mournful chorus of "Noooo..." filled the store.

A middle-aged Black woman wearing a manager's tag approached with a flashlight. She studied a tablet's screen and shook her head. "Router's out. Cash only. Lanes 2 and 4." The two guards stepped closer to the counters, hands on pistols. Were they anticipating a rush of shoplifters or a grand theft?

Phineas and Iris had chosen Lane 4. Iris edged against him. "Lucky pick. Should we buy sweepstakes tickets next time there's power—to diversify our 401K?"

She glanced at her freshly recharged cell phone as two clerks added up each customer's meager purchases on handheld calculators. "Twitter's saying the grid was just hacked," she murmured. "Adding insult to injury. Who knows how long it'll be this time?"

The elderly woman with the bag of apples arranged her goods on the counter and studied the clerk through thick lenses. An anxious look spread across her wrinkled face. The young man seemed to force a polite smile. "That'll be $33.72, Ma'am."

She lay down a twenty and a five-dollar bill and began counting a handful of change from a coin purse. "I only have $27.47." She sounded despondent and her magnified eyes glistened.

"You'll have to put something back, Ma'am."

Iris elbowed Phineas, but he'd already pulled out his wallet. He counted out $7. Getting cash was always an item on their pre-disaster checklist. He lay the bills on the counter. The elderly woman stared up at him. She offered the bag of apples. "Thank you, Sir...Please take these."

Phineas shook his head. "You keep them. We're fine."

"I'll pay you back. Give me your address."

Iris arranged their purchases on the immobile check out belt. "That's not necessary."

As the elderly woman saw Iris' items, her bulging eyes filled her glasses' lenses. "…Oooh, chocolate!" Her voice descended into a whisper.

"Trade you this for three apples." Iris slid one of the bars to the woman. A broad smile emerged. "Deal."

∼

Neat clumps of vegetables covered a portion of the kitchen countertop. Tomatoes, zucchini, carrots, and onions were destined for a summer gazpacho. Phineas scrubbed early fingerling potatoes for roasting. "Cold soup, grilled potatoes and an omelet enough for supper tonight?"

Iris looked up from last month's Nature Conservancy's colorful magazine. "Sounds fine. Nothing like serial power outages to keep the weight down."

The background hum of central air conditioning eased back to life. Phineas and Iris stared at each other. "Think this time it'll stick?" Phineas asked.

"Depends. Which country did the President last offend?" Iris powered up her laptop. "Router's back. Checking news." She slid two fingers over the mousepad. "Yup. They say it was China this time. Too bad. Their hacks are as bad as Russia's."

"Well, let's go through our prep drill for the next one. Could be soon."

"I could do it in my sleep by now." She closed her computer, ambled to the kitchen sink, and began filling empty bottles. Phineas checked his wallet to be confident he still had enough cash for the next disruption.

∼

Mateo gesticulated at Phineas from his infant car seat as Martha's silent Chevy Bolt crept down the driveway. Both hands flailed over the toddler's head, and he mouthed words Phineas could only guess at. As soon as the electric motor shut down, Phineas opened the car door and unbuckled his grandson's harnesses. Mateo bounded out. "Mateo pick potatoes." He scanned the yard. "Where Ruby?"

"Ruby's with your Uncle Jacob—at his house."

"Awww...I wanna play wit' Ruby."

"Let's go dig those potatoes, Mateo. We should have a *big* pile when we're done."

Martha came around the front of her car wearing jeans and a well-worn UNC tee shirt. "He's ready. Time to pass a family tradition down a generation." She scooped up work gloves from the back seat. "It's one I still look forward to—plunging my hands into your rich soil—and finding buried treasure. Let's go."

Phineas maneuvered the two-wheeled garden cart to the raised bed. "As always, the Irish potatoes are around the outside and are ready for harvest. Be careful of the sweet potato slips I recently established in the center. We'll harvest them in October."

"Which varieties did you plant?"

"Same as last year. Purple Majesty, Yukon Nuggets, Norland Red, and French Fingerlings."

"I love the fingerlings...so buttery."

"You get that from me." He pulled up one of the yellowing plants and the eight or nine fingerlings dangling from its roots. Martha rummaged into the soil it had come from and held up two more, each half the size of a banana.

"Let me! Let me!" Mateo hollered. He plunged tiny fingers into dark soil. "Got one!"

"Dad, you've hooked another convert, another generation," Martha murmured.

Phineas chuckled. "You can put it on the cart, Mateo."

"It's Mateo's." The child pressed it against his chest.

"Sure thing, Buddy. That one's for you, and there are more." Phineas harvested another plant laden with tubers and set it in the cart. Mateo's hands went back underground.

"So, how's life with all that's going on?" Phineas asked.

The smile for her son's delight faded. "Well, the ICE raid and its fallout has Felipe stressed out. And there's campaigning with a two-year-old. To top it off, my opponent and his big boss seem to want to get dirtier and dirtier. How do *you* think?"

Phineas draped his arm on Martha's shoulder. "You know we're here to help you take care of your little man." The image of her as an excited child digging for potatoes flashed into Phineas' memory. He swallowed to ease a thickness in his throat.

"Thanks, Dad." Martha leaned against his side. "I'm having serious regrets that I chose to run. Homelife has never been more stressful, and I put Felipe in crosshairs no one deserves."

Phineas felt anguish at his daughter's plight but immense pride that she took a stand against corruption. "Should we cancel our Italy trip? I feel bad taking your mother away from your campaign for a stretch."

"You'll be back for the last couple of months, the final push."

Mateo held up two Purple Majesty's, one in each hand. "Purple ones!" He stared up at his mother. "Waylo hug Mommy."

Phineas let his arm fall to his side and Martha accepted the potatoes from her excited son. "Good work, Mateo. Let's find as many more as we can."

Phineas studied his schedule on the doctors' workroom computer and recognized most of the names of his afternoon clinic, including his first patient, Dolly Jones. The green dot indicated that she was checked in and ready. He was mildly surprised, but pleased, that she came back as promised. She would have had to leave home well before 7 AM for the six-hour drive, and he suspected she planned to drive home after her appointment. A small child and tight budget would make staying in a motel an uncomfortable stretch. Today, she was scheduled to receive her first infusion of SYMBI-62022—or placebo.

At the opposite end of the workroom, Gabby Villalobos studied her own schedule on a monitor. She stood and buttoned her white coat. "Looks like I've got another referral for the SynMedical study. That makes four for me since it started. How many have you enrolled, Phineas?"

"I'd have to pull records to give you a precise count, but I've enrolled quite a few after the talk in New Orleans." His knees creaked as he pushed himself up from his seat. "And I'm about to give one her first infusion. Sure hope it helps her. She's had a miserable time of it." He tucked his notepad under his arm and started for the workroom's door.

"Good luck."

He paused at the patient examination room door to collect his thoughts then cautiously pushed it open, hoping Darrell Junior wasn't playing on the floor behind it again. He wasn't. Dolly was alone and studying her cell phone. She sat up straight and wheezed, her eyes wary in her round face.

"Hey, Doc. Haven't done so well after I was here. I had to go back on sixty milligrams of prednisone, but I'm not in the kind of trouble I *can* get in. I'm improving now, just still kind of noisy." She slipped her cell phone into her silver purse and stared up at him. "You're still going to treat me, ain't' you? Please, Doc!"

Phineas instincts sent him from a steady workflow mode to one of high alert. Dolly couldn't be in crisis and receive the study drug. "Let me get more information on how severe your asthma is today, and then we can decide. Okay, Dolly?"

She nodded yes but kept staring at him with anxious doe eyes.

He sat on the rolling stool in front of the computer monitor, accessed her record, and took pen and notepad in hand. "Where's your husband?"

"I sent the Darrells to the cafeteria. Didn't need their stress—and I didn't want Darrell Junior to watch me get stuck."

"I understand." Darrell Junior had probably seen too much of his mother's suffering already in his short life. "Okay, so when did you get worse?"

"Couple of days ago. It was an ungodly hot night before and we ran the A/C on high all night. Woke up 'fore dawn and had to take treatments, one after another, so I took sixty of prednisone. Took it again yesterday and today, so's I could get your new miracle drug." She took a deep breath and let it out slowly, a high-pitched wheeze coming at the end.

It reassured him that she could say as much without pausing to breathe. "Have you had any fever or mucous?"

"Naw, Doc. This ain't infection. You can give me another breathing test—if you need to."

"That's a good idea, but let me have a listen to your lungs first." He stepped toward the examination table.

She popped out of her chair and climbed onto the table. Phineas grasped her wrist and counted her heart rate. Eighty-four and strong. Then her respiratory rate. 16 and without the need to use her neck muscles to assist inhalations. He pulled his stethoscope from his lab coat pocket and listened to several deep breaths. Wheezes concluded each exhalation, something Phineas expected, and not enough to exclude Dolly from getting her first dose of the study drug.

"Okay, Dolly. Nothing on your exam tells me I can't give you the study drug today, but you need to blow at least fifty percent on the breathing test. Think you can do that?"

"Give it my best shot, Doc. I'm ready when you are." She pressed her lips together and looked like she was ready to do battle.

"I know you will. I'll send the respiratory therapist in. Then I'll be back." He resisted the urge to give her a reassuring paternal pat on the shoulder.

Phineas circled back to the doctors' workroom to hastily type the first part of his clinic note then returned to listen in the hallway outside Dolly's examination room. The respiratory therapist's voice penetrated the door. She cheered Dolly on with, "Blow, blow, blow!"

When the coaching ceased, Phineas eased the door open. The therapist rotated the portable spirometer screen toward him. "First second flow is 52 per cent. High enough, Dr. Mann?"

"It is. Dolly, do you still want to go ahead and take your first treatment?"

She punched the air, triumphant. "Hell, yeah, Doc!" A sheepish expression with a faint grin replaced her jubilation. "Sorry. I meant to say, 'yes, please.'"

Phineas couldn't suppress a chuckle. "You signed all the paperwork at your last visit. I'll send the IV team in, then the study pharmacologist. The infusion will take about thirty minutes. We'll need to observe you for two hours after, to make sure you're stable to leave."

"Bring it on, Doc. I'm ready."

JULY

"Unless someone like you cares a whole awful lot, Nothing
is going to get better. It's not."
FROM *THE LORAX* BY THEODORE GEISEL 1971

Iris shouldered her purse and tiptoed toward the door.

"You're going out?" Phineas asked. He'd gathered this month's pulmonary journals and planned to peruse them from his recliner during the scorching Sunday afternoon.

She whispered, "Mateo's down for his nap. I'm going to run a couple of errands—be back around the time he wakes up." Ruby lifted her head from her pillow and yawned.

"Seems like Martha's had an event every weekend afternoon lately." He lowered his voice.

"It won't get better any time soon." She held her hands palms up with an "it is what it is" shrug.

Phineas settled into his chair. "I've never heard of a chef who gets weekends off, but I do wish Felipe didn't have to work every Sunday."

Phineas glanced at the first journal's cover. "Glad we can help."

"When did Jacob say he'd pick up Ruby?" The dog, hearing her name, stared at Iris then let escape a low guttural groan and lowered her head onto the pillow.

"He'll be back in town Tuesday night."

"Keep a listen out for Mateo." She waved goodbye and made a quiet exit, gently pulling the door shut.

Earlier, he'd performed his monthly testing of the bees for their ever-present deadly parasite, the varroa mite. Mite counts were inching up and now approached a threshold that demanded chemical treatment. He'd been dragging his feet on this, hoping to buy time, since his options were restricted by their toxicity to the bees in July's extreme temperatures and by the mite's increasing resistances to available agents.

With the brutal weather conditions, the summer's nectar dearth, and his repeated but necessary invasion of their hives, his bees were nastier today than he'd ever experienced. Guard bees had dive bombed him over and over and managed to sting him twice through his baggy jeans before he escaped the bee yard. The whole process took longer than usual, his usual effortless skill with a hive tool sluggish and less steady today. Had to be the damned heat.

In less than an hour and despite a 'breathable' tee shirt and beekeeping jacket, he'd dripped so much sweat, that he had to peel his baggy jeans and boxer shorts off his skin, so he could take a much-needed shower.

Phineas reclined his chair partway, focused his attention on *The American Journal of Respiratory and Critical Care Medicine*, and studied the table of contents. He selected a multicenter trial from Europe and started with the dry **Methods** section. It looked like another powerful clinical study made possible by their universal health care—and not doable at an adequate scale under the fractured system in America. It was always best to start with the tedious parts of the study while he was awake and focused...

Barking. Distant furious barking followed by a burst of a child crying. He jerked the recliner upright and rubbed his eyes.

Shit. Must have dozed off.

He scanned the living room. No Ruby. He bolted to Martha's old bedroom. The portable crib was empty. A flesh and blood jackhammer began pounding the front of his chest. He bolted out the front door—left wide open.

Is someone kidnapping Mateo?

More barking. Coming from the back yard. He raced around the side of the house to find Mateo waddling toward the front of the hives. Ruby faced the toddler, blocking his approach. Beards of bees hung off the landing platforms and buzzed at high volume. Mateo, in tee shirt and diaper, took another energetic step toward the noisy attraction. "Bee house!"

Ruby charged him like a linebacker, knocked him down, and let out a furious bark. Mateo shrieked at the possessed dog. A cloud of bees hovering above suddenly descended onto Ruby. She yipped and twisted about, trying to bite her own back.

Phineas scooped up his grandson and cradled him tight against his chest. As he and Ruby raced for the shelter of the house, points of pain seared the back of his neck and his scalp.

He settled a silent and wide-eyed Mateo on the sofa to inspect him. Only crumpled dry leaves. No marks. Phineas picked crud off his startled grandson. *No need to leave evidence of my lapse.*

Phineas felt his own heart rate slowing. He wiped sweat from his temples with his palms and tried to relax. What's this? Phineas' left thumb and index finger were rhythmically rolling across each other involuntarily, as if testing the firmness of a ripening blueberry.

What's going on? No! Not this. Not now. Not when he was nearing retirement, and the gratification part of delayed gratification was in sight... How long before this would be a regular thing? How long before his face became a mask and he'd require a boost to start his legs moving...and how long before his mind began to fade? Please no! He plunged the offending hand into his pocket.

He'd seen old men wheeled into his clinic after they'd suffered recurrent pneumonias, because they couldn't swallow without choking. Men who could barely handle a pureed diet...and he'd seen men with feeding tubes penetrating their abdomens, tubes that their vacant minds couldn't comprehend. Would he subject Iris to maintaining such a man? And in the very near future, would he still be able to perform the necessary skills of his occupation?

"Waylo." Mateo was watching him. "What in pocket?"

Future misery? A steady decay in his grandfatherly existence? "It's empty, Mateo." Phineas patted his grandson's thick hair with his steady right hand. "You look fine now. And how's our good friend, Ruby?" Ruby stood vigilant, alternately licking her back and panting heavily, her tongue hanging. He patted her head. "You deserve a treat, Girl." She appeared to understand the word "treat" and sat on her haunches whining. "Come on, Mateo, let's give Ruby a treat."

"Ruby hurt me." Mateo pouted and wiped at his eyes.

"She saved you from getting stung—from *bad* ouchies. Now let's thank her."

I should buy her a filet mignon...Glad she can't tell on me. They each rewarded her with one of the biscuits Jacob had left behind.

Phineas needed to redirect his thoughts from his transient tremor—and imagined decline. Maybe it wouldn't be so dire. He *did* see only the worst cases, those poor souls referred after late pulmonary complications. Maybe it was just a weird form of a benign essential tremor—or just fatigue and stress. Maybe it wasn't what he'd first thought it was. There were other causes of tremor. He'd have to think on it later—if it happened again.

"Mateo, let's go check out your crib." He took his grandson's hand and led him to the bedroom. Before the boy could protest, Phineas grasped him under his armpits, hoisted him up, and stood him inside the enclosure.

"No, Waylo. Out!" In seconds, Mateo gripped the rim and hauled himself over and out, plopping onto the floor on his diaper-padded bottom. Ruby licked his face and nudged him with her head.

"I'm home." Iris' voice found its way from the living room. "Where are my men?"

Phineas spine stiffened. Hopefully, his failure in vigilance wouldn't be found out—and the hand thing had thankfully gone back into hiding. "Back here." Ruby sauntered from the bedroom and returned with Iris.

Mateo pushed himself to his feet. "Wayla!" He scrambled to hug her leg.

"Mateo just wake up? D'you change him?"

Phineas shook his head. "Our grandson has a new skill. Let me show you before Martha comes to pick him up." Phineas placed Mateo back in the crib.

"No, Waylo. Out!" The practiced toddler hauled himself out of his minimum-security prison with even greater ease.

Iris rounded her eyes and mouth in astonishment. "When did he figure that out?"

"After his nap. He was out when I found him." That was all the honesty he wanted to share. He slipped his now steady hand back into his pocket, in case it decided to misbehave again.

Mateo surveyed the toys in the room and settled on his Ernie and Cookie Monster figures. He picked one up in each hand, Ernie facing Cookie Monster, and showed them to his grandmother. "Go see bees with Ruby dog. Waylo seepin'."

Iris head snapped back. "Phineas, is there something you didn't tell me?"

Yes, there was, but he wasn't ready to tell her *all* of it yet, and it was painfully clear that he could never bury his secrets from her. Not with his grandson eager to sell him out.

Monday evening, Marie in her Sugarbeeter track warmups, stretched out on her sofa and studied her cell phone. Chelsea had forwarded Martha's dramatic and freshly made campaign videos. Martha looked and sounded confident and polished under the professional coaching the seasoned TV personality Chelsea could provide, and Chelsea's expert editing lined up the best clips into four dynamic and effective commercials the four women could be proud of. Marie and Iris had eagerly tagged along to witness the taping.

Before Martha's final clip, this one on the climate crisis, she went outside until her pretty face visibly dripped sweat. Then she adlibbed, "Were you hot when you went outside today? I sure was. Each of the last ten years was hotter than the last, and it's still getting hotter. What will it be like in ten years for your children, in twenty for your grandchildren? Our planet has a raging fever and it's caused by burning coal, oil, and gas. My opponent, Rex Blechmann, doesn't believe in proven science and supports more drilling for oil—including in our national parks—and more fracking for gas—even after those earthquakes that fracking has caused. And he doesn't support renewable energy alternatives in *any* form. They must not be paying him enough. I'm Martha Mann-Hernandez and I'm running for the United States House of Representatives. Vote for me on November 5th, and I *will* work to save our planet."

Marie watched with admiration as Chelsea's own spot played. Such a professional! The way she looked into the camera and the perfect changes in her voice at just the right times. During her ad, she relived her grief at the death of her husband. Tears rolled down her cheeks and into the corners of her trademark scarlet lipstick. "Rex Blechmann lied to us about the pandemic, and most of us lost someone we loved; someone who wouldn't have died if he and his fellow Republicans had acted the way scientists told them to instead of how the President dictated." She'd pressed both palms into her eyes and paused. "My husband, Dr. Ron Bullock, worked long hours to save victims of COVID-19, and I lost him to the virus. I'm voting for Martha Mann-Hernandez on November 5th, and you should too."

Martha was lucky to have Chelsea LaFever Bullock donate her expertise and energy. Lucky Chelsea was friends with her parents, and lucky Chelsea still had connections that allowed her to borrow a television facility. It had been a totally new and thrilling experience for both Marie and Iris.

Surprised to be invited to the event, Marie cleared her work schedule. Her donations and those she raised from folks at SynMedical, while individually generous, amounted to mere tokens in the expensive political world. The few at work she'd gotten close enough to approach cautioned her not to be too public there in her efforts for Democrats, since CEO Eugene Schmidt donated heavily to the President and other Republicans. Schmidt's net worth mushroomed due to the business-friendly tax laws enacted by the Republican administration. It was obvious that Schmidt's focus was on his personal bottom line more than the progressively deteriorating status of the common citizen—and the planet.

Throughout the entirety of the filming, Iris sat beside Marie and chatted with excitement—until Chelsea spoke of her husband's death, and then Iris wept a silent torrent.

Marie switched off her phone, feeling she'd joined a select cabal, even if she did bring the least to the effort. The four now seemed to move as one whenever schedules allowed. She couldn't wait until their next meeting.

⌒

On the heels of Monday's flaming sunset, a powerful storm cell developed and intensified. Within minutes, a flash and crash exploded, and the electricity died. Phineas, having drifted off in his recliner, jerked upright.

Iris retreated back from the house's front bay window and watched another lightning bolt scorch the atmosphere. "Time to light some candles—again."

Phineas rubbed his eyes. "What's that make—three times in the last three weeks?"

"I stopped counting." One by one, she applied a butane fireplace starter to the numerous candle wicks spaced around the living room.

Phineas squinted at the journal page. "Glad I still get a couple of these in print." He got up to retrieve his headlamp from their power outage section of their pantry, the one section they always kept stocked.

She settled onto the sofa and activated her laptop. "Yup. Router's out again." She clicked it off and reached for a paperback novel. "One thing about retired life, I can read what I want."

"You're tempting me to join you in fiction." He settled back into his recliner.

"Why *don't* you retire? Under this administration, NIH funding has dried up." Iris located the page with her bookmark and leaned closer to a nearby flame.

"Maybe this Phase 3 trial will be my last."

"You still getting enough referrals for SynMedical to keep it going?"

"Ever since I talked about SYMBI-62022 in New Orleans, I'm getting way more referrals than other sites." He clicked his headlamp on and found his place in the journal.

"So SynMedical should be happy to pay your support?"

"And Gabby's. The study's salary support keeps us from having to work in the ICU and clinics full time."

"You might finally be too old for those activities."

She muttered that last comment in an unexpected tone. Did she want him around more, or had she noticed he'd declined more than just aged?

"I might just be." He raised his voice to compete with the pounding noise of a downpour that was now a constant between the storm's fireworks. "Hope this rain doesn't last long. The pond's already high."

"Before I lost the connection, I was reading about the fires in Alaska. You remember Pike's Lodge in Fairbanks, where we stayed when we first arrived on our trip last summer?"

"Sure do. Window air conditioning didn't work in that first room, and it was hot as Hell at night in June up there next to the Arctic Circle." Despite the exhausting flights across the continent, five time zone changes, and a 1 AM check-in, he'd tossed and turned trying to sleep in the swelter.

"Well, Pike's Lodge burned to the ground along with half of Fairbanks."

"Including those stuffed grizzly bears and wolves that greeted us in the lobby?" He'd had no prior appreciation for the size of those beasts, until he found himself standing slack jawed with them staring down at him.

"The article showed a map of fires in the state." She frowned. "Fire fighters are overwhelmed. Hundreds of forest fires all over, and they go under the tundra and smolder for months, only to flare up again. More heat. More carbon dioxide. And the black soot covering what snow's left absorbs even more heat from the sun."

"Glad we saw Alaska when we did. Might be too late now."

For the next hour, they settled into their reading, Iris by candlelight and Phineas by his trusty headlamp. The rain's drumming on the skylights was deafening. Iris closed her novel on a bookmark. "My eyes are too old for this. I'm going to bed."

"I'll join you." Phineas put down his journal.

She shone her flashlight beam on Ruby. The dog was stretched out on her pillow, eyes closed, breathing deeply. Her feet twitched from a dream chase. Iris nudged the sleeping dog with her toe. "Come on, Ruby. Time to go out and pee." Ruby startled, lifted her head, and blinked several times before she glared at Iris. Then the sleepy beagle allowed her head to settle back onto her pillow before she sighed deeply.

"Ruby. Time to go out." Iris set the flashlight on the floor. "So, this is how it's going to be?" She bent over and hoisted the sleepy dog onto her four feet and herded her toward the door then retrieved the flashlight. Ruby sauntered toward the house's main entrance and yawned. Iris cracked the door open and shone her light outside. The deluge's din intensified as watery 'cats and dogs' bounced off the front steps.

"Come on, Girl. Go pee." She nudged Ruby again. "Then you can sleep all night."

Ruby stared up at Iris' face, all the while inching her back legs into an arched position over Iris' foot. The canine rebel began to squat, when Phineas alertly scooped her up and boosted her out the door and into the downpour, rescuing Iris' foot.

"Ruby, let's not undo your good deed with Mateo." Phineas felt instant guilt and wished another option existed.

Ruby stared up at him with round brown eyes that said, "and after all I did for you, Phineas?".

~

This time the power company required only two days to get the grid back up. Outages after violent storms were now frequent enough that, as soon as rain and winds receded enough to safely launch restoration efforts, companies' repair manpower and logistics teams were ready to go, ready to sell more power.

After Phineas' tiring day at work and Iris' countless tasks helping Martha, they settled back into their evening routine of checking news postings across the dining room table, she on her laptop and he on his iPad. He turned his screen to face her. "Recognize this place?" The image was of a beach house next to the ocean. The surf lapped at its front porch.

She shook her head. "Should I?"

"I'm pretty sure it's the place we used to rent when the kids were young."

"That place was up on a dune and third row from the beach." Iris seemed puzzled.

"Exactly. The first two rows are gone."

She put her thumb and index finger on his screen and spread them apart to blow up the image. "I'm guessing the other wealthy owners got insurance payouts when their fancy second homes submerged...Imagine if you had no insurance, and you lived in a tiny home near the rising ocean, and you survived day to day. That's what's happening to poor folks all over the world. Much of Bangladesh is gone...No longer exists."

She glared at her screen. "Not another one!" She turned it so he could see the headline.

Republicans Look to POTUS' Son as VP Running Mate

Iris groaned and closed her eyes. "Not another one of that family in office—especially *that* creep. How many endangered species has Junior murdered?"

"You just know that this president wants to keep running things, keep having his rallies, keep feeding his enormous ego—and to stay out of a New York jail."

Iris focused back on her laptop's screen then slapped the table. "Shit. He's trolling Martha again."

"Who?"

"The President. He tweeted that when the power went out from Hurricane Chastity, Felipe served spoiled food. Said people 'should watch out if they eat immigrant food'. Then he reminded his followers that Felipe was married to Martha, and she's a Democrat running for a house seat."

The claim blindsided Phineas. "Did you hear that anyone got sick?"

"None of us heard anything. Her opponent posted that a man called their office with a stomachache after he ate there. Didn't mention that he ate for free, of course, and probably just ate too much." Her voice began to rise.

"Or that the 'immigrant food' was French cuisine. They have any medical documentation?" He doubted there'd be objective proof, since the administration made up whatever message suited them.

"Of course not, but that doesn't stop them from defaming him—and her by association." She closed her laptop. "I can't read any more of this crap."

Why had they settled into a routine that, in recent years, only provided daily glimpses at misery? "Politics has always been dirty. Just more tools available to the really dirty." He began scrolling his finger up his iPad screen. "Damn!"

"And what new misery did *you* find?"

"The President is again pushing his tax credits for spraying poisons for ticks and mosquitoes." Phineas felt queasy with every reminder of this toxic threat to his bees—and to insects in general, and now that all too familiar sensation was returning. Nausea was just one of the many symptoms insecticide exposure caused. He suspected his was in sympathy with his six-legged livestock.

"Here's a video clip of him." He rotated his iPad so they could both watch the President speak from the Oval Office. Phineas squinted and adjusted his reading glasses.

"My fellow Americans, so many mosquitoes...so many after all that rain—couldn't play golf yesterday, there were so many...So many." His voice trailed off. "YUGE clouds of 'em. Horrible! Could hardly swing a club! Got in my eyes and ears—I'm still itching!" He jutted his jaw and vigorously scratched his double chin.

"I made a tax break for you good people, a tax credit actually—the best kind of tax break, a tremendous one, if you help control these pests. Call your pest control service and have 'em spray—have 'em spray everything. Keep the receipt. We'll cover it. Then you can go back outside without gettin' eaten alive. And those sprays kill ticks too—the nasty little bloodsuckers.

"Let's keep America great. Great like the last eight years. Take it back from the nasty bugs—just like we did from Democrats, Antifa, and those other protester pests. It's our land. Ours...And may God bless you."

Phineas paused the clip and lifted his eyes from the screen. Iris looked furious. "That's terrible, Phineas. He's pushing covering the country with even more poisons than we already have."

"What did you expect? His knowledge of ecology is limited to what he thinks is good for his golf courses, and he has no clue of the dire consequences of his ignorance." Ignorance, overconfidence, and power. A toxic triumvirate.

"Can you do anything to protect your bees?" She was studying him.

"If I knew when someone was spraying within three miles of here, I could prevent them from foraging with netting for a little while, but I can't do that for long, or often—and no one ever warns us when they're going to spray." The queasy feeling began wringing out his gut.

"So, we just wait?" Iris reached across the table to place her hand on his.

Hidden under her palm, his thumb and index finger began rubbing together almost imperceptibly. He pressed them tightly together. "And we hope his party is replaced in the election." He pointed at the screen. "Notice anything about his face today?"

"It still nauseates me." Her neck muscles twitched. Had she gagged?

"Look how *round* it's become. I wonder if he's been on steroids for his red meat allergy—his Alpha Gal Syndrome—or for something else...Or he's just gotten really fat on chicken nuggets."

⌒

Phineas recognized Marie's white Tesla exiting his driveway. He stopped his truck on the street and turned off NPR before he opened his driver's side window. The moist heat crashed over him like heavy surf. Marie stopped opposite him and lowered hers too. Her butterfly shaped sunglasses flashed a reflection of the blazing red evening sun. She offered a smile. "Late clinic today?"

"You've seen my typing skills. Had to finish my notes." And that hand tremor thing slowed him down today. At least he was all alone and out of sight battling it this time. Phineas checked the rearview mirror for approaching cars then absent-mindedly rested his arm on the truck's door panel. "Ouch!" He jerked his arm off the hot metal. "So, what have you women been up to?"

"More strategizing and planning, and we rehearsed Martha for her upcoming debate." She gestured at posters and roadside election signs filling her back seat. "And reloaded my stock to replace what the rednecks keep pulling up."

"Elections are getting dirtier and meaner."

"They follow their leader. Until he's out, it'll only get worse." A car crept up behind her. "Whoops. I'd better move on, and you're bound to be hungry. See ya." She gave a compact wave and turned her attention back to the road ahead. Before her window closed Phineas heard her command, "Siri, take me home."

Phineas raised his window, relishing the air conditioning running full blast. The empty driveway told him that he'd missed Martha and that Iris'

Prius would be resting on the cooler concrete slab in the garage. One day soon, he'd organize the mess of gardening and beekeeping supplies in his half and start keeping his old truck protected inside. Or he could finally trade for a plug-in electric vehicle, an excuse to lobby Iris for solar panels on their roof. Of course, his new ride would have to be another truck for hauling soil, mulch, and his other gardening necessities. He pocketed his key, stepped back into the swelter, and hustled into the house's welcome 80-degree air conditioning.

Iris occupied her usual spot at the dining table. Her open laptop was surrounded by piles of handouts, campaign buttons and voter registration forms. A wine glass contained the remnants of a white, and an empty one sat across from her. The tall thin bottle suggested it had once contained a vino verde. A few carrot sticks remained next to a small bowl streaked with hummus. She paused her typing. "You just missed Marie."

He leaned in to plant a kiss on her cheek. "We exchanged 'hellos' on the street. So, Martha was here? Marie said you worked on the debate." He used one of the carrot sticks to wipe up the hummus remnants. His stomach had growled in clinic as he laboriously typed.

"Martha had to leave a couple of hours ago to pick up Mateo."

He wished he could have been here to see his daughter. One more reason to think about retirement. "So, Marie's been here for hours?" The fiery spice in the hummus surprised him. He stole a sip of Iris' wine and swished it over his palate.

"According to her, when she's not in her office, it's assumed she's working elsewhere. She's given Martha's campaign a lot of hours." Iris closed her computer and looked up at Phineas. "And we've really enjoyed her company. We've become good friends."

Could that become a problem for him? "Does she say anything about making other friends since she moved here?"

"She hasn't mentioned it. With all her time working on the campaign, I'm guessing that she's mostly just gotten to know us outside of her job. She seems thrilled when Martha, Chelsea, and I invite her to meet." Iris' focused work face began to relax. "She might still be lonely."

"Well, it's kind of you to include her."

"Actually, Phineas, we really *like* her. She's always agreeable and no nonsense. It's gotten so it wouldn't feel right without her being here."

He couldn't put his finger precisely on why Iris' words unsettled him. "Okay. I'm sure you'll keep in mind that she oversees a good chunk of the funding that pays my salary." Maybe that was the reason for his vague discomfort. *Yeah. That makes sense.* He pulled out a chair and sat. "Has she said any more about her life?"

"A few tidbits. Nothing very deep. After she left, I realized that she was mostly asking us for stories about our lives. It's like she's absorbing our times…as if she's filling holes in her own past."

"Maybe she had some rough times growing up." Phineas' eyes locked onto Iris' brilliant blue gaze. She was always adept at bringing *his* worries out into the air—way better than he was at knowing hers. Had she guessed some painful secret Marie wanted to hide?

She pushed her chair back and dropped her hands onto her lap. "Well, whatever happened, she seems to have done well for herself and become a successful and very pleasant young woman, and we're lucky to know her."

Were they? Phineas wondered how well they really knew her.

He opened Apple News on his iPad and scanned the headlines. "Southern District of New York Attorney Missing." *What's this?* He tapped the screen and read. Fresh intrigue. "Iris, did you see the headline about the New York district attorney who's been working on the financial fraud cases against the President? The article says she's gone missing."

"Oh? Foul play by the administration's henchmen?"

"Seems she was vacationing with her family in Vermont on Lake Champlain, and none of her family came back from their day of boating."

"That's scary. Think the President arranged for her case against him to disappear if she does?" She reopened her computer and logged back in.

"Possibly. That would also send a warning to her replacement." He read further. "They speculate that maybe she crossed into Canada for protection and to hunker down and prepare for January, when he's no longer president, and she has the authority to bring charges." Phineas switched his screen to the Duck Duck Go search engine for a map and confirmed that Lake Champlain did indeed extend into Canada.

"Let's hope that's what happened. If it is, you know POTUS will be even more desperate to keep power." She turned her screen around to show a picture of the President's son kneeling proudly over a magnificent antelope he'd killed. "Can you believe the leading Republican candidates are the Vice President and the President's horrible son? You know they'd be puppets with *that* former president behind the scenes."

"He's never behind the scenes, and they'd have pardon power. If Republicans win, we'll be stuck with his presence in the White House."

"Unless the Southern District can win their case. I read a while ago that he won't be protected from it by his successor's federal pardon power." She closed her laptop.

"Then he'll do anything to stay in office—even try something desperate to cancel the election." Phineas forgot the hunger he'd felt just minutes ago. His appetite had melted away.

The wine buzz made Marie thankful for her Tesla's computerized safety and navigation features. Carrots and hummus barely dented the alcohol's jolt on her empty stomach. She let the ghost in her machine park them near her condo, while she mentally reviewed her current food inventory. Maybe a Lean Cuisine or two in the freezer. She hadn't polished off the Chinese takeout from two days ago. She really needed to start enduring the chore of regular grocery trips, but shopping for one reminded her of the isolation she hadn't felt until her mother's death.

As heat waves rose from the asphalt, she gingerly tiptoed to the thin strip of grass between the parking lot and building and planted a Mann-Hernandez for Congress sign.

Her condo's smart thermostat had thankfully anticipated her arrival, but the bright white empty inside of her refrigerator was a shocking reminder of the desperate state of her provisions. The paper carton from Chinese takeout contained several tablespoons of rice and drab snow peas. Her freezer offered one box of frozen peanut chicken with rice noodles. 300 calories. A half empty clear plastic pistachio ice cream container tempted her more. She set it and a spoon on her oak dining table then took out her cell phone to order delivery of a supreme garbage pizza. Plenty of calories there—and she could freeze what she didn't eat.

While Marie contemplated the new Mann family information she'd gleaned, she savored the first spoonful of ice cream and waited for dinner to arrive. Two glasses of a wine variety designed for easy drinking during summer weather loosened Iris' tongue. She almost come to tears describing the devastating impact of Phineas' murder charges so many years ago. From him being led at dawn to jail in handcuffs, to Iris' mother putting her family home up as bail, to the months of pretrial agony—all while a pregnant, exhausted Iris financially supported the three of them in a city struggling to recover from a devastating hurricane. And all Phineas could do was meet with his lawyer, rehearse, and anticipate. Louisiana's infamous Angola State Prison constantly loomed in the back of their minds.

During her mother's preterminal suffering, revenge on the man who arranged her mother's public humiliation felt like a fitting pathway. But did her absent father deserve blame for his daughter having to grow up constantly on the move to obscure locations? No. The mother she thought she knew brought cruel desperation onto him and his family. Today, Iris' recounting touched Marie with new guilt for her mother's actions and reasons to forgive her father.

If the Manns found out who her mother was, would Marie lose her new closest friends? Her new family?

Her mother had given instructions for her ashes. She'd wanted them poured into the Mississippi in New Orleans. The May trip there revealed that the once mighty river was a stinking mess choking in human waste, so the urn went back into her suitcase for the trip back. North Carolina was the last place they lived before her mother became a felon. This would be where the ashes should stay, but where exactly?

Her earlier hunger melted away, and the ice cream and air conditioning together delivered an unexpected chill. She screwed the ice cream lid back on and headed to the bedroom to change into the familiar comfort of her Sugarbeeter track warmup.

What if she'd given up her college scholarship and stayed in Chinook, Montana? Could she have had a life like Ada, who married her high school boyfriend and settled into farming and making babies? Of course, that would have required a girl to *have* a steady boyfriend, and her mother always managed to scare off any boy her daughter dated before he got close. She thought back then that her mother was just being overly protective, but she now knew that her mother was protecting herself from curious outsiders. She pushed her daughter to be the best student possible—good for the scholarship—but bad for a social life. In Chinook, academic success did not get a girl dates.

Would she have found happiness married with a houseful of kids in Montana?

The college gymnasium was packed for the evening's town hall style debate that WUNC agreed to host and televise. Even with massive air conditioners pumping nonstop, a gym's sweaty, acrid odor clung to the crowd pouring in from the sunbaked parking lot. Phineas shivered as his perspiration evaporated under the frigid air blowing directly down on him from vents in the ceiling—air refrigerated from electricity generated by burning government subsidized low quality coal. And the President still claimed that wind power caused cancer, repeating this absurd mantra so many times that his base believed it as an established fact.

Phineas and Iris had arrived early and located folding chairs set up beside the speakers' platform at the far end of the cavernous space. He watched the double doors at the entrance. Would the debate's security presence be enough tonight? More and more potential voters poured in and were forced to stand around already claimed seats. At least there were metal detectors at the entrance.

Chelsea arrived soon after they did, sporting a tee shirt with RBG emblazoned on its front. She made it a point to chat with the young woman moderator, who appeared surprised and excited to see a legend in the field being so friendly to her. Chelsea took her seat with the Manns, whispering, "I told her how much I admired her work, and I didn't need to tell her whose corner I was in."

Martha, elegant in a robin's egg blue dress and matching high heels, turned Mateo over to Felipe's care and stood at the lectern on the left of the makeshift stage arranging her notes and adjusting the microphone. Mateo immediately protested being picked up by his father and insisted on being put down, at which point he raced to Iris' lap. Felipe, having replaced his kitchen jacket with a French blue dress shirt, hustled behind. The circumferential crease in his glossy black hair provided evidence of his recent wearing of a chef's toque blanche, and his cheeks were shaved smooth, his usual five o'clock shadow sent down the drain.

He extracted a colorful book from Mateo's cloth bag of supplies and pushed the bulky sack under the chair beside Iris then dropped onto it. He handed her the book. "Thank you so much for all the help you've given to Martha and me." His usual melodic voice sounded tense as he reached across Iris to shake Phineas' hand.

"No need to thank me. I get to hang out with Mateo." Iris gave her grandson a gentle squeeze. "And Martha's ready for this." She glanced at the book's cardboard cover. Creases formed across her forehead. "Uh oh."

Mateo jammed a finger at the title. "Un Gallo Rojo!"

"Sorry. Meant to give you an English one." Felipe reached under his chair for the sack.

"Hey, no problemo, right Mateo? This little man can teach me." Iris' face relaxed into a grin.

Phineas cleared his throat and murmured, "looks like the enemy has arrived."

Rex Blechmann took manly strides across the stage platform. Tanned with a salt and pepper crew cut, he appeared purposefully casual in a red checkered button-down shirt and jeans. Cowboy boots tucked beneath his pantlegs completed his idea of a cultivated image. More than a head taller than Martha, he extended his leathery paw to her and leaned into her space. Her spine stiffened in defense of it. They exchanged words that were drowned out by the crowd. Finally, Blechmann retreated a step and said loudly enough for at least the front row to hear, "May the best man win."

Iris brought her mouth close to Phineas ear and whispered, "What an asshole!"

"No, Wayla." Mateo pressed a reproving finger to his grandmother's lips.

Marie emerged from the crowd and slipped into one of the seats Phineas had protected with campaign posters. She was down to the last of the flyers she'd been passing out. "I hope she's not too nervous. I'd sure be. Her opponent looks like he's about to enjoy a meal."

Phineas knew of husbands experiencing their wives' pregnancy symptoms. He imagined absorbing anxiety from his daughter in her first public debate like he had way back when her team played for the state high school soccer championship.

Marie sat up like she'd been poked with a stick. "I see Jacob." She pointed toward the far entrance where his recognizable bearded face rose above the masses. He appeared to be mouthing "excuse me" and weaving his way through by turning sideways and parting the sea of assorted hairstyles, bobbing scalps, and bright red caps. Conversations throughout the hall competed loudly enough to make Phineas consider covering his ears.

"WUNC thanks everyone for coming out tonight for our townhall debate," the loudspeaker announced. The words failed to penetrate the ruckus.

Rex Blechmann reached into the leather briefcase at his feet and produced a cowbell and a claw hammer. After three raucous clangs, the crowd's faces turned to the stage and ceased their chatter. He raised his instruments over his head and whooped, "Thank you, Y'all, and thank you, WUNC!"

Jacob plopped down into the chair next to Marie, the last empty seat anywhere. "Phew! Well, that's not exactly the way Martha would want to start this thing."

WUNC's plump, dark-haired moderator sat at a folding table facing the candidates with her back angled to half of the audience. Short stacks of index cards were arranged on the table. She leaned into her microphone and sent her voice into the loudspeakers on the sides of the stage. "Good evening! I'm Monica Louis from WUNC's evening news. Welcome to our townhall debate between Republican candidate, the incumbent Congressman, Rex Blechmann, and Democratic challenger, Martha Mann-Fernandez. Thank you everyone for your attention." Louis paused and surveyed the crowd. "WUNC staff members are circulating with more cards for your questions, and they will bring them to me throughout the evening. Each candidate will be given sixty seconds for an initial answer, and then subsequent responses will be limited to thirty seconds, so, candidates, be concise. There's a lot to cover."

"Our first question is to both of you and has to do with guns. Congressman Blechmann, you may answer first. What actions do you plan for the year 2025 regarding assault weapons and high-capacity ammunition clips?"

He flashed whitened teeth in a broad smile and swiveled his head side to side surveying the audience. "Well thank you, Monica and WUNC, and thank you all you fine American citizens for coming. ...That's an easy one for me. I'll keep my answer short. Our forefathers gave us a second amendment for a reason. We're doin' just fine the way things are now. If you feel you need both a hunting rifle and personal protection, well, you've got both covered in one instrument right there. He pulled a thick, bright red pocketknife from his front pants pocket and held it up. It's like a Swiss Army knife." Raucous yells and moderate clapping were interspersed with several boos. Blechmann struck his cowbell for silence. "I want to hear Ms. Fernandez's answer."

Monica Louis, with her mouth still close to her microphone, pivoted sideways to face the entire audience. "Please hold comments and applause until the end of the debate. Ms. Mann-Fernandez, your answer?"

Martha's knuckles blanched as she gripped both sides of the lectern. "Thank you, whoever asked this question. ...Our forefathers wrote about the right to bear arms after state militias united to defeat an oppressive foreign regime, and the weapon then was a single shot muzzle-loaded long rifle, *not* a high-capacity rapid-fire instrument designed for the military and used during our present times for frequent acts of terror.

"My position is that we need a mandatory assault weapons and high-capacity ammunition clip buyback program administered and enforced by the federal government. Full value to the owner at first, then 25% less every six months. After two years the penalties for owning these begin and then grow. I suspect Mr. Blechmann wouldn't still feel the need to own a weapon of war, if his neighbor didn't also carry one."

Smirking, he interrupted her answer. "It's not *my* neighbors I'm concerned about."

"And do you *need* a weapon of war to shoot a deer?" Martha pressed on. "As a fourteen-year-old, my father killed a deer with a bolt action rifle. Are your hunting skills so much worse, that you have to compensate with a semiautomatic killing machine? And do *we,* the American people, want these terrorists' weapons roaming around in our fields and woods—and invading our schools while our children desperately try to find cover under their desks?"

Cries of "Right on!" and "Tell it!" competed with scattered boos and curse words.

"You go, Girl!" Chelsea exclaimed.

Mateo sat wide-eyed watching his mother from Iris' lap. Phineas leaned close and murmured, "starting this with a bang, and she did it well."

He noticed movement at the crowd's front row. One of the red caps climbed onto the edge of the stage. The stout man scrambled to his feet and brandished a long, dark hunting knife. Men in fluorescent green security vests approached cautiously toward the stage. The intruder had too much of a head start. Phineas tried to bolt from his chair to intercept the man, but his once nimble legs felt like they needed a boost to respond to his will. His thumb and index finger began their rhythmic rubbing. *Please, not now!*

The more agile Felipe zipped past and reached Martha's lectern in time to face down the man. Felipe ripped the microphone from its stand and swung it on its cord at the man's face. With the assailant's attention focused on dodging the swirling microphone, he paused his charge and pointed his weapon at Felipe. Jacob circled from behind and, towering over the distracted knife-wielder, wrapped him in a bear hug, and pinned his arms to his sides. Felipe let the microphone drop and grabbed the immobilized arm holding the knife in both of his powerful chef hands then brought it down hard over his raised knee. The arm deformed with a crisp crack. Red hat screamed in pain and his knife tumbled to the floor. Security was suddenly there to relieve Jacob and, one on each of the attacker's shoulders, began a rough escort of the howling attacker toward an exit. Distant sirens outside the gym increased in volume.

Jacob kicked the knife toward a third security employee's feet. It skittered across the floor and made a sound like stacking china saucers, a distinctly non-metallic sound. "Here you go, Sir. Glad you finally made it here."

A line of the bright green vests formed in front of the platform. Monica Louis approached the oldest looking man among them, who appeared to be in charge, and asked, "Do you feel it's safe to continue?"

The man scanned the audience. "Should be now."

Felipe kissed Martha's cheek and rejoined their family. Martha raised her hands over her head and clapped. Many in the crowd followed her lead. She bent to retrieve the microphone from the floor. "Is this thing still working?" Her voice reverberated off the walls.

"We hear you." and "Go on!" The crowd answered her.

She put it back in its holder and clapped again. "Let's give a round of applause for my husband and my brother!" Loud clapping. "And now... to my opponent, I'll say this..." She pointed a finger at him. "It's safe now.

You can come out." Blechmann rose up from a half-crouch behind his lectern. Laughter rose to a crescendo and filled the hall.

"She learn that from you?" Phineas whispered to Iris. His left hand was now behaving itself. He'd shoved it deep in his pocket, lest it start up again.

"Definitely from the women on my side of the family."

His inability to respond to the danger his daughter faced was crushing—and a new reason, beyond the new sporadic tremor, to make an appointment with a neurologist. He'd set up the consultation right after their Italy trip. And he'd keep that consultation a secret. Iris and Martha had enough to worry about. When he had more information, he'd tell Iris about it, though now he was even more certain what the diagnosis would be. Eventually, he might require medications, just not yet.

His reverie evaporated when he spotted a familiar pair of black suits moving along the periphery of the crowd toward the far exit. "Iris. Look at those two in the suits over there." As though the taller of the two had heard those words, he turned and paused long enough to lock eyes with Phineas. "Meyers and Richter!" Meyers offered a quick thumbs up then melted into the crowd.

Iris gasped. "What are *they* doing here?"

"Who, Wayla? Who?" Mateo tried to follow her gaze.

"No one you want to know, Mateo...No one you *ever* want to know." She hugged him to her chest.

A stooped elderly man parted the crowd with his walker and shuffled ten paces behind the men in suits. Vinnie DiCenzo gave Phineas a single, emphatic nod before continuing his urgent pursuit. Theresa strode close behind her husband, protecting his back.

Monica Louis announced the conclusion of the debate, and Felipe was once again the first to reach Martha, while Phineas and the rest of the family stood in line for their turns at congratulating her on a stellar performance. Mateo let go of Iris' hand, scrambled by everyone, clung to his mother's leg, and commanded, "Up!" She caressed his dark locks and obeyed.

"Ms. Fernandez." Her opponent's voice came from behind them.

"Mr. Blechmann." Her voice demanded respect.

His bronzed brow was lined with creases. "That was a cheap shot."

"Nothing you wouldn't do. And, by the way, why *were* you hiding from your constituent? Were you and your Swiss Army knife afraid of him?" She offered Blechmann a crooked grin.

"I'd just looked down at my notes. It...It all happened so fast."

"Uh huh." She cocked her head at a slight angle. "You've been telling your followers that my U. S. born husband here, a lifelong citizen of this country, invaded from Mexico. You *know* that's a bold-faced lie."

Felipe kept his fists by his sides.

Blechmann took a step back to a safer distance. "Nothing personal. That's politics. Talking point from the party's leader. Say it often enough, and they believe it." He shoved his hands into his jeans' front pockets and rocked back on his boots' heels.

Felipe raised clenched fists half-way to a fighter's position.

Martha looked like she also considered punching Blechmann. "How can you look at yourself in the mirror, especially after sucking up to *him*?" Her upper lip curled in obvious disgust. "And he'll no longer be your leader after the election. Your lies will follow you."

"Don't know about that." Blechmann's smug smile morphed into a sinister sneer. "With the Senate and DOJ in his pockets, he may not be going anywhere."

The Republican's words sent a chill through Phineas.

～

Below the high-intensity parking lot lamps, only the half dozen cars of Martha's family and campaign staffers remained. Iris and Phineas reached theirs while the younger members of the team lugged bins of campaign material outside. Iris waved when she spotted Felipe carrying

Mateo through the building's heavy metal door. She yelled, "tell Martha to text me in the morning. I need to take Phineas home. He has an early start tomorrow."

The route home on the rural roads was inky black except for the twin beams from the Prius' headlights. At each bend, they spotlighted fields of withering corn, soybeans, or tobacco plants.

With the car's air conditioning on high, Phineas' worry over Martha began to fade. Her performance had been solid. Nothing to worry about there. But then, while he studied the road, another concern surfaced. "Notice anything different about driving down these backcountry farm roads tonight?"

Iris appeared deep in thought. "Not really. What am I missing?" She snapped her head up to a full vertical posture.

"It's what isn't there that's missing. When we came to North Carolina, if you drove down a country road like this, your windshield would be pelted with a blizzard of bugs. Yours hasn't been hit once. It's like an insect ghost town."

"You're right, but I hadn't thought to complain about not having to wash it."

"And when's the last time you saw a firefly?" He turned his head front to back, searching the darkness beside them.

"Can't remember. Maybe last summer?" She sounded exhausted.

"I've seen several studies looking at quantities of insects, and their total numbers are falling at an alarming rate."

"Uh huh. That can't be good." She was humoring him.

"I've been watching our yard. Haven't seen a firefly all summer. The butterfly bush and butterfly weed used to be covered with swallowtails. None. And milkweed brought in Monarchs, and moonflowers humming-bird moths, and on and on...I'm not seeing any of them anymore."

His finger and thumb gently rolled against each other. He slipped his hand into his pocket, lest it misbehave more noticeably in his sudden emotional state.

"And all the creatures that feed on them—the birds, frogs, lizards—and all their predators—all downstream casualties. If this insect apocalypse is coming from pesticides, where do the toxins end up? The soil? Our water? Our food? And what about the devastating effect of no pollinators on food production, at a time of such terrible shortages?"

She sighed. "It's been a long day, Honey, and we're both tired." She clearly wasn't in the mood for a lecture on the environment, one she'd heard from him before.

She eased the car around a corner. "Armadillo!" There, in the headlights' beams, the armored creature's shell reflected from its encircling bands of white dots. It raised its head to stare at them from the center of their lane. Iris jerked the steering wheel to the right and swerved two wheels onto the road's shoulder before she guided all four back onto pavement. Phineas turned to watch the miniature four-legged tank continue its unhurried passage into darkness.

He whispered, "Why does an armadillo cross the road?"

"Funny man." Iris glare shifted into a hint of a grin. "That's not the first time I've had a close encounter with one of those buggers. They could do some serious damage—woke me up though."

"Another consequence of climate change. They've moved north from Texas. I read they'll probably keep going all the way to New England."

She groaned, "Ugh" then eased the car through an intersection and into a neighborhood of identical blocky houses, each a few feet from the next. "Back in civilization, but this is still unfamiliar territory for me. Remind me when we're near that turn I missed before. I'm mentally running on fumes."

The beams lit up a garish yellow poster on a corner lot proclaiming:

MOSQUITO PRO
WE'LL GIVE YOU
BACK YOUR YARD
Approved for Tax Credit

A competing hot pink company sign across the road reflected her high beams, and another, and another—sprouted up beside each driveway likes mushrooms after a downpour.

⌒

Marie and Jacob practically staggered to Felipe's Nissan LEAF, loaded as they were beneath armloads of signs and rolled up banners. Felipe was bent over its back section under the flipped-up door. His head snapped back. "Phew! You might want to stay back a moment. I'm changing Mateo. My Nino's dropped a stinky load."

They stepped back until Felipe expertly rolled diaper and wipes into a plastic bag and tied it shut. "He expressed his opinion on Martha's opponent...Long day for him. Glad he had a diaper on."

Mateo sat up and yawned. "Casa, Papi."

"I know you're tired, my little man." Felipe scooped him into his arms. "Let's get you settled in your car seat, and we'll go home as soon as your mother's ready."

"Here I am." Martha joined them, waving to a handful of college-aged supporters, her head held high like a seasoned legislator. "Thank you everyone. Good work tonight." She opened the LEAF's passenger side door and watched her departing workers scatter toward their cars. Felipe lowered the car windows in the still hot night, and Martha climbed in.

Standing next to her Tesla, Marie turned to Jacob and said, "Well that was fun. Have a good rest of your week." Time for her to slip away before he had a chance to ask her out again—and she had to beg off—again.

His smile sagged. "Marie—"

Marie froze. A dark grey Hummer barreled into the parking lot and came to an abrupt stop, tires squealing, blocking Felipe's car. Three men in black ballcaps and camouflage garb spilled out. Two brandished aluminum baseball bats. The third, an older man with a full white beard, cocked his head and growled, "So, you think you can break my American friend's arm and just drive away, you lousy immigrant?"

Felipe lay on his horn and inched his vehicle forward. A bat took off the mirror next to Martha and left wires hanging.

Jacob reached into the back of his red pickup truck and grabbed a long-handled shovel. He took three long strides toward the second bat-wielding man, who was now level with the driver's side, and raised his weapon.

"Hold it right there, Sasquatch." The older bearded attacker pulled a pistol from the back of his belt and pointed it dead at Jacob.

Jacob stopped, the shovel over his head, poised to swing.

But then, from behind the Hummer, a man appeared, wiry and nearly invisible in a black suit and tie. He leveled a semi-automatic pistol at the three and exclaimed, "FBI! On your knees. Put the gun on the ground. Hands behind your heads."

The two aluminum bats struck the pavement with resounding clangs, and White Beard, gun still pointed, shifted his attention to a second black suited man, this one's suit stretched over burly muscles. The burly FBI agent said nothing, only displayed an identical pistol in one hand and a badge in the other.

White Beard slowly squatted and placed his pistol on the pavement.

Burly FBI rasped, "He said, 'on your knees. Hands behind your heads.'" Menacing tones.

White Beard and the two bat-wielders knelt and clasped their hands behind their heads.

Wiry FBI extracted a cell phone from his jacket pocket. "FBI at the college gymnasium parking lot. We need police here now for an assault with a deadly weapon." He provided more details then pocketed his phone.

When Jacob asked, "Mind if I put this shovel away?" Marie jumped.

"Go ahead," Wiry FBI responded. "As soon as the police arrive, we'll be turning everything over to them." He and Burly FBI kept their weapons trained on the three kneeling men.

Burly FBI stepped closer to White Beard and hissed, "You'd better tell all your friends that this family is off limits. Any of you get even close to them, and we'll be on you like stink on shit."

"Don't take this the wrong way." Jacob dropped the shovel in his truck bed. "We're glad to see you, but I'm puzzled why the FBI is conveniently here to rescue us."

The agents glanced at each other. The wiry one murmured, "Just be thankful we happened to be in the neighborhood." They offered nothing more.

⌒

Marie sat at her dinner table and reviewed the excitement of her first in-person political debate and the night's terrifying assaults from Martha's opponent's base. The worst of it ended up being that Felipe's car was damaged, and that little Mateo had witnessed violence. Martha was unable to contain the previously sleepy dynamo in his safety car seat when the police sirens and flashing lights approached. The toddler exploded with a burst of renewed energy, gesticulating, and exclaiming at all the excitement.

After talking with the police, Marie was so shaken it took her two tries to correctly instruct her Tesla's Siri to bring her home. Still, she had to admit that witnessing drama in person was better than sitting home reading or watching one of the infinite offerings on her ultra-high-definition TV.

But why had the FBI materialized at the scene like guardian angels? Jacob once asked her about the FBI. Were agents of the Republican government watching Martha or Felipe? It seemed a stretch for it to have anything to do with her mother's ancient misdeeds—or so she hoped.

And who has a shovel at the ready? Jacob explained that he kept tools for maintaining his scores of hives and their stands, and then he joked about not firing up the chainsaw in the truck's large, locked toolbox. The man was full of surprises. A rabbit out of his ballcap next?

She took a bite of the turkey sandwich she'd tossed in the refrigerator earlier. The deli had finally been able to get their hands on blessed avocados again. Most of the California orchards had burned up in recent years. Maybe these delicacies were from Central America. The familiar taste and texture pleased her palate.

She opened her laptop to scan the news. Nothing yet about the debate. Under the usual daily headlines of White House bluster were more storms and wildfires. A cluster of blazes in Montana near where she went to high school caught her attention. She opened an article about the fires in that area and scanned the images. Her eye caught the word "Chinook" in a caption under a grouping of pictures.

She clicked on an image of a sooty family checking into an evacuation facility. The father's haggard expression conveyed pure anxiety and weariness. The mother of the six children looked familiar. Marie expanded the image. *My God! Ada!* Her best friend in high school. The caption indicated that they waited to hear whether their home and sugar beet farm were incinerated by the blazes. They'd barely outrun an approaching wall of flames only hours before.

Marie pushed her sandwich away. She hadn't checked on Ada on Facebook for too long. She opened Ada's page. It was flooded with "thoughts and prayers" and with countless offers to help from family, friends, and churchmates.

Marie began composing her note. First, more thoughts and prayers for her Mormon friend, then an offer to help that felt hollow. Ada's people were proud and probably wouldn't accept her charity. Marie blinked back tears and sent a wish that they could still be close. Ada was family once, so long ago. Family.

She lifted her Sugarbeeter team warm-up jacket from her top dresser drawer and draped it over her shoulders, as loneliness engulfed her like a sudden downpour. She'd tried to convince herself that she should think of her circumstance as a blessed solitude—a respite from her hospital work—and that she should savor it, yet what she felt now was the isolation of an orphan, and she was tired of it.

⌒

A walker clanked on the linoleum floor, distracting Phineas from typing his patient notes. He spun around to see who entered the clinic workroom after hours.

"Well, hello, Vinnie. How's it going?"

"Fine, Doc." His old detective friend shuffled to the seat next to Phineas and settled into it with an accompanying sigh. DiCenzo's black pants were flecked with short, white hairs. "Afraid I didn't get much for you on those government suits. We kept our eyes on 'em and followed 'em out of the gym."

"You get a new cat, Vinnie?"

"Nothing gets by you, Doc. You'd have made a good detective." He gave his pantlegs a few token brushes with his hand. "Theresa adopted a ball of fur from the shelter. He and I are still sorting things out."

"Did you get a chance to talk to the agents?"

"For a little bit. Theresa enlisted them to help me get my walker into our trunk. Pretended we were helpless. The tall one—the one you said was Meyers—told his buddy to wait while he helped us." DiCenzo pulled out a pocket-sized notebook. "Theresa makes me write everything down. She did most of the talking. You know how good she is with small talk."

Phineas chuckled at the image of his octogenarian investigative team interrogating federal agents without them knowing it.

"Doc, she's here with me today...was right behind me but stopped to share some cookies with the housekeeping guy. Probably still talking with 'im." DiCenzo studied his notes. "First Theresa complimented 'em on how well they were dressed. Then she thanked them for helping. Asked if they enjoyed the debate. Got only one-word answers out of 'em."

"They've been tight-lipped with me too."

"Then she commented on their government plates—like she thought it was the coolest thing. Gave her an excuse to ask if the two men were there as part of their job." Dicenzo tilted his head forward. "Meyers gave her a look like she'd guessed right—so, she asked if the job was protection for Congressman Blechmann."

"You married a clever woman, Vinnie."

"You know it, Doc. And here she comes now. Hey, Honey. Doc and I are just getting started."

Theresa, in a blue silk blouse and cream-colored slacks crossed the room in silent, graceful strides. She held up a brown paper bag with its top neatly folded. "Brought you oatmeal cookies, Phineas. I hope you don't mind I shared some with Jeremiah out there."

Seems everyone knows I like oatmeal cookies. "Of course not. He and I go way back. Thank you." He could smell the cinnamon already. "How are you?"

"Lovin' life, Phineas. You?" She pulled up a chair, opened the bag, and handed him a fragrant cookie.

It was still warm. "Fine. Heard you got a new cat."

"Vinnie told you about Orso Bianco already? He leave me anything to talk about?"

"We were just getting to the part where you asked Meyers why he was at the debate." Phineas realized how hungry he was and took a healthy bite. Delicious. Buttery and sweet. Just the right spices.

"Such a nice man. Really helpful. Once his partner got in the car, Meyers opened up a bit more." She lowered her voice with the last sentence. "Said that it was hard to keep public events secure—and they wanted to make sure Martha and her family were safe too."

Phineas forgot about the tasty morsel in his mouth and swallowed. "He definitely mentioned Martha's family?"

"No question. Surprised me too. Maybe he wants to keep one of you ready for something important. Like you said he said before."

Vinnie reached for the paper bag. "Doc, you don't mind if I have a couple, do you? The smell is terrific." Theresa narrowed her eyes at her husband and handed him just one. Vinnie lifted the cookie to his nose and sniffed. "So, just as Meyers was about to leave, Theresa asked if he knew your family very well."

"And?" Phineas leaned forward, begging for an answer.

"He didn't say anything, just gave her a little smile. Then got in the car and left."

Phineas was past creeped out. What was that something that he should be ready for, and when would that be? "Well, they came back to the gym parking lot after the debate ended."

Vinnie's mouth hung open, purposed for his first bite. "Really? We left when they did. Figured they might get suspicious if they saw us circle back. You learn anything else?"

"Iris and I weren't there. We'd already left. Some more armed right-wing thugs with baseball bats came after Martha and Felipe in the parking lot. The agents interrupted them and turned them over to the police. Then the FBI guys split without saying anything useful."

Vinnie already wrinkled forehead took on deeper furrows. "Seems like they're looking out for you and yours."

"But why? What do they want from me?"

The three exchanged glances in silence.

AUGUST

"Never have we so hurt and mistreated our common home
as we have in the last two hundred years...Reducing green-
house gases requires honesty, courage and responsibility...
Those who will have to suffer the consequences...will not
forget this failure of conscience and responsibility."

POPE FRANCIS ENCYCLICAL

Phineas eased his truck out of traffic and into their neighborhood. He'd
tolerated his long day at work with the promise of a soothing sit watching
pollen-dusted forager bees land at their hive entrances, the baskets on
their hind legs packed with warm shades of pollens from the asters and
goldenrod beginning to bloom. Clouds of the youngest bees would hover
in their first orientation flights, imprinting lessons on how to find home.
Others would beat their wings at the hives' entrances to ventilate the
muggy insides. In August's early evening swelter, bees cling together and
hang off the bottom boxes like beards and, like him, they try to chill out.
He parked in the driveway and headed straight for his hives.

There were no bee beards. The familiar hum was gone. Only silence.

He could count the number of bees in flight on one hand. The ground in front of his three colonies, usually green grass and weeds, was transformed into a golden carpet. He knelt next to it. Tens of thousands of honey bees lay still. An occasional trembling worker crawled a few steps at a time over piles of her deceased hive mates. Brilliant white corpses of pupae dotted the eerily vacant hive entrances.

As Phineas lifted the outer and inner covers off the closest hive, his hand began its now familiar, bothersome shaking. He tried to ignore the constriction in his throat and pounding in his head. He needed to understand this devastation.

A lonely worker staggered across the top of one of the frames. Gone was the usual phalanx of guard bees displaying their protective stingers. Phineas extracted a frame from the middle. More pupae and larvae hung from their cells. *There.* In the center. A circle of a dozen rigid bees, the queen's retinue, surrounded her. Her tiny tongue protruded toward one of her feeders, stilled in the act of accepting nutrition. The queen's abdomen had been inserted into an empty honeycomb cell before she died. She was poisoned while laying an egg, while dutifully maintaining the colony.

Pesticides! His bees foraged on plants sprayed with poisons within the three-mile radius of his apiary.

Those offensive roadside signs claimed this or that company could sterilize yards from all those nasty insects and allow you to sit without swatting, have a cool drink without scratching. Their employees were supposed to spray only near dusk, after foragers returned to their homes, but Phineas saw their trucks at all hours of the day. Homeowners wouldn't want them spraying during happy hour.

Every day now, Phineas frowned at the growing troops of novice unlicensed pesticide applicators, tanks of chemicals on their backs or in the beds of pickup trucks that displayed mottos promising death. Death to all with six or eight legs, including the important pollinators, the beneficial insects and arachnids that feed on true pests; and the wiggly worms and caterpillars that would become songbirds' lethal meals. The President's tax credit for spraying increased demand for poisons to such levels that pesticide companies barely kept up.

One more reason to hate the man. As if one more was needed. The President attacked his daughter and her husband. He promoted violence and encouraged his deranged base to arm to the teeth with military grade weapons. He mocked and stepped on the downtrodden over and over. And the planet Earth was disintegrating at an accelerating pace with no hope of reversal—all due to that man's ignorance, neglect, and direct actions. Oh, how Phineas loathed his so-called Commander-in-Chief.

Both hands now shook, and his knees felt so weak he had to sit on the supporting timber between his hives. Was he feeling the toxin? Or was he feeling the sudden cataclysmic loss of all the fuzzy little creatures he nurtured for so many years?

He pulled out his cell phone and called his son.

"Hi, Dad. What's up?"

"Death. My bees are dead." He struggled to hold back a flood of emotion. The accumulation of all the misery and death he'd witnessed over so many years had finally eroded his wall of professional stoicism.

At length, Jacob asked, "When did they last look okay?"

"Yesterday—this morning." Phineas wished his son could be there with him.

"Has to be pesticides. Freeze a couple of frames and a jarful of bees, and I'll get them tested."

"What else could it be?" Phineas tried to think diagnostically.

"Nothing really."

Case closed.

"Testing could get you compensation, maybe," Jacob offered gently.

"Does that include pain and suffering?" Phineas bent forward, elbows supported on his knees.

"Sorry, Dad. Probably not." Jacob's voice trailed off.

"I'm feeling pretty shaky—and nauseated. Those poisons the companies are using—could they physically harm me?"

"I doubt it. The LD50, the lethal dose, for a person would be way higher than you could get from touching your foraging bees and beehives." He cleared his throat. "Dad, I probably don't need to tell you that you shouldn't harvest their honey."

Phineas found his handkerchief in his back pocket, dabbed at his eyes, and wiped his nose. "Too bad the lethal dose was so low for my girls...I'll miss them...and their honey." Were his beekeeping days finally over? Had the President shut him down for good? Phineas' backyard was no longer a nurturing environment for raising bees when deadly threats to them loomed just down the road.

Iris had avoided the apiary when the bees were alive, but she pitched in with the somber cleanup after the state inspector examined the scene and collected samples. And yesterday she was on her hands and knees with him weeding and harvesting vegetables. Once, he caught her watching him, like she was assessing him for damage. At dinnertime, she stayed nearby while he prepared it rather than busying herself elsewhere.

God, how he loved that woman!

Phineas poured off the boiling water and shocked the blanched green beans with an ice water slurry. The aromas of minced garlic and ginger simmering in olive oil in a cast iron fry pan filled the kitchen and dining area. He again drained the beans and tossed them into the pan with the fragrant blend before sprinkling salt, pepper, and the tiniest pinch of hot pepper flakes.

Iris looked up from her laptop with a broad smile. "Whoa, Phineas! That smells amazing."

"Had to find something else to do with beans, since we've had them almost every night for weeks." He tried to return her cheer. "So, what's in the news?"

"A bit of good news for a change. The latest polls have Martha with a narrow lead over the 'Gallo Rojo'. Don't you just love the name Mateo provided for her opponent?"

"It does fit him. As long as our grandson translates gallo rojo as red rooster and not red cock."

"He's only two, Phineas." Iris giggled, something he hadn't witnessed in a while. "And the polls also show gains for Democrats in several swing states, for the house and senate candidates. Phineas, how about pouring us each a glass of wine to celebrate the moment?"

He surveyed the wine rack in the pantry and slid out a Primitivo. "This one should hold its own with dinner." He peeled the foil, delivered the cork, and sniffed it. Not musty or tainted. He poured an ounce and swirled it around the goblet, inspected its 'legs', and inhaled the bouquet. He finally tasted it and began contemplating its notes. "Blackberries and pepper. Perfect."

"Am I going to get some before it goes by?" A comic pleading look.

"It's still breathing." He poured her a share and hoisted his glass. "To Martha, and to democracy. May we see it again soon." They clinked and sipped.

She set her glass on the table and studied her screen. "Phineas, it says that after another attack of hives from Alpha Gal, the President fired his chef."

"Did they say what he ate? Did the chef screw up, or did POTUS cheat on his diet?"

"Maybe some of both." A puzzled expression. "It says the President was savoring the smell of barbecued beef brisket, but then ate gelatin in a fruit salad. Can those do it?"

"Absolutely. Gelatin comes from horses' hooves, so that could cause a reaction. Did he have to go to the hospital?"

"Yup. And they gave him an adrenaline shot at the White House."

Phineas chuckled. "Bet he was tough to deal with after that." Hard to imagine that man more jazzed up than usual. "Glad I wasn't his doctor."

"So, climate change is responsible for our president being unable to sniff a brisket or eat Jell-O. Pretty pathetic." Her eyes opened wide at something on her laptop screen. "Phineas, the New York district attorney that went missing was spotted in Toronto. CNN speculates that as soon as the President leaves office, she is planning to come down hard on him for tax evasion and falsifying bank documents. They say she could even send him to a New York jail."

More good news? "Should we have another toast to that?"

"Why not?" She raised her glass. "Salud."

Phineas followed with a healthy swallow. As the warm liquid trickled from mouth to stomach, disturbing thoughts seeped in. "I wouldn't count on anything with him. He could create chaos in his remaining four months. Somehow screw up the transfer of power."

Dolly Jones had transformed into someone else. Even young Darrell Jr. had evolved. He perched on the examining room's extra chair and was thumbing through a children's' book, the kind with the thick cardboard pages. His clothes were washed, hair combed. Dolly's own hair was now a uniform blond and restrained in a trendy ponytail. She wore a red sleeveless blouse, clean jeans, and bright white athletic shoes. She'd applied makeup to a slimmer face, and her ankles were thin. In the two months since her first visit, Dolly Jones had blossomed into an attractive young woman.

"Sorry Darrell Sr. couldn't make it today, Doc. He had to fix an 18-wheeler, so it could head to the coast with a load of per'shables."

"So, you made the long drive on your own? How've you been doing?"

"I had Darrell Jr. for company, Doc." A broad grin emerged like a sun-rise in a clear sky. "I'm better, Doc." She nodded enthusiastically without taking her eyes off Phineas' face. "Haven't needed my rescue nebulizer since the second dose of your drug. Got my prednisone down to a real low dose too. My Doc back home says it's like a miracle."

"That's wonderful, Dolly. To be truthful, we're still not sure if you're getting the drug or a placebo solution."

"I know I'm getting' it, Doc. My life ain't 'zactly been full of miracles, so I wasn't 'spectin' much." Her smile disappeared and her eyebrows pinched forward. "You're not gonna stop it anytime soon, are ya?"

"The agreement when you entered the study was that after there's enough data to show it's safe and effective, the company will provide it to you at no cost for at least a year. By then, hopefully, it'll be readily available."

Her face relaxed. "Les you an' me pray that nothin' happens to ruin it for me." She closed her eyes, folded her hands, and her lips prayed silently. Darrell Jr. rested his folded hands on his book and studied her, his lips moving with hers.

⌒

Phineas had just settled into his evening seat at the dining table across from Iris when the headline flashed across his iPad screen. Every muscle along his spine and in his throat tightened.

U. S. BOMBS NORTH KOREA

He clicked the link and said, "Oh my God, Iris, listen to this," commandeering Iris' attention away from her laptop screen. "Two waves of U. S. stealth bombers sent missiles into North Korea installations. The first wave eliminated known and suspected nuclear weapon sites. When the Korean military tried to respond to the first attack, a second wave of U. S. bombers followed and destroyed previously unknown locations identified by satellite imaging. The President announced that the joint chiefs were confident that North Korea's nuclear capabilities were eliminated, and their conventional military defenses crippled."

Iris' hands fell from her computer keyboard onto her lap. "Why? Why now?"

"Why? He's doing what a weak president does to try to look like a strong president. He wages war." His left thumb and index finger began rubbing against each other. He slid his hand under the table.

The next article reported that hours before the bombing attack, a powerful U. S. naval fleet moved into the South China Sea. China immediately lodged a protest in the United Nations and mobilized its mainland military forces and sent its own ships toward the U.S. fleet.

Iris shifted her focus from her husband back to her laptop screen. "Pundits are speculating that the President's handlers have decided that he's shifted production of so many critical tech components back stateside that he no longer needs China's manufacturers. He can rattle sabers at them now, not just tariffs." She focused on her screen with a horrified expression. "What if he reinstates the draft? Could Jacob be drafted?"

"Jacob's a bit too old for that, unless we go into World War III."

"You don't think this president isn't desperate enough to do that? Where's the Vice-President during this? Can't he be the adult in the room? And what about all the advisors? Are they *all* now just sycophantic lap dogs?"

Iris tapped her touchpad and return key. A familiar jarring voice came from her laptop's speakers. She turned it at an angle, so Phineas could also see the screen. The President's round face filled much of it, as he hunched over the podium in the White House press room.

"My fellow Americans, when I first took this office, I promised I would eliminate the threat of a nuclear North Korea." His focus shifted from the teleprompter to his audience. "I told that to their prior leader. Then I told it to his disgusting sister when she took over that nasty country. Today, I kept my promise. On my order, I wiped those weapons off the face of the earth. And I did it with zero casualties on our side. Zero. We flew in, and we flew out. They didn't know what hit 'em. Let this be a lesson to Iran and other two-bit countries. You can't scare me by claiming you've got nukes."

He closed a black folder on the lectern and momentarily puckered his lips while staring at the camera. "I'll take a few questions, then it's back to the situation room." As the image backed up, he pointed a stubby finger and smirked. "You. Failed New York Times. Go ahead. Give it your best shot."

A middle-aged man in a suit stood. "Mr. President, what is the likelihood that China will respond with a military action against one of our bases, or that, because our forces will have to concentrate more on the Pacific theatre, today's action will embolden Russia to further advance its military takeover of the Baltic States?"

"That's a nasty question, but I expect nasty questions from your people...China knows better than to start anything with us. We don't need 'em for anything anymore. My programs got rid of our need for their factories...What was the other question?"

"Russia advancing into the Baltic States."

"Who cares about 'em? When did they ever do anything for us? The Baltic States? Who cares about Serbia? Let Russia have their problems." He pointed at a young woman with long blond hair. "Next question. Who are you with?"

"CNN. Mr. President—" She rose from her chair and held up a notepad.

"Well, you're an improvement over that nasty guy CNN used to send. What can I do for you, Honey?"

Her shoulders sagged when several pairs of eyes in the room glared at her. Had CNN sent a pretty female, figuring POTUS would approve? "Mr. President, what is the likelihood that after today's action, Russia will provide advanced defenses and technology to Iran, allowing them to finally become a nuclear power?"

He furrowed his brow and again puckered his lips, this time like he was coming in for a kiss. "I talked to Russia's leader. A tough guy. Told me that won't happen, an' I trust him." He stretched his arm out and pointed to his right. "Last question. You. FOX News. Go ahead."

"Thank you, Mr. President. Our polls suggest that the American people were hoping for a strong display of our military power, and that it will help get your supporters to the polls in November. Do you believe today's action will help your vice president become your successor and continue your important work?"

"I'll answer that later, since it looks like we're gonna postpone the 2024 elections—until I make the world a safer place." He waved and flashed a mouthful of bright white teeth framed by fleshy orange cheeks. "That's all. Lots of work to do. Have to keep America great!" The image shifted to a news studio where a panel of talking heads waited behind a long semicircular desk.

Iris closed her laptop, creating a sudden vacuum of silence. "Jesus, Phineas! Did he just announce he's going to stop the election?"

"Sounded like it. Sounded like he won't give up power."

"Why doesn't he just go play golf full time?" She yelled this time, clearly exasperated.

"He plays plenty already." One reason for not giving up power was clear. "It's New York's case against him. As long as he's in office, they can't prosecute him for all his crimes before he took office—he won't give up power, and no one's stopping him. The Republican legislators let him do what he wants."

⌒

Marie's monitor displayed the identity numbers and demographics of those currently enrolled in SYMBI-62022's Phase 3 trial. She was studying them for the umpteenth time. She opened Phineas Mann's subject panel, by far the largest of any of the sites. Thirty-seven as of last week. She clicked on one of his latest entries and found a thirty-year-old woman, an organic farmer with multiple hospitalizations for status asthmaticus. The next subject was a sixty-one-year-old male, forced into retirement from his factory job after countless absences due to asthma flares. Both were stuck on daily prednisone at study entry. She read several more. They could be anybody she might pass on the street or in a store.

It was almost time to take a lunch break from her plexiglass prison. She was ready for some hot, moist outside air and a break from the artificial cool air she worked in, the cool air that was maintained by consuming gobs of energy generated by burning coal. The coal polluted the air, warmed the planet, and created more cases of severe asthma that would need their new drugs. *Damn!*

Uh oh. Trouble coming? Schmidt, in a corporate warm-up suit, glided directly toward her through the office's clear floor to ceiling tunnels. *Must be on his way to the gym.* She hoped that meant he wouldn't stay in her cubicle long. He knocked once and, without waiting for her to answer, pushed his way inside. His caterpillar mustache quivered with excitement.

White roots, like tiny legs, anchored it and revealed that he hadn't kept up with his Just for Men applications.

"Have a seat, Sir." She felt obliged to gesture at the lone chair in the corner. "Looks like you're keeping fit."

"There's no other way." He dropped into the chair, shifted his weight onto its front edge, and leaned closer. "I hope you're ready for the biggest thing in your career." He stared expectantly.

"Well, that sounds exciting, Sir. What do you have in mind?" Exciting for him might mean trouble for her.

"A huge opportunity for your drug and our company." He seemed to be waiting for her to seem thrilled.

"I'm all ears, Sir. Tell me more." She'd never taken acting lessons. Maybe that's why her response felt so flat next to his exuberance.

He obviously didn't perceive her lack of enthusiasm. The caterpillar's ecstatic head and rear ends curled upward. "They want us to give SYMBI-62022 to the most powerful man on Earth."

She was supposed to be certain who that was. Amazon's founder? Tesla's founder? Maybe a politician. Rather than guess wrong, she'd play coy. "No! Really?"

"You've got it." He glanced at the empty cubicles surrounding hers and whispered, "the Chairman of Medicine at Walter Reed Hospital wants us to *give it to the President.*" Schmidt leaned back and pressed his fingertips together.

Oh shit! Easy for you to say. You won't be the one giving it, and it was still being studied, still in Phase 3. "You mean they want to enter him in our trial, Sir?"

"Oh, Marie." Her CEO smirked. "That's not how real power works. They want us to *treat* him."

"You want to break from the trial protocol?" She was new at the business, but she knew this wasn't right.

"*They* want us to. And *they* get what they want." His stare seemed to be trying to break her down.

"So, we send a dose to Walter Reed for them to administer?" She hoped for an easy option.

He appeared disappointed in her. "Of course not! You and our Principal Investigator will deliver the dose and administer it personally." He wasn't whispering any more.

Phineas Mann wasn't going to like breaking protocol. Given the chance, he'd say, "That's not how a study is run."

She cleared her throat. "Have you told our Principal Investigator?"

"Day after tomorrow. That morning, you'll take a limo to pick up Walter Reed's Chairman, Dr. Smith, at RDU. I'm on my way to the airport now, but I'll fly back in time to meet you and him at Mann's office." His eyes narrowed. "I'm counting on you to make this happen. No hiccups. This could help us get early FDA approval—and valuable publicity."

"And if Dr. Mann isn't available for the trip to Bethesda?" She hated to prick Schmidt's balloon.

"Then he's off the trial, and we'll pull his funding." A dark cloud replaced his earlier childlike excitement. "We'll get his younger associate to take over. The younger ones are always hungry enough. Remind me who she is."

"Dr. Morales-Villalobos."

"Oh…That's not good. The President may draw the line at being treated by an immigrant."

"She was born in the U. S., Sir." *She's as American as you are.*

"But she won't look like one of his people." Schmidt sprung to his feet. "Just make sure Mann is on board and has the right attitude. Remember, Marie, this is a huge opportunity for us." He opened her door, pivoted, and commanded, "I'll see you, Dr. Smith, and Dr. Mann the day after tomorrow at UNC." His fluorescent shoes carried him down the narrow, translucent corridor and out the exit.

~

A small envelope with neat handwritten addresses rested on top of Phineas' office snail mail in his desk's in-basket. 'Dolly Jones' headlined the Tennessee return address. He reached into a desk drawer for his hand-carved, mahogany letter opener and slit the envelope open. A card slid out with "Thank You" scrolled on the front inside a golden frame. He opened it to a neatly printed note.

Dear Dr. Mann,

My life has been so much better since you put me on your new drug. I may soon come all the way off prednisone, and I hardly ever need a nebulizer treatment. Now I go whole nights without wheezing! I can keep up with Darrell Jr., even when he plays outside—and his Daddy is just so pleased with me!

God bless you, Dr. Mann, and everything you do. I'm praying for you—praying for you EVERY DAY.

Your new best friend,
Dolly

Phineas leaned into his chair's mesh back and reread the card. It had been a while since he'd had a note like it, and its plain heartfelt words made him feel better about his work than all the congratulations he received after his state-of-the-art asthma lecture at the national convention in New Orleans.

He expected an afternoon of trudging through a solitary review of consent forms, entry data, and detailed patient intake examinations attached to the study checklists. Each short pile of papers on his desk represented one new patient entering the Phase 3 SYMBI-62022 trial. Eight more since last month's review. His laptop sat open in the center of the piles, with the same data in digital form, already entered by an assistant. Paper *and* bytes. Fault tolerant records that he, an overly compulsive investigator, required, especially if his memory might not be what it used to be. Was it? He hadn't noticed a difference. Had anyone?

Focus on the work, Mann.

He scooped up the first pile, the one at two o'clock on his desk's wide clockface.

His phone chimed once, and the division's administrative assistant's light flashed. He pushed the speaker button on the decades old telephone, a dated remnant when requested upgrades were long forgotten during recent years' tight academic budgets.

"Hi Grace."

"Dr. Mann, I have Dr. Marie Porter here with another doctor and two other men. They say they need to speak with you."

Two other men...Were they from the FDA? His recent stresses pushed him straight to his most dire professional concerns. Had someone had a deadly reaction to the drug? Were they going to shut down the Phase 3 trial?

His stomach lurched. There would go his last research funding.

And he was too old to spend day after day, seeing patient after patient on a clinic, ICU, or ward assembly line. So many, like Dolly, were not able to afford prohibitively expensive asthma drugs, and so many more had no insurance at all. Evenings of laboriously typing clinical notes and reviewing lab data on the ever-present electronic medical record that never allowed a doctor a break from work. Maybe now *was* the time to retire.

"Is the conference room available, Grace?"

"It should be, Dr. Mann. Shall I ask them to wait for you there?" She had used her friendliest voice. They must be standing right in front of her.

"Yes. Thank you. I'll be right over."

"I'll offer them coffee and water."

He rose and put on a freshly laundered white coat. *Might as well look like a professor.* He took a deep breath and released it from puffed cheeks through pursed lips. Did his career executioners await him in the barren chamber?

He cracked open the conference room door and paused to scan the faces of its occupants clustered at one end of the long table. *Richter and*

Meyers! Why is the FBI here? And who is the middle-aged guy in the suit? Grace had said, "another doctor."

Marie, in a black pinstripe business suit and conservative make-up, had taken the seat at the head of the table. Her familiar wide smile displayed a muted rose-colored lipstick. She'd left a matching print on the rim of a Styrofoam coffee cup. A silver glint flashed off her ever-present cross necklace. She offered a compact wave from the hand that rested on a closed black binder in front of her. "Dr. Mann, thank you for meeting with us on such short notice."

"I had just started going through more new patients' records for your trial." He nodded once at the familiar FBI special agents, whose faces maintained a lack of any expression or recognition. *Nothing to see here.* Their eyes were trained on his.

"Fantastic!" Marie responded. "Glad to hear how well you're doing with it." Her raised voice and careful enunciation startled him and suggested she was performing for the others.

Having Richter and Meyers study him made the hairs on the back of Phineas' neck lift. "So, how are *you two* tied to SynMedical?"

A subtle smile emerged on Meyers' narrow face. "You're almost through with us, Dr. Mann. We're done vetting you and *almost* finished delivering you safely to what you're needed for."

Marie cleared her throat loudly enough to yank Phineas' attention back to her. "Let me introduce Dr. John Smith, Chairman of Medicine at Walter Reed Hospital."

Whoa! Must be something important for him to be here. And it seemed doubtful he was here to shut down the trial. Phineas offered his hand and Dr. Smith stood to give it a vigorous shake. "It's an honor to meet you, Dr. Smith. What can I do for you?"

The door opened a sliver, then enough to admit a short, spry bald man in immaculate athletic shoes. His navy-blue suitcoat was draped over his arm, and a polka dotted Carolina blue tie hung loose under his unbuttoned dress shirt collar. And the mustache. Like something that might crawl across a sidewalk on a warm fall day. The little man exclaimed, "Traffic from RDU is worse than ever. Good thing the limo driver brought me lunch. What have I missed so far?"

Marie Porter vacated her seat, gesturing to the new arrival that he should occupy it. "Dr. Mann, have you met Eugene Schmidt, CEO of SynMedical Biopharma?"

Schmidt approached and Phineas shook his hand, trying not to appear surprised at the sudden powerful assembly. "I haven't yet had the pleasure. What brings you to Chapel Hill, Sir?" *Is he an MD too? No. She'd have called him "Doctor" if he was. This Schmidt has to be a business guy.*

"Call me, Gene, Dr. Mann." He looked around the table. "Let's sit and talk. If you're asking why I'm here, I'm guessing you haven't gotten to the purpose of this meeting."

"I'm curious to hear it." *More than curious.*

Schmidt clapped once, appearing almost gleeful. "Excellent. Dr. Smith, why don't you explain to Dr. Mann why we're here?"

The Chairman of Medicine at Walter Reed Hospital cleared his throat. "We have an...an important patient we'd like you to treat with SYMBI-62022."

Realizing he'd been slouching under the weight of an uncertain future, Phineas now sat erect. He was used to doctors referring their patients for treatment with experimental asthma drugs, but never a doctor of such importance. It seemed the moment to clear his own throat. "Please tell me about your patient, and why they should receive 62022." *Must be really important, if the FBI has to 'vet' and 'deliver' me.*

Smith glanced at the ceiling. "Figured you'd ask—glad you did. Shows you're a careful clinician."

Phineas kept his focus on Smith's grey-green eyes. The darker puffy semicircles under them suggested the Chairman hadn't slept well lately. And why was a VIP from Walter Reed patronizing him?

Smith glanced at Schmidt then back at Phineas before he continued. "Over the last several months, we've exhausted the usual asthma treatments, including recent courses of the two newest FDA approved and indicated biologic agents and had no success at controlling this patient's symptoms or allowing a reduction in a daily high prednisone dose." He looked from Marie to Schmidt. "Our pulmonary chief has been communicating with the scientists at SynMedical Biopharma and has come to believe SYMBI-62022's mechanism of action offers the best chance for our patient. We've waited until you had experience with the drug, but now we want to try it next."

So far, that sounded reasonable to Phineas. "Did he say that your patient has a dominant eosinophilic phenotype?"

Schmidt made a 'T' with his hands, the timeout signal. "Whoa. Please explain."

"That's the subgroup of asthmatics with dominant allergic features, whether or not we can identify a specific allergy. SYMBI-62022 specifically targets the eosinophil blood cell's precursor cells in the bone marrow—thus reducing their population—and subsequently an asthmatic's inflammation."

Smith vigorously nodded his head. "Our pulmonologist *and* allergist confirmed that our patient does have that phenotype."

So far, Smith was making a strong case for their patient to enter the trial. The tension in Phineas' back eased. This wasn't about ending the study. "When can this patient come here so I can review their case and enter them in the trial? I'll be glad to see them right away, and we can then randomize them to drug or placebo."

The muscle above Smith's jawline twitched. "We just want you to treat this person, outside of the trial."

Six years ago, the President had rammed through legislation that allowed drugs not yet FDA approved, even those still under study, to be given in "desperate" cases. "Compassionate use" was the euphemism used, and he promoted it as "the right to try" law.

Then along came COVID-19 and the President's denial of its infectivity and danger—until he got it—and got acutely scary sick. The cocktail of experimental drugs he immediately received was followed by his rapid improvement and return to his campaign and its maskless mass gatherings. The President concluded, based on his own individual rescue, that all the drugs he'd taken were miracles and that further study was unnecessary. He'd pushed those drugs into production and widespread use. The opportunity to determine which of those drugs helped and how much was—in effect—gutted.

Phineas had never agreed with the legislation and was horrified at its total disregard of scientific method. There were good reasons to go through graduated study protocols before allowing new drugs to be prescribed, and the terms "desperate" and "compassionate use" usually applied to hopeless Hail Mary cases when the patients were too sick to benefit. False hope and futility bequeathed at the end of a life.

"So, you want to break our protocol?" He had to try to dissuade them. "That could undermine all the work done thus far on this important Phase 3 trial." He couldn't keep his voice from rising.

"In this case, it's a necessity." Smith lowered his, like he was trying to instill calm.

"But why here? One of the study sites is Johns Hopkins, and that's just down the road from Walter Reed." Perhaps Phineas could divert his involvement.

"At Hopkins, they've only enrolled a handful of subjects so far—hardly any experience with the drug." Smith kept his calm voice. "You here have, by far, the most experience giving SYMBI-62022. How many have you treated now?"

Phineas' hopes began to sink, and yet he admitted with more than a bit of pride, "We've enrolled thirty-seven and treated twenty-nine of the subjects at least once. Of course, you know only two thirds received the drug." He performed a quick review in his head. "I believe we've given at least fifty total monthly doses of either drug or placebo, so probably thirty-four doses of drug since the trial began in March."

Smith leaned forward, his crossed forearms resting on the table. "Any adverse reactions yet?"

"One had anaphylaxis. Since the drug is given by IV infusion, the allergic reaction was immediate. The subject responded quickly to epinephrine and diphenhydramine." Phineas was glad he'd been right there, the one giving SYMBI-62022. "Of course, that subject had to be dropped from the study."

The CEO's eyebrows arched upward. "Diphenhydramine?"

Definitely a business guy.

"Benadryl." Marie Porter and Phineas answered in near unison.

Schmidt fidgeted in his chair. "Can you tell if you're seeing much benefit?" His caterpillar flexed up at the ends.

Phineas was sure he still looked upset, so he forced a smile. "Sure. Some say they're better. Some have even come way down on their prednisone doses, but we don't know yet if they're getting the drug or placebo, since it's a double-blind study."

"So, our drug *must* be helping." The fuzzy black insect squirmed hopefully.

"Sometimes patients on placebos improve in drug studies. We think it's the extra care and attention they get during it—or it's the well-known placebo effect."

Marie opened the black binder. "Dr. Mann, why don't you explain how all that study data is gathered under the watchful eye of a central observer?"

An ambush. Phineas had to force himself to stay composed. "All drug studies have someone elsewhere, not a study investigator, who collects and analyzes data points from all of the trial sites in real-time. It's in case statistical analysis shows they have enough subjects treated to prove benefit or futility—or to detect safety issues." He took a breath. "We're not even close to having enough data points for them to say anything conclusive about SYMBI-62022 yet."

FBI Agent Richter sat up like someone had poked him. "Where's this central observer with all the data?"

"I'm not privy to that information," Phineas was glad he could truthfully answer.

"I'm sure we can find that for you, Dr. Smith." Schmidt used what must be his most soothing tone. Richter smiled and settled back in his chair.

Phineas clenched his fists under the table, out of sight. *This Schmidt could jeopardize all the study's hard work and its validity, and it's his drug!*

"Our patient is too busy and important to come here." Dr. Smith turned to face Phineas. "We'll let you know when we need you to come to Walter Reed to treat them."

Who is so damned important? Washington has to be crawling with 'important' bureaucrats. "Talk to me then, when you decide something." Despite the bomb dropped on him, Phineas somehow now kept his tone even, his frustration mostly concealed.

FBI agent Meyers finished writing in his notebook, clicked his ballpoint three times, and glanced at his watch. "Dr. Mann, you were told back in April that you might be called on to serve your country." He and Richter grinned like third graders with a shared secret, a disturbing look on grown men in black suits.

Eugene Schmidt bolted from his seat, came around the table behind Marie, put his hand on her shoulder, and bent close to her ear. "This could be a fantastic opportunity for us." She cringed for an instant at his touch then acknowledged his enthusiasm with a nod and a grin.

Or a terrible mistake.

Schmidt displayed a broad toothy smile—like another third grader, one clutching a full bag of Halloween candy. "Thank you, everyone!"

Phineas kept his seat. "Gene, might I have a few words with you and Marie?" Breaking a trial's protocol to serve a VIP clashed with Phineas' nature—and just felt *so* wrong.

"Got to run." Schmidt gave a brief half wave. "Need to get to another meeting." He took a step toward the door. "Marie can pass on your words." He disappeared without another sound, his flashy running shoes gleaming.

"Thank you, Dr. Mann. We'll likely see you soon." Dr. Smith followed Schmidt into the hall.

Richter paused to say, "I suspect *we'll all* see you soon." He lifted his eyebrows twice, as if to say, "Hah!" Meyers slipped out behind him and closed the door.

Marie stared at Phineas in the suddenly quiet room, its stillness a suffocating vacuum.

"You know more than you're telling me." He broke the silence.

She drained what was left of her coffee, stood, and scanned the room for a trash can, then tossed her cup in one under the wall's antiquated viewing boxes for x-ray films. She paused to inspect the boxes' perimeters then ducked her head to peer under the table where Meyers and Richter were seated. Finally, Marie lowered herself into the seat across from Phineas, and whispered, "I don't see how they could possibly have bugged this room, since they didn't know we'd be here."

His neck muscles tensed even more than before. "Bugged?"

"They can't know what I tell you, and I've got more to tell." She seemed eager to divulge more.

"Maybe we shouldn't have this conversation." *Immediate retirement is sounding better and better.*

"Dr. Smith and SynMedical have already worked out a plan and a schedule."

Damn! "And it requires me?"

"Oh yeah." She appeared to be organizing her next words. "In two weeks, we're to be transported to Walter Reed to administer the drug. We'll spend the next night there, to be sure everything went smoothly, then they bring us home."

"That's not going to work for me."

"We'll need to make it work."

When did this young woman get so bossy? He stifled his irritation. "Before then, Iris and I are flying to Milan and staying for a month. We've bought tickets and leased a villa in the North. Already paid for." And Iris was really looking forward to the trip, as was he.

"Not a problem. SynMedical will buy new tickets and reschedule your rental. I'm sure we can fly you first class and arrange a limo in Milan.

Want us to rent you a car too?" She began jotting on a sticky note in the Phase 3 binder.

She has deep pockets. He'd been outmaneuvered. "Why not just do the treatment earlier?"

"Our patient has to be elsewhere before then, and his schedule is packed."

"*His.* So, our patient is a man. Who? Do you even know?"

Marie blinked extra and pressed her lips together, a clue Iris had coached him to look for. She could always tell when he or the kids were withholding information.

Marie cracked open the door, peered into the hall, scanned both ways, closed it softly, and retook her seat. "You can't tell anyone—even Iris," she whispered.

"Agreed."

"POTUS." She watched him expectantly.

"Excuse me?"

"We are going to treat the President." Her words hung between them.

Phineas' earlier coffee soured the back of his palate. "That explains a lot." The pieces were coming together.

"Go on."

"It explains his physical appearance when he has to appear in public. And his increasingly erratic behavior—something I hadn't thought possible, until he did it—from all the steroids he's taking."

"So, you'll participate willingly?" She sounded determined.

He stared back. "From what you've told me, neither of us can stand that incompetent narcissist. And to be honest, I hate the man. Never thought I'd hate someone I've never met...but he's made that happen."

"That doesn't answer my question." She drummed her fingers on the conference table.

"I've treated patients who were disliked by their caregivers, or they had family whose behaviors were despicable. But doctors have always forced themselves to pack that baggage away when providing care...Yet, for *this* man..."

If he refused, they'd ask Gabby. At this stage of her career, it would be impossible for her to say "No." He couldn't do that to her, nor could he send her to that horrible man's bedside. She didn't deserve that kind of abuse.

"But you'll do it?" Marie obviously needed to close the deal.

"I don't see that I have a choice." The realization that his hands were tied infuriated him and sent a churning into the pit of his gut. He'd agreed to provide special care for a wealthy VIP who disdained the common man.

"Actually, we both could walk away. But they'd just get someone less experienced to do it—and—consider this: if treatment helps, a steady stream of *generous* NIH funding for you will likely follow." Marie settled back in her chair with a triumphant smile. "You'd be set."

She considers me up for sale? "Now that statement makes me feel like a whore."

She winced. "Sorry." His being so offended must have caught her completely off guard. "I'm *really* sorry I said that...You're truly the *last* person on the planet I'd want to offend...That...That would hurt *me* too much."

Strange comment from a co-worker. "Oh? And why do you say that?"

"Never mind. Forget I said it." Her cheeks were aflame.

What is she not telling me? Since he'd met her, she'd revealed precious little about herself. He wasn't going to let this one go. He couldn't. "You can't just say these things and then shut down." He leaned across the table into her space, glared into her eyes, and shouted, "What are you not telling me?"

She shrank into her seat and blinked like she was trying to hold back a torrent. His aggressiveness had shattered her defenses. "I...I don't want... to hurt my father." Her voice was low and thick.

"Thought you didn't know him." *Wait. What is she saying?*

"I do know." A whisper. "You're...You're my father."

All the breathable air left the room. "What did you say?" He almost choked on his words.

Her whole body appeared to stiffen, and she sat taller, her hands pressed on the tabletop. "You...are...my...father." A steady, forced monotone.

Come on now. "Impossible."

"She said you'd say that." Her voice dropped off again.

"She? And who is *she*?" He tried not to yell this time.

Marie's eyes glistened. "My mother, obviously."

Her mother died from cancer. That was all Marie'd ever said about her.

"Who was your mother?" He yelled again.

Marie retreated back against her chair, like she anticipated an explosion. "My mother was Angela Portier." Another whisper.

Jesus Christ! The silver cross on her neck. *Could she really be...?* "Angela Portier was your mother?" He *had* seen that cross before. He'd seen it flash in the dark, fetid Baptist Hospital hallways after Hurricane Jezebel in 1985, and he'd seen it in UNC's ICU before the racist terrorist had threatened him, his family, and UNC hospital in 1998.

Marie nodded slowly, her intense stare taking in his reaction.

Jesus! "I never..." The lung specialist couldn't get a breath.

"She said you'd say that." She sniffed and swallowed. "She said that one time, during the days and nights after Jezebel, she went to your office to get orders." Marie continued in a rush. "She said you'd been without rest for days and were on your back in a deep sleep, nearly comatose in total darkness. She told me it was like she was drawn to you by a spell."

"That's impossible. She made that up. I would have known." *Damn! That was so long ago, and those days and nights were pure hellish chaos.* He'd blocked that miserable time from his memory, but infidelity was something he should remember.

Even in the months before the hurricane, overwork and sleep deprivation had sent him to bed so tired some nights, that when he woke up the next morning, he couldn't remember if he and Iris had made love, or if his fuzzy memory of the act was a deep sleep dream. Most of the time they hadn't. He'd plunged into an exhausted sleep before she had time to turn off the lights.

"Of course, you'd say that." Marie's face was stone. "Do you really think she'd lie on her deathbed?"

"She hated me." *Didn't she?* "She had to have told you this to inflict more misery on me."

"Believe me, I've seen the YouTube videos, and what your lawyer did to her on *60 Minutes*. The public humiliation—and no one would hire her after that." Marie cleared her throat. "Mom said she fell in love with you before she hated you. More than a crush. She'd cherished every minute she'd worked with you...before Jezebel."

A single tear dribbled down her cheek into the corner of her mouth. "*This* is why I didn't tell you. And is the thought of having me for a daughter *that awful*?"

Christ! This day just can't be happening. "Marie, I admit I *had* enjoyed working with you...but you can't be my daughter."

She smeared a comet tail of eye shadow across her temple. "Had? You said that like we're done."

Maybe we are. "We'll have to figure that out after Bethesda." How could he work with her? His hand tremor started up and was worse than he'd ever seen. He hid it under the table. Did Marie notice?

She rummaged through her purse, found a tissue, and pressed it into her eyes. Seeming more composed, she stood and gathered the Phase 3 binder into her arms. As she grasped the doorknob to leave, she spun back around to face him, her hair twirling over her shoulder. "I'll send you the trip details."

Phineas sat alone in silence, staring at the conference room door then rose to his feet and marched down the hall to his lab. After breaking the seal on a fresh Biobag box, he covered his shaking fingers with sterile gloves and extracted two of the red plastic Biobags. He concealed them behind him and returned to the conference room, where he fished around in the trash until he found a cup smudged with rose lipstick.

～

When Phineas stepped into the air-conditioned lobby of the Chapel Hill Police Station, flashes of memory roared back to his first meeting with Detective Vincent DiCenzo to report the racist bent on revenge. Zebediah Jefferson. Phineas would never forget the name of the UNC Bomber. Bored after his NYPD retirement, it was DiCenzo's first North Carolina case, and his office in this building was still barren. The terrifying events of the case would cement Phineas and his lasting friendship.

Nothing had changed in the grey concrete building's lobby except the names on the wall and the person behind the desk. The young Black woman seated there called out, "Sir, can I help you?"

He slipped his backpack off his shoulders and firmly gripped its strap. "I'm supposed to meet Detective Vincent DiCenzo here. Have you seen him?"

"He's the older man with a walker, right?"

"That's him. Is he here yet?"

"Not today." The mention of DiCenzo made her smile. "I'd offer you a private place to wait for him, except he doesn't have an office."

"I can wait here." The cushioned chair next to the windows was worn past any semblance of firmness. Phineas sank so low into it that he wondered if he'd be able to get back up without help. He rested his backpack and its precious contents on his trembling knees.

The automatic door slid open, and the familiar clank of the red metallic walker preceded Vinnie DiCenzo. Phineas had to rock forward twice to get his weight over his feet enough to stand. Was it the low chair, or was he stiffer?

"Hey, Vinnie. Over here. Thanks for coming."

Vinnie's shuffle accelerated to a pace Phineas hadn't seen in a year. "No problem, Doc. Glad to help, and it's good to have something to do." The same words he'd said in 1998 when he first met Phineas. DiCenzo waved at the young woman. "Hi, Dorothy. You doin' okay?"

"Yes Sir, good to see you again. Now, who can I get for you?"

"Detective Thomas. Should be around here somewhere. Said to come right in."

She pushed three buttons on a phone that looked like a relic. "I have Detective DiCenzo and..." She raised her eyebrows at Vinnie.

"Friend." DiCenzo answered.

"Friend." She listened then hung up. "He'll be right down."

A middle-aged man pushed open the stairway door. His red hair was neatly combed, and his green eyes were magnified behind thick lenses in black frames. A striped bowtie and the white pocket protector in his short-sleeved white shirt advertised meticulous. When he smiled, dimples formed crescents in a sea of freckles.

"Hey, Vinnie. Good to see you. And you must be the famous Doc the Beekeeper." He offered his hand to Phineas. "We still owe you bigtime. I'm Jim Thomas from Forensics. How can I help you?"

Doc the Beekeeper. Still? Clearly, there hadn't been a crime nearly as monumental for the Chapel Hill Police since that crazy day in 1998. He shook Thomas' soft hand and asked, "Is there somewhere we can talk?"

Dorothy answered for him. "First floor conference room's available."

"Thanks, Dot." Thomas gestured toward the hallway. "This way, Doc."

DiCenzo leaned on his walker and stepped, advanced the walker, and stepped until he reached Room 105. Phineas fought imagined future images of himself depending on a walker. How long would that be? He held the door open for DiCenzo until the detective dropped into one of the four seats. Phineas placed his backpack on the table and unzipped it. He removed two red Biobags, labeled "A" and "B", that still emitted the faint fumes of a Sharpie.

How to explain. Phineas had rehearsed his words on the way over, but now they seemed to be stuck in his throat. "My oral swab is 'A'...the other, 'B'..." He swallowed. "...is a coffee cup from a woman who claims to be my daughter." His next words rushed out in a torrent. "It's impossible. I—I never touched her mother."

"Sounds like we can finally return the favor, Doc, for all the lives you saved in '98." Thomas picked up one of the sealed, plastic bags and studied it. "I can keep your name off these and have the DNA run right away. We'll take care of you. You're a legend around here, and Vinnie..."

"I try to help out when I can." DiCenzo glanced at the ceiling.

Thomas chuckled and tipped his head toward Vinnie. "He listens in on our tough cases, and he's helped solve more than one crime. All for donuts and coffee. We owe him too."

Still embarrassed, Phineas responded, "Thank you, Sir, and thanks, Vinnie."

"Don't mention it, Doc."

Thomas pulled apart the seals of each of the Biobags, peered inside, and carefully resealed them without touching their contents. "You want me to run either of these through the national databases—you know—23andMe and criminal? We can see if hers matches another father—and we can even find *your* long-lost relatives."

Options Phineas hadn't considered—and wouldn't Marie be legitimately furious when she learned he'd analyzed her DNA without her permission? "Let me first ask her if she wants you to try to identify her real father."

And the other offer? "I'd have to say a definite 'no thanks' to enlarging my family tree. I'm satisfied with the relatives I know. I don't need more." All he needed now was to find out that he was third or fourth cousin to some infamous character. Life was complicated enough.

◦

As Iris and he began dinner, Phineas put down his fork. His appetite was missing in action. "There's been a change in our departure date for Italy."

Iris looked up from her plate of grilled salmon, okra, and freshly shelled, blanched, and sautéed black-eyed peas that Phineas had just prepared. "Not a delay, I hope, I'm eager to get out of this brutal North Carolina heat and into the Italian Alps."

"A two-day delay. I have to go to Bethesda for the SynMedical study."

"Awww." She looked as disappointed as she sounded. "Did you change our flights?"

"They did. They're making it up to us by upgrading us to first class—and by having a limo pick us up in Milan—and they adjusted our villa dates."

She seemed to perk up. "I could get used to that kind of treatment. Maybe I won't feel so crappy when we land this time." She speared a forkful of okra. "Do we leave as soon as you get back to Chapel Hill?"

"We leave together from Dulles Airport."

"And how do *I* get there?"

"They're driving us all to Bethesda from here and putting us up in a hotel."

"And who's *they*?" She studied him like she suspected he hadn't revealed something vital.

He squeezed a slice of lemon over his piece of the salmon fillet. An errant squirt of the juice hit his cheek and stung his eye. "SynMedical." It wasn't easy to keep his tone matter of fact. "Since Jacob's housesitting, I'll let him know of the change in dates." His voice trailed off.

"Is there something you haven't told me? Wait. Who's '*us all*'?" She was still staring at him.

Indeed, there was. "Marie will be riding with us."

"Good. Finally get my chance to learn a little more about her." Iris' words were light, her tone agreeable, but she kept her focus on his eyes and probed deeper. He was well accustomed to her entering his mind through his pupils, then into his soul. She knew there was more. "But what *else* haven't you told me?"

He hadn't given her enough, and his efforts to spare her were failing. "She dropped a bomb on me today." It came out in a rush.

"Oh? What?" Lines deepened next to her icy blue eyes. "Bad news with their funding?"

"Worse." He cringed in anticipation. "She believes I'm her father." There. He'd said it.

"WHAT?"

"Her mother's dying words—but Iris," he reached for her hand. "It's impossible...I was *never* unfaithful to you."

She drew her hand away. "And just *who* is her mother?" Her words singed him.

"*Was*. She's dead." He trembled in his core, like a child caught in a misdeed or a lie.

"Okay, who *was* her mother?" Still hot.

He had to say it. "Angela Portier." He could barely hear his own words.

"What did you say?"

"Angela Portier." Louder.

"Angela?"

Hearing Iris utter that name made it a thousand times worse.

"When did you—?"

"I didn't." He lowered his voice. "Angela's supposed to have claimed it happened in my office after Jezebel."

"And?"

"It...didn't...happen." He couldn't tell if Iris believed him.

"Can you prove—?"

"DNA tests already in the works." *Those tests better...*

Iris pushed her plate away. "I hope you can." She drummed her fingertips on the table with such force that the tendons stood out. "Will the misery from Angela never end?" She stared up at him. "Maybe Marie's not the sweet person we thought and carrying out a scheme to avenge her mother."

"I...I don't think she's been plotting to hurt us. She was really broken up when I said I couldn't be her father." The image of Marie's visible heartache when he'd rejected that possibility flashed through his thoughts. "I think she just wanted to have a family...our family. To be part of it."

Iris exhaled slowly through pursed lips, and her body language seemed to shift from rage to pity. After a while, she said, "If that's true, I feel sorry for her. She may be as much a victim of her mother as you are." She narrowed her eyes at him. "—*if* you can prove it." The bomb had hurt her too. Collateral damage.

Something smacked the dining room window and startled them. A half dollar sized collection of azure feathers remained on the glass, the remnant of a bluebird's fatal head-on collision with the invisible pane.

Iris stood and studied the ground underneath the window. "Pretty incredible."

"What?"

"Angela coming after you from the grave."

⌒

Marie pounded the table with her fist. She didn't mean to reveal it. He forced it out of her. She was afraid he was going to explode.

She poured her second glass of chardonnay, her first alcohol in weeks, and it wasn't helping. She'd ruined everything. Her connections to her new family and closest friends. Her job. Would he even work with her now? Could either one of them be comfortable with the other ever again?

A shiver of panic and despair crept down her spine. She hurried to her bedroom and opened the dresser drawer, the one protecting her Chinook Sugarbeeter warmups, and slipped on the pants then the jacket, which she pulled tight over her chest. There was a frayed spot she hadn't seen, a new seam separation near the elbow. She'd have to mend it later. An easy job for someone who had to learn to sew as a kid.

The outfit again prompted memories her of her high school teammate and friend, Ada. How was she doing after that horrible Montana fire? Marie had only received a brief, polite thank you when she offered assistance to Ada on Facebook. Would talking to her now help? Marie had entered her friend's contact information, gleaned from Facebook, in her cell. She stared at it and paced for several minutes before she gingerly touched Ada's number. It rang twice.

"Hello?"

The question meant Ada hadn't entered her number in her contacts. Ada didn't know who was calling. Would it be best to hang up now?

"Ada, this is Marie." She really needed to hear a friendly voice.

"Marie?" Ada's pitch rose. "From Chinook High?" A squeal.

"The same. How are you? I've been worried about you." Marie collapsed into a chair at her dining room table.

"Oh, you know how things are here. We just figure out what's next and move on. Nothing changes in Chinook." Ada's voice sounded *sooo* familiar, *sooo* comforting.

"Are you back in your home now? How's your family?" Family. Would she still have one after today? Or had she ruined that?

"Oh sure. We're back home. It was a mess, but everyone helped clean it up." A silence. "But we lost the beet crop. We're hoping the crop we planted after the fire pays enough to cover the loans." Her tone was somber now. "It's always year to year. You know how it is."

Ada's parents had always been working the figures, figuring out how to pay for the next season's seeds and fertilizer. "I can help," Marie offered. "I'm just getting settled here in North Carolina, but I can help tide you over." For now, at least. After today, would her position at SynMedical be in jeopardy?

"You could help by moving back here. We need a GP. Since Old Doc Pickett died—and that was three years ago, we have to drive all the way to Havre, and they only have a clinic two days a week. The doctors change each time. Whoever can come from another town that day. Sometimes it's a nurse practitioner. At least she's really good."

Moving back to Chinook, to a town most young people abandoned. There'd be Ada, but that would mean giving up on marriage or having her own family. "I need to see how things work out here a while longer, Ada... but it's great to hear I'd be needed." And setting up a practice in a small town...the onerous loans, the leases, employees. Reimbursements probably wouldn't cover it all, especially with the patients mostly uninsured beet farmers.

"It'd be so great if you'd come home, Marie. I'd love to see you!" A crash. "Josiah, what have you done?" A child wailed in the background. "Marie, I've got to go now. Got to clean up a mess. Let's talk again real soon."

"Let's do that. We can Facetime then. Sound good?"

Ada giggled. "Give me warning, so I can look decent and have the kids organized."

"I'm sure you'll look great. I saw your picture in the news. You haven't changed."

"You're kind—or going blind. Talk to you soon?"

"You bet. Go take care of your son. Bye." Marie blinked back tears and sipped wine.

She should have kept the secret from Phineas. Taken it to her grave. He'll tell Iris, and she'll be furious. She sure as hell won't want a woman claiming to be Phineas' long-lost daughter around. And he'll have to tell her. He won't be able to resist her probing his certain mood change.

Then there's Martha and Jacob. Jacob. At least she won't have to deflect him asking her out anymore. He won't want to have anything to do with her. She's going to really miss feeling desired by someone desirable. Kind of eccentric and goofy, but fun, and *sooo* easy to be with. Easier than all the driven medical and corporate types she's dated. Not the least bit pretentious either. Yup, she'd miss him. Now that she'd made her big reveal, seeing him would be history.

Her face toppled into her hands, and she pressed her palms into her eyes to stanch the coming flow. *Oh hell, Girl. Let it go. There's no one to see you.* She let her head settle onto crossed arms on the table, and her chest heaved with misery. *What have I done?*

Would knowing for sure one way or the other make it worse? It couldn't get any more painful for her—but might for Phineas and Iris though, if it proved what her mother claimed. Of course, according to Mom, he was incapacitated. Maybe a *victim* of a theft of something of immeasurable value. There. She admitted it. She might be the product of a moral crime, and Mom was a serial criminal.

How could she leave it uncertain? She *had* to eventually find the courage to ask him for a DNA test then deal with the results. As much as she wished just to be included in their family, it would be better for all if her mother had lied with her last breaths. But nobody lies on their deathbed—do they?

⌐

"Jacob, sorry that most of the tomatoes have gone by. Still some Romas left. They're best for sauce." The heat index was past 120, but Phineas was out in it, standing in the center of his garden area, where he pointed at each bed. "It's too early for sweet potatoes, but there are plenty of Irish potatoes and butternut squash in the basement. Peppers and black-eyed peas are still coming in."

"I'll be sure to forage back here when I'm too busy to get to the store, or if they're out of decent produce again." Jacob scanned the yard twice, his head swiveling to look from one corner to the opposite. "Hey! Where'd Ruby go?"

"She was running the perimeter of the deer fence, like she always does when she first gets here." The beagle was usually so busy in Phineas' backyard that her presence was never a question. "I hope I don't have a hole in the fence."

They started at the left end post and hurried along the fence, inspecting it along the ground as they advanced. There, in the deepest, quietest corner, telltale loose soil was sprayed back in a fantail of freshly dug red dirt. Above it was a short linear rent in the black-brown plastic fencing material. Phineas bent to probe the defect. "Squirrels and rabbits bite through it sometimes. Ruby must have dug below to make it big enough for her."

Jacob slapped his temples with both hands. "I knew she had it in her, but it's the first time I've lost her. Better find her before she gets in trouble—and I get in trouble with her owner."

A soft baying from the west barely reached them. Phineas met his son's startled stare. "Jacob, you take your truck north of the main road, and I'll take mine south, and we'll check the neighborhoods west of here where that came from. We'll find her."

They drove along the country road in the direction of the sound and split up where neighborhoods branched off. Phineas rolled slowly with windows down and listened. Nothing but the sound of a passing car out on the main road. He stopped across from a well-dressed man emptying his mailbox. "Sir, have you seen or heard a beagle recently?"

The man extracted an envelope and a magazine from the depths of his mailbox and closed it. "Heard one in that direction when I first got home, maybe five—or ten minutes ago." He pointed farther down the neighborhood's entrance road. "That breed does like to run, don't they?"

"My first time with a beagle. Always had Labs. Thanks." Phineas continued along the road, turning in and out of short cul-de-sacs and listening. A dead-end sign warned he approached the neighborhood's wooded limits.

He shut off the engine, got out, and called, "Ruby! Ruby, where did you go?" He started to climb back into his seat, when he noticed that something shook the dense leafy undergrowth below a roadside stand of beech trees. A black and brown head emerged.

"Ruby! Come here girl." He hurried toward her. The runaway beagle panted, advanced two wobbly steps into the low weeds, and collapsed, her eyes glassy. He knelt next to her and stroked her shoulder. Her muscles quivered from her neck to her tail. She vomited and emitted an explosion of foul diarrhea.

"Oh, Ruby. What have you gotten into?" Phineas pulled out his cell phone with his shaking left hand and used his steadier right one to contact Jacob. "I've got her, but she's sick. I'm taking her to the emergency vet's office on Weaver Dairy Road where we used to take Stella. See you there." When he scooped up the stiff hound, she suffered a fleeting whole-body convulsion. *Hang on, Ruby...Please.* He laid her gently on the passenger seat and sped the several miles, alternating glances at the road and Ruby. Her breathing was ragged.

Phineas braked into the closest parking space next to the brick building. He cradled the unconscious dog in his arms, pushed through the double glass doors, then yelled at the receptionist, "Emergency! I need the vet now."

She looked up from her glass-enclosed workstation. "Name please." She sounded bothered.

Phineas knew the layout well enough to ignore her and, without hesitation, invaded the back-clinic area, where he guessed the vet was at work.

"You can't go back there!" the receptionist shouted after him.

In the back part of the clinic, a young woman with bleached blond hair emerged from one of numerous doors lining a hallway. 'Jennifer' was stitched over the chest pocket on her pink scrubs, and 'CHAD' was tattooed across her wrist.

"I need the vet now," Phineas demanded.

"I'm the vet tech. What have you got there?" She placed her hand on the dog's shoulder and another whole-body tremor followed. "I'll get the vet right away." She stepped behind a counter and through another door.

He paced with Ruby in his arms and stole a glance at his watch. As he reached the far side of the room and turned, Jennifer re-emerged with a slim thirty-something dark-haired woman in shamrock green scrubs, a woman too young for Phineas to have met during their Lab Stella's visits so many years ago. A stethoscope hung around her neck.

Jacob burst through the entry door. "Dad, how's Ruby?"

The veterinarian stared up at the sudden intruder with a surprised expression. "Dr. Mann!"

"Do I know you?" Phineas responded then held up the comatose, panting beagle. "Please, Doctor. I think Ruby may have been poisoned."

She pointed at an open door down the hallway, where a stretcher, hanging bags of intravenous solutions, and oxygen tanks were at the ready. Phineas hurried to lay Ruby on the stretcher. The vet gestured her thumb at Jacob. "I meant him, Dr. Mann, the bee professor. I took his class on bee diseases at State's Vet School." She approached the stretcher and studied Ruby. "I'm Dr. Romano. Now, tell me about your dog."

Jacob placed his large right hand gently on Ruby's head. "She dug out under the fence and was gone maybe an hour at most. My dad found her—like this—in a neighborhood nearby."

Dr. Romano shone her penlight in Ruby's eyes and used her stethoscope to take a quick listen to Ruby's chest. "I need to insert a tube in her airway so we can breathe for her until she's better." She opened a black valise on the counter and removed items familiar to Phineas' ICU work: a metal laryngoscope and a long clear plastic breathing tube. The vet rolled Ruby onto her back, advanced the blade of the scope into her mouth, and inserted the tube. She removed the metal blade and attached a clear plastic resuscitation bag, the size of a Nerf football, to the tube. Phineas held his breath as the vet squeezed and released it. Ruby's chest rose and fell. Phineas exhaled along with her. Dr. Romano positioned Ruby back on her side.

Phineas was impressed. "You're good at that. I'm a pulmonologist, and you did it better than we do." He hid his left hand in his pocket to conceal its shaking.

"Hmph. I should be." She glanced at him. "We do this all day long for surgeries. Jennifer, you take over squeezing the bag."

"I can do that—if it'll help," Phineas offered.

A hint of a polite smile came and went on the young Dr. Romano. "It's probably been a while since dog lab in med school. Jennifer does this for me every day."

The veterinarian listened again to Ruby's chest and abdomen, examined her eyes through a lighted hand-held ophthalmoscope, and finally inspected and palpated every inch of her body. "No signs of snake bite." She stretched and flexed the dog's stiff legs. "I agree she probably got into some poison. Her tiny pupils, muscle tremors, and coma point to an insecticide, probably an organophosphate. We've been seeing more of it since our Commander-in-Chief told everyone to spray their yards. Ruby might have found a container and drunk from it or eaten something heavily doused with it."

Dr. Romano tied a rubber tourniquet onto Ruby's front leg and found a vein for an intravenous catheter. She withdrew a syringe of blood "for tests" and set it on a nearby metal table before attaching a bag of intravenous solution to the catheter.

"Will...will she get better, Dr. Romano?" Jacob's eyes glistened under the brilliant fluorescent lights.

She opened a drawer in a cabinet beside the stretcher and lifted a small medication box, from which she removed a glass vial. "She's in luck. Just last week, we had to send two similar cases to NC State's emergency clinic, so we started stocking the specific antidote." She drew the organophosphate antidote into a syringe and injected it slowly into the fluid line then removed another syringe, this one filled with a clear liquid, from the box. "We also give a dose of atropine," she explained as she injected it. She dragged a stool up to the stretcher and sat. "This may take a little while."

Jacob remained stock-still, like a wild animal in the road with a vehicle's high beams speeding at it. "But she will get better?"

"I believe she will, Dr. Mann." Dr. Romano offered a hopeful smile up at him.

He took a deep breath and let it out slowly through pursed lips. "Thank you, Dr Romano. Thank you so much."

"That's what we're here for." She returned her attention to her stricken patient on the stretcher and wrapped the catheter with a protective gauze bandage. Jennifer printed 'Ruby' on a label and stuck it on the syringe of blood. Jacob and Phineas stood back and stared in silence. Minutes later, Ruby's feet jerked rhythmically, like she was sleepwalking, a handful of steps at first, then vigorously. Her forehead wrinkled and she blinked hard. Her neck muscles contracted, like she was gagging.

Dr. Romano murmured, "I think the antidote is starting to take effect." When the dog tried to lift her head and roll onto her stomach, Dr. Romano put one hand on Ruby's chest and the other on her head. "It's definitely working. Our diagnosis was correct. The drugs wouldn't help anything else. The specific agent is called pralidoxime or 2-PAM." Phineas recognized the name from critical care board review courses he'd attended and not from any patients he'd treated with it.

The veterinarian now had to forcefully hold the dog on her side. "I think we can take the tube out." She slipped it out of Ruby's mouth and helped her onto her stomach. Ruby coughed and pushed herself into a sitting position. Blinking repeatedly, she surveyed the room's occupants and let out one soft, hoarse bark, then another.

Jacob stepped to the side of the stretcher and put his hand on Ruby's back. "Ruby, you're back—good dog!" She nibbled on the catheter's bandage.

Dr. Romano chuckled. "I think she's out of the woods, but we need to watch her for a couple more hours, at least, in case she requires more atropine. You want to wait with her, or leave her with us overnight?" Her words came out in a rush. She sounded elated, almost giddy, with her miraculous success.

Jacob scratched behind Ruby's ears. "I'll wait. Dad, you can go home." Ruby let out a soft, contented-sounding groan.

"I'll stay with you for a while." Phineas lowered himself into one of two chairs along the wall and took out his cell phone. "And I'll let your mother know where we are.

"Jennifer and I need to see some other patients, but we'll check back periodically." Dr. Romano stepped toward the door. She paused and peered up at Jacob triumphantly. Ruby was licking his hand. "So, Dr. Mann, still teaching beekeeping to vets?"

Jacob looked up from Ruby, his worry wrinkles now gone. "Every spring semester."

"I liked your novel." She cocked her head at an angle and glanced at his hand. "You single?"

He blushed and cleared his throat. "Thanks. Yup. Still single."

"Well, I guess we'll have to arrange follow-up here for Ruby real soon." She winked at him and glided out of the room.

Jennifer spoke over her shoulder as she trailed her. "I'll send in someone from our front desk to get your information."

Phineas leaned back and crossed his legs. "So, Jacob, that sounds like an appointment you'll want to keep."

"Yeah. I'll be sure to bring Ruby back...for Ruby's sake." Jacob sighed. "I sure wasn't getting anywhere with Marie."

Not when she believed he was her half-brother. Would the DNA tests confirm it? Would they add yet another unexpected layer of complication to all their lives? The results were promised to be back tomorrow, so he could forget about sleeping tonight. In three long days, he'd share those results with Marie, whatever they revealed.

⌒

The day of their trip to Bethesda was sweaty hot at dawn and blistering hot as noon approached. Phineas clicked his cell off and pocketed it. "Should be here any minute." Three suitcases and two backpacks stood in a row in front of Iris and him next to their driveway, enough for Bethesda and Italy.

Jacob reeled in the slack in Ruby's leash as she retreated onto grass and away from the heat waves rising off the baking asphalt. "A whole month in Italy. I'm seriously jealous. And jealous that you get to first travel with Marie. She's always keeping me at arm's length—says it's company rules with your study."

Phineas raised his eyebrows. "Maybe Dr. Romano will ask you out when you go back there. She doesn't seem like the shy type—and that would be less complicated."

"We'll see. Well don't worry about the house. Ruby and I are looking forward to housesitting and having a fenced yard, complete with recent repairs, except for that big storm coming this way." They'd all watched the Weather Channel an hour ago. The strengthening Tropical Storm Nancy was predicted to glance off the Outer Banks before proceeding north. Its threat to Chapel Hill was mostly heavy rain with chances of flooding and power loss, but Virginia, D. C., and Maryland were in the center of Nancy's projected path.

Phineas tried to tamp down the tension he felt over the anticipated confrontation with Marie. "Depending on how things go, we may escape to Europe more in the future. You can come stay with us there."

The black limousine turned the corner on their street. Its fresh wax job glistened in the blinding midday sun. Iris murmured, "The neighbors will think we're getting uppity." She wiped expanding dots of perspiration from her forehead with a crumpled tissue.

The driver, a slim white man in a short-sleeved white shirt under a plain black tie, exited the car. "Afternoon, Folks. Want to keep your backpacks with you?" He popped open the sizable trunk and came around to load the suitcases.

Phineas gripped the strap of his backpack. "Yes, Sir. Thanks."

"There are beverages and snacks in the back, and Dr. Porter had me pick up lunches." Their chauffeur opened the passenger side back door and stood next to it. Marie Porter stepped out into the heat wearing casual clothes and a somber expression. She held a white cardboard deli box. "Everybody ready?" She turned toward Jacob and offered the box. "Hi, Jacob...You doing okay? Want a lunch?" Her voice trailed off as she offered it to him.

"Envious. And you?" He took a step closer and further tightened Ruby's leash. The dog's head was tilted back as she sniffed at the offering. "I never turn down food. Thanks." He lifted the box high enough that Ruby's vertical leap fell short.

"Fine...truthfully, a bit nervous. Be glad when the tomorrow's work is over." She was still speaking softly.

"Oh? Must be serious stuff."

She appeared to force a half smile but said nothing.

The transient wrinkles between Jacob's eyebrows hinted at his curiosity. "Well, look after Mom and Dad—and when you get back in town, I'll be staying here—if you happen to get bored."

"Thanks. Nice of you to offer," she mumbled.

"And make sure you get back before the storm gets close. I checked a few minutes ago, and my folks' flight should depart the day before it hits D.C."

"I should be back in Durham by then...Well, shall we head out? It's awfully hot out here." Her brow already shone enough to reflect the intense overhead sun.

Iris and Phineas took turns hugging Jacob, then Phineas followed Iris and Marie into the limo. He shouted out through the open door, "Call or text if you have questions, Jacob—or even if you don't." The chauffeur closed the door.

Phineas sank into the spacious leather back seat next to Iris and fastened his seatbelt. The driver navigated his lengthy sedan through a careful three-point turn in the driveway and back into the street. The vehicle's welcome air conditioning blasted a distracting noisy wind.

Marie cracked the inside window open long enough to ask the chauffeur to lower the fan then sealed the three passengers back in. "We have a variety of sandwiches, chips and cookies for the trip, whenever you get hungry." Her offer came in the same monotone as a flight attendant.

Phineas lifted his backpack onto his lap and unzipped it. "Thanks, Marie. Maybe in a bit." The three shared tense glances. As the limo merged onto the highway, Phineas broke the awkward silence. "I told Iris what you told me."

Marie's head snapped fully upright, and her distressed eyes brought back a reminder of the deer Phineas regretted shooting as a teenager.

"You...you promised you wouldn't tell anyone."

"I said I wouldn't talk about our work in Bethesda." He reached into his backpack and extracted folded papers clipped together. "The other thing involved her."

Iris bent forward and placed her hand on Marie's knee. "This doesn't have to drive a wedge."

"You're...you're not angry—just knowing who my mother was?"

"I have no reason to be. That's in the past, and you're your own person." Iris' voice was gentle, soothing.

Marie closed her eyes and released a slow exhalation. "That's such a relief. I was afraid you wouldn't want to have anything to do with me."

"Marie, we like you, and we have an idea what you've been through." Iris sat back and clasped her hands together.

Phineas handed Marie two pages stapled together. "Please don't take this the wrong way."

"What's this?" She stared at the first page, then flipped to the second. Her furrowed brow suggested deep concentration as she sank back into the seat to study the papers. "Who are Person A and Person B?"

"Those are their DNA tests. You can see A and B are clearly not related." He waited long enough for her to confirm his interpretation of the results then, in a firm voice, added, "I'm A and you're B."

"You...you had me genetically tested?" Her face drained of color to a ghostly pallor.

His gut tightened. Had he just now created another enemy? Yet he could not allow Angela revenge from beyond the grave. "Your mother's claim forced my hand."

She shifted to the edge of her seat. "How? When...?"

"Your coffee cup."

"Without my permission." He hadn't seen her angry before. Was she now?

Would he be able to work with her again? Would she somehow try to sabotage him professionally? "We *had* to know, and I may have saved you subpoenas, lawyers, and a public event—not to mention considerable expense." Phineas handed her one more sheet of paper.

"And what's this?"

"Here's a list of every man that I can think of who might be your father. These men were also in Baptist Hospital during Jezebel." He watched her scan the list. "I starred the few I thought the most likely. I can help, if you'd like, to pursue your father."

She shook her head. "No. I'm not interested in asking any of them for their DNA."

"It so happens that I have a friend who knows a guy who can see if your DNA matches any of the millions submitted so far by 23andMe and other companies, and in the national criminal databases. Or it could match a family member of your father."

"A friend who knows a guy...sounds like a Mafia movie—and criminal databases? Yikes! I don't need that kind of relative." She seemed alarmed at the thought.

"It could narrow the possibilities on that list—maybe to one man—or maybe even point to someone outside of Baptist Hospital."

"Not now...I'm not ready."

Iris unbuckled her seatbelt and slid over next to Marie. She put her arm around Marie's shoulders and let her crumble into an embrace. "Marie, this doesn't have to change things with us. You're always welcome in our house."

Marie's shoulders heaved while grief—or was there also relief? — gushed out of her. Phineas had expected he'd feel relief but was surprised by a silent sorrow after he disproved the existence of a second daughter, one he'd made every effort not to claim.

The three travelers settled into their rooms at the Bethesda North Marriott then met in its lobby at 6 PM. They watched through the floor to ceiling windows for their limousine to return to transport Phineas and Marie to the NIH. When it pulled up to the hotel's entrance, Iris deposited a peck on Phineas' cheek and said, "You two get done what you need to do at the NIH. I'll find dinner and see you later on, and I want to catch more of the China news."

Minutes earlier, in their hotel room, she and Phineas were shocked by the CNN announcement that the Chinese military had overrun a degraded North Korea and simultaneously expanded their naval presence further in the South Pacific. In a video recording, the Chinese president proclaimed that "as long as the current reckless dotard" occupied the White House, the United States risked global war. Phineas resisted the urge to tell Iris that tomorrow, he would treat said "dotard" and abet his frightening reign.

Their familiar friendly chauffeur stood at attention while he held open the car's back door and announced, "I have boxes with lasagna from Mama Lucia's, and there's a bottle of Reserve Chianti." When he caught sight of Marie's blotchy face and her attempt to hide it, he tilted his head forward and appeared concerned.

Phineas set one of the boxes and a bottle of water next to him before he buckled in across from Marie. "Shall we save the Chianti for our trip back to the hotel?"

"I guess so, but I could do with some of it now…and I'm not that hungry."

"Start on the wine now if you want, but I've got a lot of records to read and a facility to check out." His full attention would be required.

"I'll wait. Sometimes I forget that I'm still a medical doctor and should be able to function as one." She studied her cell phone for word from Walter Reed's chairman.

He pinched off a forkful of lasagna and, despite stop and go traffic, managed to guide it into his mouth. Even so, he had to pluck a hanging string of mozzarella from his beard. The pasta was al dente and the sauce tasted like fresh tomatoes. "This is good lasagna. Have some."

Marie's eyes looked empty, her lids past puffy under freshly applied makeup. Her eyes revealed the magnitude of her losses—her mother—and today her imagined father. "I'm sorry for all you've had to go through." *All by yourself.* "We're a team, Marie. I'm glad to have you working with me on this, and I hope to not need all your hospitalist's skills. Let's get this done and get out of Maryland." He bit off the edge of a portion of crusty bread.

She nodded agreement and held up her cell. "Dr. Smith just texted to confirm that he'll be there tonight and tomorrow."

"This could be very good for your career."

"Or bad. I must look like Hell. I hope I can fix my eyes by morning."

"You look okay, and you'll be perfect by morning." He knew he was a terrible liar. He glanced out the window at massive brick buildings. "Looks like a hospital campus. We're probably getting close. Eat something. Please."

She shook her head. "I'll wait."

⌒

Trailing Phineas out of the limo and onto the pavement at the main entrance to Walter Reed Hospital, Marie carried a small cooler in one hand and her briefcase in the other. All business now, she seemed to have rallied from her earlier traumatized state. "I'll text you when we need you to pick us up," she instructed the chauffer.

"I'll keep the tiramisu on ice." He closed the door behind them.

Phineas shouldered his backpack. "I could learn to enjoy being treated like this."

"We need to find the Ambulatory Surgery Unit. Dr. Smith should meet us there with the records."

A uniformed young man at the visitors' information desk drew a stepwise line to their destination on a map and handed it to Marie. They hiked what felt like two city blocks and rode two escalators before they spotted the unit's sign. Its heavy metal double door entrance was locked. Marie rapped her knuckles on it. No answer. Phineas pounded on it with the soft edge of his fist. A muffled voice came from within. The door cracked open and revealed the Chairman of Medicine in a business suit. He waved them in then flipped a bolt to seal the entry.

When Marie caught Dr. Smith studying her face, she bowed her head. He cleared his throat. "Sorry. I was in the back working on a summary of the pertinent history for you." He beckoned them to follow him down a dimly lit hallway. "Glad you asked for this facility for the treatment. It's safer and more secure than the clinic." He opened a door into a wide-open surgical suite with four medical procedure tables around the perimeter, each able to be separated by curtains.

Phineas began scanning the room. "In my experience, if you don't prepare for problems, that's when they happen."

"I brought the drug." Marie showed Smith the cooler.

His face lit up. "Excellent. I'll get it to Pharmacy and have it here, ready to mix, when you arrive in the morning."

Phineas chose the nearest alcove and confirmed oxygen outlets and locations of stored intravenous access equipment. "Now, where's your code blue cart?"

Dr. Smith gestured at a chest-high, bright red metal toolbox on wheels in a corner on the far side of the suite. Phineas rolled it against the wall behind the procedure table before opening and closing drawers, memorizing contents. He removed a rigid laryngoscope, attached a blade, and confirmed the light worked. "Dr. Smith, is there a flexible fiberoptic laryngoscope or bronchoscope, in case I need it?"

"Please call me John. Anesthesia has both. I'll have a bronchoscope here in the morning." He flipped on a computer monitor that hung from a mechanical arm above the head of the procedure table.

A whirring tone rose in pitch and captured both men's attention. It came from Marie charging the defibrillator that rested on the top of the cart. "Thought you'd feel better knowing this works too." She appeared satisfied and turned the power off. "It hasn't been *that* long since I shocked someone."

Dr. Smith adjusted the computer screen to face them. "I have to confess that it's been quite a while since *I've* shocked anyone. Let's hope we don't have to even *think* about that tomorrow. Here's the patient's clinical record." He offered Phineas a rolling stool and lowered the monitor to that level. Smith continued, "I'll summarize if you'd like, Dr. Mann, while you begin reviewing it."

"Thanks, John. Please do, and you can call me Phineas." Phineas lowered himself onto the stool and familiarized himself with the digital record links. The patient's identification was in the form of a complex password.

"Our patient is a 78-year-old nonsmoking, nondrinking male," Dr. Smith began, "without prior history of pulmonary or allergic disorders until April, when he developed Alpha Gal Syndrome after a tick bite. Despite avoiding mammalian meat, he has had new-onset difficult and potentially life-threatening asthma, controlled only with prednisone at unacceptable levels."

"What doses, John?"

"As much as 60 milligrams—never less than 20 milligrams a day—and that's in addition to the standard maintenance asthma medications. You can imagine the side effects."

Yeah. The side effects. On full display in the news. "I see the newest drugs on his list. Any help?"

Smith shook his head. "Unfortunately, he's failed trials of the newer FDA approved injectable biological agents."

Phineas switched screens to review the lab flowsheet. "I see his Immunoglobulin E levels and eosinophil counts were elevated when this all began, suggesting a probable allergic contribution. And I see that routine serum allergy panels were negative. Any clues about unusual allergies the panels might have missed?" He was intrigued by the mystery of what trigger was behind this case of difficult asthma.

"At first, we blamed the Alpha Gal allergy and expected his asthma to get better once he stopped eating red meat. That didn't happen."

"Any other ideas about allergies?"

"One of our allergists correlated his asthma flares with days using a tanning lotion. Of course, they said he should stop using it. Then our people studied its chemical components. Some are natural extracts." He paused as if trying for dramatic effect. "As a scientist, you'll appreciate this part. When they did 3-D modeling of the components, one of them resembled the Alpha Gal antigen. Then our allergists demonstrated that his Alpha Gal antibodies react with that substance."

"Fascinating, but why didn't he get better when he stayed off the lotion?" Phineas rotated on the stool to study Smith's face.

Smith shrugged. "They speculated that he's absorbed so much of it over the years that his fat stores are loaded with it, creating a self-perpetuating allergic reaction, that started with the tick bite…Then, to prove their hypothesis, they did a fat biopsy and demonstrated the allergic antibody binding with it there."

Allergic to his own fat. What price vanity?

Phineas looked Smith dead in the eye. "And you believe this patient— that he's not still exposing himself to either the lotion or the occasional cheeseburger?"

A twitch above Smith's jaw line. "Have to. We don't have a choice." This patient would never give him one.

"Well, given that assumption, his treatment regimen appears to have been logical and appropriate. He is therefore a candidate for SYMBI-62022, and if asked, I'd enroll him in the trial." Phineas returned his attention to the screen and selected more clinical files for review.

"We appreciate your willingness to treat outside the trial," Smith said.

Not willingness, but strong-armed into potentially jeopardizing the entire trial if something goes wrong. Phineas rotated on the stool to again level his gaze at Smith. "It's not how I'd have chosen it...but here we are."

"Here we are." Smith cleared his throat. "I'm going to tell you who the patient is, and you'll better understand why we're at this point, but I'm guessing a smart guy like you has figured it out."

Phineas stole a sideways glance at Marie. She stood stone-faced beside the crash cart. He returned his full attention to Smith.

"Dr. Mann, tomorrow morning you will be administering SYMBI-62022 to...the President of the United States." Smith's final words were delivered in the same cadence as the Sergeant of Arms annual announcement at the State of the Union address.

Trying to seem surprised, Phineas assumed an erect posture and fully opened his eyes. "Glad there won't be any extra pressure on us." He longed to ask Smith if he was still sure about those cheeseburgers.

⌁

During the limo ride back to the hotel after the Walter Reed rehearsal, Marie could think of little to say to Phineas. They'd shared bread and uncorked the wine. He seemed to be doing his best with steady chatter to try to cheer or distract her. She gave him the tiramisu to enjoy later. Too rich for her twisting guts.

Back in her room, she wrapped herself in her comforting Sugarbeeter warmups and heated a portion of the leftover lasagna in the microwave. The bottle of Chianti was more than half full. She peeled the clear plastic cover off a hotel room glass and filled it.

When he'd handed her the DNA results, she felt empty, alone, and hurt that he'd wasted no time and gone to such ends to prove that she wasn't his daughter. Would he have been ashamed of her, if she was? With a felon for a mother, did she not measure up to his standards? Was *her* DNA inferior to *his*? At least he saved her the pain of asking for *his* DNA—and she would have had to, eventually. She would have dreaded that difficult request.

Knowing that she wasn't Phineas Mann's daughter, her mother's long-ago humiliation now made her mother's relentless drive for revenge even more understandable. As her mother's surviving defender, should *she* now consider taking up that bitter inherited quest?

No.

He was only defending his sacred marital bond. There'd be no more vengeance.

Her mother had lied to her, made her a pawn in a foul scheme, and given her false hope for a family she'd learned to respect and care for, only to embarrass her in front of them. Phineas Mann had done nothing to deserve more misery from Angela Portier, whose ashes remained in a Durham condo's closet, a grim presence and reminder. Those ashes had to go. She'd take care of that on her return. Chatham County's polluted Haw River would take her mother's remains to the Atlantic and disperse them.

Working down Phineas' list to find her real father just didn't seem worth it. She'd found Phineas Mann and thought she found the one she wanted. And Iris, her hoped for stepmom. Iris has tried her best to be a source of comfort as long as she's known her, even during today's painful ride to Bethesda. Iris is the reason Phineas pursued the truth with such vigor, to demonstrate his fidelity to her, to prove his unfailing love over the totality of their relationship. That had to be it. It wasn't that he considered his wannabe daughter an outcast. And even knowing the lie her mother claimed, Phineas and Iris weren't acting like they planned to reject the daughter as a friend.

She took a sip of Chianti.

And there was Jacob...definitely *not* her brother. She'd not met a man quite like him, comfortable in his unique skin. He was nothing like the types she'd dated and lost interest in. Her mood lifted. He'd pursued her since the day they were tied together by his spirited beagle. Now, she could let him. There was no longer a need to deftly parry his advances—*if* he was still interested.

She took a hearty swallow of Chianti and studied her reflection in the mirror over the desk. *Girl, you need some work!* Her eyes were someone else's, a tragic soul's draped with pink, swollen lids.

She set down her glass and dialed Room Service. "Hello. I'd like to order a tossed salad for room 732 with lots of extra sliced cucumbers, vinaigrette on the side...and a bucket of ice."

The next morning Phineas almost bumped into Marie when he exited the hotel. She offered him a tall paper cup. "You take yours with milk, right?" She looked professional in the morning light in charcoal grey pinstripes and just enough makeup. Her eyelids appeared remarkably less puffy this morning, and her mood seemed almost upbeat.

"Yes, thanks. You sleep okay?" He'd not only ironed his white dress shirt and Carolina blue tie but draped a fresh white coat over his arm.

"The Chianti helped. Here's our limo. Ready?"

"Hell, no." He forced a smile. "But let's go anyway."

Their chauffeur opened the limo door. "Warm croissants and maple-glazed doughnuts in the bakery box." When he saw Marie's composed face, his approving smile confirmed her recovery.

The fragrance of maple sugar brought back memories of Phineas' Vermont youth. "Definitely a doughnut for me." His stomach growled in agreement.

"Maybe later for me." Marie passed him the box.

He popped open the lid and inhaled deeply. "Sure you want to do this on an empty stomach?"

She nodded. "My guts are in a knot. Don't want to chance throwing up on our patient."

Not that he doesn't deserve it.

To Phineas' surprise, the limousine soon eased into the entrance drive of the elegant Weichert Suites and stopped. The chauffer hurried around the front of the vehicle to open the building's all glass main door. Eugene Schmidt stepped out in a tailored black suit, scarlet tie, and polished wingtips.

"You didn't expect the boss to miss this, did ya?" Marie murmured.

Schmidt joined them inside and settled into the seat between them. Phineas offered him the bakery box. "Greetings, Gene. Nice suit. Pastry?"

"It's not every day you get an audience with the President." His recently blackened mustache puckered with interest as he stretched his neck to peer at the baked goods. "What have you got?"

"I haven't eaten *all* the maple doughnuts yet. Like one?"

⁓

The ambulatory surgical suite alcove was as Phineas and Marie left it, except that now a fiberoptic bronchoscope occupied a shelf next to the head of the procedure table. The slender black instrument was in a sterilized sheath and attached to a light source. He flipped on its light and looked through the eyepiece. "Works fine. Good to have it, just in case," he said to Marie.

A middle-aged woman in a short white coat pushed through the entrance door. She held a tray containing the glass vial of drug powder, a 20-milliliter syringe, and a 250-milliliter bag of fluid. She approached Phineas. "Dr. Mann? I'm Janet Hicks from Pharmacy. Would you like to watch me mix the SYMBI-62022?"

"Thanks, Janet. Please proceed." She wiped each hub with alcohol then drew fluid from the bag into the syringe and injected it into the vial, dissolving the medication. She next drew the drug solution back into the syringe and injected it straight into the bag of fluid.

Phineas felt like he should hold the bag high, bow his head, and murmur a prayer.

"And Dr. Mann, as requested, I left a new anaphylaxis kit in the top drawer of the crash cart."

"Perfect." He suspended the bag on one of many ceiling hooks over the head of the table and opened the indicated drawer. Two Epi-pens, intravenous Benadryl, and a hefty dose of intravenous steroids.

Mise en place.

Iris had once joked that she would have that French cooking phrase etched on his tombstone. Everything in its place, one last time.

Marie looked up from her phone. "He's rolling down the hall now."

Schmidt positioned himself next to the entrance doors. Phineas slipped on his white coat and buttoned it. The doors burst open and admitted two men in dark suits. They scanned the room. "All clear," one announced.

Phineas recognized the next two suits: Richter and Meyers. The taller Meyers winked. "Dr. Mann, ready to serve your country today?"

"Agent Meyers, I'm confused. You FBI or Secret Service? Just curious."

"Think of me as both today."

"I told those damned generals to let me bomb that nasty guy in China," a familiar voice muttered in the hallway. "And how come no breakfast today? Christ, those pills make me hungry."

"We'll bring you whatever you'd like as soon as the treatment is finished." Dr. Smith's voice.

"Eggs. Three of 'em. Over hard, not runny—with hash browns and white toast, buttered. And jelly—apple jelly—and you got any real bacon? Not that phony turkey stuff." The voice was now just outside.

Dr. Smith, in a long white coat, led two more agents in suits, one in front and the other pushing the President in a wheelchair. A navy-blue windbreaker partially covered a white golf shirt that stretched over his torso. A red cap crowned his swirled, golden hair. The disturbing orange tint on his cheeks and prominent jowls was only modestly lighter than the images Phineas recalled seeing over the years.

"Someone tell me who all these people are," the President commanded.

Schmidt stepped in front. "Eugene Schmidt. CEO of SynMedical

Biopharma. Our company developed your treatment." He held out his hand.

The President offered a minimal wave from his lap. "We're doing you a big favor. This could be *yuge* for you. Don't forget that when you write checks to the party." He checked his cell phone. "You staying at my hotel?"

"No Sir. I—I stayed near here."

"Big mistake. Don't do it again." He jabbed a thumb in Phineas' direction. "Who's he?"

"Dr. Phineas Mann, from the University of North Carolina," Dr. Smith answered. "He's an asthma specialist and Principal Investigator studying the new drug."

"Phineas. Never met a Phineas. I'll call you Phinny."

Phineas winced. "I've never heard that one."

"How about Finman? That's a good one. Damn, I'm good at nicknames."

Only my friends call me Finman.

"Need to get you a red tie—and a hat." His eyebrows flexed down, dragging deep crows' feet with them. "You like my postponing the election, Doc?"

Phineas head snapped back. "Well, Sir—."

"Never mind." He struggled to sit erect when he spotted Marie. "Someone introduce the pretty lady."

Schmidt cleared his throat. "Dr. Marie Porter works for us and is coordinating the Phase 3 study with Dr. Mann."

"She can coordinate with me later." He leered at her from his wheelchair.

"Mr. President, Dr. Mann and I will be monitoring you before and after your treatment." Marie, somehow poker-faced, maintained an all-business tone.

A momentary, suggestive raise of his eyebrows. "Good. Good. See that you do...Well, let's get this over with. Wanna get in some golf before the storm hits, and hafta to act presidential. Probably a nasty one with the name Nancy." He kicked up the wheelchair's footrests. "Someone stand me up. Seat's too damned low."

The two agents took an arm each and, with soft grunts reflecting their effort, lifted him to a standing position. Two halting steps had his buttocks on the surgical table. They lifted his legs and rotated him ninety degrees. Phineas pushed the Raise Head control button, allowing the President to recline at a forty-five-degree angle.

Dr. Smith stepped to the patient's side. "Mr. President, when we get you off prednisone, your leg muscles should get stronger."

"They'd better. Got to get on and off a golf cart. And I can't catch the first lady anymore—not even close."

A middle-aged Black woman in a short white coat pushed open the door and announced, "Johnson. Intravenous Team." She pushed a cart with supplies. "May I enter?"

One of the agents inspected the cart's contents and nodded toward Dr. Smith, who waved her in. "Thank you, Ms. Johnson. Please proceed." He approached the President. "Sir, let me help you with your jacket. Ms. Johnson will start your intravenous line."

The patient's eyes opened wide at her approach and at her display of syringes and catheters. "Wait a minute! Why isn't one of you doctors doing the sticking?"

Phineas couldn't help grinning. "Sir, you want someone who puts a whole lot of these lines in, not one of us."

Ms. Johnson remained matter of fact as she prepared her equipment, inspected her patient's arm, gloved up, and took the protective sheath off a two-inch catheter over a hollow needle. Her hands were rock steady.

Her patient stared at the sharp device like it was a gleaming dagger before he looked away. "This part makes me squeamish." His lips formed a snout. He flinched when she stuck him. Dark blood filled the catheter's hub. She flushed the device with saline and secured it with strips of tape.

"There. All done, Sir. Have a nice day." She wore a relieved smile and rolled her cart out of the room.

"Mr. President, I need to examine you now." Phineas showed him his stethoscope.

The President waved at the cluster of black suits. "You guys gimme some privacy. Go stand in the hallway."

They filed outside, except for Meyers, who maintained his position. "Mr. President, one of us has to stay. I'll look away."

"Whatever. Go ahead, Doc." He stared up at the ceiling like he was inspecting its construction.

Phineas' examination revealed upper and lower dentures, a troubling narrow throat with a thick neck, and scattered wheezes. Bruises splotched thin forearm skin, and both legs were swollen. His patient's abdomen hung over his belt and displayed numerous stretch marks, signs that confirmed heavy steroid use.

Marie handed Phineas EKG stickers, which he attached to both arms and legs. The rhythm was regular at ninety beats per minute. He placed an oximeter probe on his patient's index finger. Acceptable at ninety-five percent.

Phineas briefly considered crossing himself but said a quick silent prayer instead. "We're ready to proceed with the treatment, Sir." He readied the intravenous line from the bag of SYMBI-62022 solution. Marie nodded silent approval from beside the Code Blue cart.

His patient held up his free hand like he wanted to pause the proceedings. "Wait a minute, Doc. You're a Republican. Right?" The rim of paler skin over his baggy eye sockets wrinkled extra when he squinted at Phineas.

"I'm a doctor, Sir." *And I wish I were somewhere else.*

The hand went down followed by a deep sigh. "You don't wanna screw this up, Doc. Remember, I got guys who love me." His lips trembled before he puckered them. Among all the news images, Phineas hadn't seen this defeated and frightened expression.

Phineas plugged the line into the catheter, opened the valve, and activated the programmed pump. "Some patients say it tingles a bit. Let me know if you feel any discomfort." SYMBI-62022 dripped at the expected steady rate and filled the intravenous line.

"So far, so good, Doc." He closed his eyes and let his head sink back into the thin pillow.

Phineas listened to his patient's lungs again. No change. The President reached across his abdomen with his free hand to scratch above the intravenous site on his arm then slid the hand over his chest. Phineas lifted the edge of the golf shirt and saw soft pink patches rise and coalesce across his patient's abdomen and chest.

Shit!

Without uttering a word, Phineas turned the pump infusing the SYMBI-62022 off, closed the valve, and opened the top drawer of the crash cart. He inserted the needle on the Benadryl syringe into the IV line's port and injected its entire contents.

"This should help the itching, Sir. It might make you a little sleepy." Phineas reached back into the top drawer. "And I'm going to give you a shot." Phineas pushed an Epi-pen needle into his patient's thigh through the pants' fabric.

"A shot? Why?" His words were thick. "Ouch. Damn!" Frankly hoarse.

"You're having a reaction to the treatment, Sir. I'm trying to stay ahead of it." *Now what?* His left hand had commenced its maddening pill rolling tremor, its involuntary thumb to index finger tango. *No! Not now!*

He said another silent prayer and tried to suppress his left hand's independence by using it to massage the thigh injection site. He readied the syringe containing the massive dose of steroids and pushed it as a bolus into the intravenous line then replaced the SYMBI-62022 bag with a liter bag of saline solution. He adjusted the valve to wide open and the pump to its maximum rate. The President's lips were puffy.

"Lips are numb. Can you fix that?" Each breath in made a honking noise and each breath out sounded like a braying donkey. He stared at Smith with eyes that were bloodshot saucers. "Smith! This is your fault!" Barely a frightened whisper.

Marie arranged an oxygen cannula under their patient's nose and exchanged a worried glance with Phineas. He opened the container with the laryngoscope and endotracheal tubes, clicked the blade of the metal laryngoscope into the 'light on' position, and set it on top of the cart. His hand shook while he injected more epinephrine, this time as a slow push into the intravenous line. Multiple extra heart beats danced across the monitor screen. "Marie, draw up something for sedation. I saw midazolam in there." The automated blood pressure cuff deflated, and the screen displayed 80/50. *Shock.* Phineas pulled on sterile blue nitrile gloves.

Smith began pacing back and forth next to the table. "Should I call the Code Blue Team?"

Phineas shook his head. "Do you think that mob would get through Secret Service, or add anything? Better that we handle this for now...We need an open airway to keep him alive long enough for the epinephrine to work."

The patient's terrifying breathing sounds escalated to louder honks, his taut neck muscles visibly contracting with each breath. His arms flailed in the air in front of him then clutched at his neck as he mouthed the two words Phineas dreaded most, "Can't breathe!"

Now barely a sound from the lips that had spewed loud hate for more than eight years, ordered children into cages and stormtroopers onto city streets; and this ignorant man behind those lips botched the management of the pandemic that killed so many friends.

Let him go!

For eight years this man had, with help from foreign hackers, twice stolen the presidency, encouraged the ruin of the environment, and pillaged and violated everything sacred. This corrupt man had attacked his daughter, promoted saturating the country with poisons that wiped out his honey bees, and almost killed the dog, Ruby. This man lay dying in front of him.

Let him die!

Phineas struggled to focus on the crisis that was his to lead.

Revenge is not mine.

Not one particle in his makeup allowed him to deny someone needed care. He couldn't suppress his reflex compulsion to temporarily deny death a decaying soul. He asked Marie to inject sedation into the IV line.

"I gave 3 mg of midazolam," she announced.

Their patient released the grip on his neck, and his arms slipped into positions along his sides. Phineas, hoping to conceal his infuriating tremor by keeping his hands in motion, fished out his patient's dentures and placed them on the code cart then grasped the metal laryngoscope in his unsteady left hand and an endotracheal tube in his dependable right. He inserted the scope's rigid blade over a swollen and protruding tongue and peered down the President's throat into heaped up pink flesh.

"Can't see vocal cords—too much swelling. Wish the damned epinephrine would start working." He removed the scope as his patient made a sluggish grab for it. "Give him another milligram of midazolam. I'm going to try to intubate him with the bronchoscope." Phineas' heart pounded in his ears on top of—alarms! The oxygen monitor alarmed as the President's level plunged. The competing EKG alarm heralded frequent frightening five to ten beat bursts of a dangerous ventricular tachycardia.

"I gave him amiodarone for his heart rhythm." Marie reported in an even tone that reflected her experience in emergencies. She flipped the cardiac defibrillator power switch to 'on' and began charging it. Its whirring added to the cacophony of multiple dinging alarms. She grasped the two handles, lifted the paddles, and looked ready to use them.

Phineas slipped the endotracheal tube over the flexible fiberoptic bronchoscope and inserted the combination into the patient's mouth. He'd done this in the ICU many times as a younger doctor when he wasn't fighting an active rebellion in his left hand, the hand he always used on the control knob, allowing him precise control of biopsy forceps with his right. "We need to get him an airway, and I don't want to cut a hole in his neck." The last emergency tracheostomy he'd participated in had been a messy event many years ago on a sad man who arrived too late.

"Step away from the President."

Agent Meyers planted himself between Phineas and Marie, his

semiautomatic service pistol drawn. "I said *step away*." He peered down the level barrel at Phineas.

This can't be happening.

"Can't. No time."

"This is God's will. Let him go. The world will be better off," Meyers barked through the alarms.

"No time to debate now." Phineas peered into the lens of the bronchoscope. Air bubbles were coming up from the lower airway. He pushed the scope deeper in pursuit of their source, past the obstructing edematous throat tissue and epiglottis. *There.* Swollen vocal cords. The opening between them leading to the trachea, the opening that would give a chance to save a life, was at most a few millimeters. The shaking in his left hand made it difficult to keep the scope's tip where it needed to be and impossible to keep the darker tracheal target in a steady view before his tremor fumbled it away.

"My daughter deserves a country and a planet where she can live—and enjoy living—and he's ruining it." Meyers' voice was more beseeching than commanding this time. He held out his open left hand. "Think about it. This *has* to be God's will."

"Can't talk now." Phineas switched the bronchoscope from his left to his right hand and advanced the now steady tip to where he could see the vocal cords up close. When he began pushing it into the tight space between them, he felt resistance. *Too tight. Must get through to his trachea—and his lungs.*

"I asked you months ago if you would serve your country. Step away and you'll be doing that—and serving the whole world," Meyers pleaded.

I see trachea! The lens on the tip of the bronchoscope had threaded between the vocal cord blockage into wide open trachea. Phineas carefully advanced the endotracheal tube over the scope, keeping the fiberoptic instrument in place and using it as a guide to deploy the lifesaving breathing conduit to where it could deliver oxygen. "Almost there." The infuriating alarms still saturated the space around him.

"Sorry about this. I don't want to hurt you." Meyers' agitated voice penetrated the chaos. "Last warning. Quit now."

Phineas took his eye off the eyepiece in time to see Meyers lift the gun over his head, the butt end turned to strike a blow. If he let go of the bronchoscope and gave up on saving his patient, he might have seconds to dodge the assault.

Marie was staring, the whites of her eyes fully exposed. Would his being struck down give her a final satisfaction?

Suddenly, an even louder alarm pierced the air—a Code Blue. Smith hugged the wall next to the alarm switch.

Meyers' head swiveled to glance at Smith.

Marie slammed the defibrillator paddles onto opposite sides of Meyer's exposed neck and suit collar. The agent's body convulsed.

BANG!

The pistol fired the one shot before it flew out of Meyers' flailing hand and sailed across the room. At the same instant, the plastic bag of SYMBI-62022 exploded and showered Phineas and his patient. Meyers crumpled to the floor. The air stank of gunpowder and burned wool.

The double doors burst open, and a rush of dark suits stampeded into the unit, pistols drawn.

Phineas withdrew the bronchoscope from inside the properly positioned endotracheal tube, attached the manual breathing bag, and pumped oxygenated breaths into the President. After the first few breaths, his patient's oxygen level corrected to 97 percent and heart rhythm settled at 120 beats per minute with normal appearing, regular electrical complexes on the screen. The automated blood pressure cuff indicated a healthy 110/70. Between the breaths he administered, Phineas used the table's sheet to wipe drops of the offending investigational drug from his patient's exposed skin.

Marie knelt over the fallen FBI agent. "He has a pulse." She bent low to place her ear next to his mouth. "He's breathing."

"What the hell did you do to my partner?" Agent Richter hovered over her, panting.

She rolled the unconscious Meyers on his side. "Disarmed him. He tried to prevent us from saving the President. You should arrest him."

"Why would he do *that*?" Richter's shriek was almost inaudible over the still blaring Code Blue alarm.

She glanced up at Richter, her arched eyebrows suggesting disbelief that he had to ask such a thing. "Isn't it obvious? Is it *that* hard to understand? Climate change. War. Ruining our country. So many reasons." She pointed at Meyers. "Ask *him*!"

Meyers began moaning. His eyes fluttered open, and he reached for the empty holster under his arm. "What...what happened?"

Smith turned off the maddening Code Blue alarm. "Arrest Agent Meyers." Richter scowled and secured a handcuff on one of his partner's wrists then the other.

Eugene Schmidt rushed into the room. "What the hell happened?" But then, as he took in the bizarre scene, his lips formed an 'O', and the black caterpillar outlined a semicircle above it.

Marie rose to her full height and stared down at him. "Severe anaphylaxis. We almost lost him. Dr. Mann saved the President's life."

Phineas glanced sideways at them. "Marie had as much to do with his rescue as I did—and with *my* rescue."

But the Code Blue alarm had done its work, and now a tidal wave of white coats was breaking against the wall of black suits inside the procedure room's entrance doors.

Smith positioned himself in the center of the medical invasion and yelled, "Code's over. ICU attending and resident, you stay. The rest of you, thank you. You can go back...Nothing to see here."

Phineas was giving the President a breath every five counts. The accursed tremor had become almost undetectable, and the President's hives and lip swelling seemed to finally be resolving. *Better late than...*

The President began to move his hands and feet. Phineas spoke to Marie. "He's coming to. Let's give him another milligram of midazolam and keep him sedated, so we can leave the tube in until we're sure his airway's swelling has fully resolved."

The two Intensive Care Unit physicians froze and stared when they reached Phineas' side. He motioned for the resident to take over squeezing the ventilation bag. "I'm Dr. Mann, and this is what it looks like. Our President had an anaphylactic reaction to an infusion of an asthma medication...We almost lost him, but I suspect the tube can come out in a few hours in your ICU—once his angioedema has completely cleared." He searched the code cart and located the plastic collar to secure the precious breathing tube in place.

Schmidt grabbed Phineas' sleeve and tugged. "You're going with him." Schmidt's bristly mustache was writhing.

"Of course." Phineas suppressed an urge to lash out at the bossy and self-important CEO.

"Well, I'm pulling the drug. Cancelling the trial. This is terrible for us. If word gets out that we want to sell a drug that nearly killed the President..."

It was early evening before Phineas felt he and Marie had finished all they needed to do and could leave Walter Reed Hospital. During the preceding hours, they'd stood in the ICU at the President's bedside until all visible signs of anaphylaxis had completely resolved. Then, before Phineas removed the endotracheal tube, he taught the resident and intern how to be confident that there was no residual airway blockage.

With the President's sedation wearing off and the return of his voice, he'd rambled off a steady stream of nonsense. Phineas pressed his lips together, and gave a subtle head shake to signal to the young doctors that they shouldn't reveal their amusement at their intoxicated Commander-in-Chief. At least the President's breathing remained stable, even better than when Phineas first examined him.

Phineas finally collapsed into a cushioned chair in the hospital lobby. Exhaustion trumped the adrenaline that had fueled his day, and he appreciated no longer having to make decisions and give orders. Marie also seemed to relish a silent moment, as she opened her briefcase and extracted her laptop. He allowed his eyes to close.

"Time to go, Phineas." She was standing a few feet in front of him. "Sorry your nap wasn't longer." Their limousine waited at the entrance.

"I'm sorry. Didn't expect to doze off." His knees creaked as he pushed himself out of the low seat.

"No problem. I might have done the same if I hadn't been documenting our day for SynMedical."

He took off his white coat and folded it over his arm. "We ought to celebrate one thing." Had she had the same happy thought he'd had?

"What's that?"

"We won't have to come back here monthly. If your drug had worked, the President would insist we personally give all his doses."

"So, after tomorrow, we're done with him?" she asked hopefully.

"After we see him tomorrow morning—if he's in good enough shape to be discharged, and he *should be* after the huge dose of steroids I gave him." He followed her through the double doors.

She spun around toward him and exclaimed, "Halleluiah!"

"Well, you two seem happy," their limo chauffeur observed.

With the tense moments behind them, Phineas asked, "What's your name kind Sir?"

"It's Fred, Dr. Mann." He stood at attention in front of the open back door. "Got you a selection of hoagies, pasta salad, and beers on ice—and brownies—as requested. Long day. You two *have* to be hungry."

You have no idea. "Famished, Fred. Thanks."

Marie and Phineas climbed in and buckled their seat belts. Phineas flipped open the cooler's lid and extracted two cans. "Nice! You remembered my favorite IPA."

Marie clicked her can open and took a long pull before she lowered it. "I figured you probably won't be able to get it in Italy."

"Somehow, I'll survive." He reached back into the cooler. "What do you like on a hoagie?"

"Turkey, if you find one." She sipped more beer then smacked her lips unexpectedly as if she was savoring an exquisite offering. "Today wasn't what I had in mind when I left hospital medicine for the pharmaceutical industry."

"And I'd been figuring drug studies would be less stress than ICU medicine. Who knew?"

Marie closed the inside window to their driver. "It's amazing how little the President remembered once the midazolam wore off. He was even loopier than usual."

"It would be better if he did remember. At least he'd know what we did to save him." He handed her a long sandwich wrapped in white paper. "Nearing death can change a man, even if being impeached twice didn't."

"You know nothing's going to change him."

"Unfortunately. ...Maybe I shouldn't have tried so hard." He could have failed to place the tube, and no one could honestly fault him. Few doctors would have succeeded, especially battling an uncooperative hand.

"That's not in your DNA."

"Or yours." Phineas blushed. "Whoops! Sorry. Didn't mean for *that* to come up again. ...You okay?"

She probed his eyes. "I'm fine...as long as I can still be friends with you...and Iris...and your family."

No way she'd been thinking revenge. That saga was finally over. It *had* to be over. "Absolutely—especially after all we've been through together."

She began laughing, softly at first, then right out loud.

"What's so funny now?" It was a relief to hear her laugh.

"Just picturing when you took out his endotracheal tube, and he said he wanted to give *me* the Presidential Medal of Freedom—while completely ignoring you. You're the one who saved him. I just defended you."

"And don't forget what he said to you after that." Phineas tightened his lips over his teeth like they were gums, and he was toothless. "Mebbe da Surgeon Gen'ral. Ya wanna be ma Surgeon Gen'ral?" He relaxed his lips and spoke with his normal voice. "Think he likes to have young women around him?"

"You think?" She took a bite, chewed, and swallowed. "Of course, to work for him, I'd have to bleach my hair—and I'm not about to do *either*."

"Looks like our study could be over—and my support with it." He took in a deep breath and let it out slowly. "Might be time for me join Iris in retirement." *Time to retire before I make mistakes that harm someone—if this neurologic thing progresses.* He read his sandwich's label. "Genoa salami, Mortadella, capicola, and provolone. Perfect preparation for Italy."

"We have other drugs in the pipeline that could interest you." She put her sandwich down on its wrapping paper. "I said we—if Schmidt still has a job for me." She tilted her head to one side and shrugged.

"Gene Schmidt won't dare let you go. T'would displease POTUS—and besides that, if word got out that he fired the SynMedical doctor who helped save the President...just imagine the press. Believe me. You're *golden*."

"Maybe I should bring up the subject of a private office when I get back—and just maybe next year I'll kick Schmidt's ass in the 5K—show them what I can do if I want to." She swallowed another mouthful of beer.

"That'll be sweet." He typed on his cell. "I let Iris know we're on our way."

"Find out what she'd like from our stash."

"Definitely the brownies." Iris always savored a good brownie. He recognized a shopping mall a few blocks from their hotel.

Marie asked, "So, they're expecting us back at 8 AM in their ICU?" She wrinkled her nose.

"Yeah. Let's hope we can get in and out and send our president back to the White House quick before he fires someone." He tipped his can up and swallowed. "Whew! There's some herbs and spices in this sandwich. Iris will let me know about the garlic."

"Fire someone besides Meyers?"

"Huh! You just never know who's willing to be a martyr for a cause. Thanks again for saving me from a beating. *That guy was serious*."

She shuddered. "My God...Glad I didn't kill him...There was no time to think."

"I've been thinking about Meyers. In the big picture, maybe he was right...but somehow...I just couldn't stop...being a doctor."

"Phineas, you saw what kind of shape the President's in. He can't live *that* much longer."

⌒

The next morning at the Walter Reed ICU entrance, two unfamiliar agents in black suits greeted Marie and Phineas with a handheld metal detector. The unit was now mostly empty except for the ICU medical team rounding on a handful of patients on the far side, sequestered away from the secret service agents stationed in front of the President's room. He reclined on his bed with its head raised and wore the same white golf shirt. FOX and Friends blared from the flat screen suspended on the wall opposite him. When he saw Phineas and Marie, he yelled over the television's noise, "Great guys on FOX. Great." He grabbed his red ball cap from the bedside table and carefully arranged it on his dyed and lacquered coiffure. "Get me outa' here. Feel like a caged animal."

Phineas pondered the question of how much hairspray reached the presidential lungs each morning. Was that part of his asthma problem? An issue to raise with Dr. Smith. "It's not exactly jail here. How about I examine you first?"

"Talk louder. Can't hear you." The President pressed the remote's mute button. He'd missed the jail comment.

"How about I examine you? You feeling better, Mr. President?"

"Way better. Breathing tremendous. Gotta get more of that new drug. Tremendous." More than the usual fractured and pressured speech. Steroids? Adderall?

"Sir, you hardly got any of the study drug. Only enough to trigger an allergic reaction. We had to give you a massive dose of steroids. *That's* why you feel better"—*for now.*

"Feel like Superman. Superman. Great night. Musta' tweeted a hundred times."

"Let's see what you sound like." Phineas held up his stethoscope then methodically applied the instrument to his patient's chest and neck, where he found lungs free of wheezes and none of the residual harsh sounds of a swollen larynx. "And let's see your throat. Open. Now tilt your head back. Good. Swelling's all gone."

"So, I'm outa' here. Gonna play golf now. Hit those links like nobody's business. Feel like Superman." He raised his eyebrows suggestively at Marie, who returned a stony stare.

Can't wait till I'm "outa' here" too. "You should really take it easy for the next few days. You do understand that you almost died yesterday?"

"There'da been hell to pay." He gave Phineas a "get my drift" look.

Where you'd be. "I won't stand in the way of you leaving the hospital." Phineas held out his hands, palms up, conceding a gesture of surrender. "Do you have follow-up arranged with your specialists here?"

The President waved a dismissive hand. "Got people to do that. Great people. Lots of 'em. Gotta hit the links now. My own course, National. Great course. Tremendous. Superman."

"Don't you want to get back to the White House before Hurricane Nancy gets to Washington?"

"Nasty Nancy can wait. Nasty, nasty Nancy. Gotta hit some balls. Hit 'em like Superman." He pushed the bedside table away and struggled to shift his legs over the bed's side.

Phineas and Marie exchanged glances and shrugged. *It's your funeral.* They stepped back to give him room.

The President looked Marie up and down. "You stay in touch."

The corner of her mouth twitched.

Limo chauffer Fred was waiting for them at the entrance. "Back to the hotel?"

"Yup. We'll be checking out, Fred," Marie answered with a serene smile. "Dr. Mann will need a ride to the airport, and after that you can take me back to North Carolina. I checked and flights are still leaving on time. I'm sure the airlines want to get their planes far away from Washington ahead of the storm."

She glanced at Phineas. "Remind me. What time's your flight?"

"Not till 5:30. It's a red eye across the pond. Hopefully we'll snooze most of the way, now that we're in first class—thank you very much."

"I can either hire you another limo to the airport for later, or Fred and I can take you into the city for lunch and a quick site-seeing tour, then drop you and Iris off at Dulles in time for your check in."

"I like the latter idea. I'll text Iris."

"Tell her to take her time. After my interaction with POTUS, I feel like I need another shower and a change of clothes. We should still be able to get out of here safely ahead of Hurricane Nancy."

"One more thing, Marie."

"Yes?" She looked surprised, as if she thought she'd arranged every detail.

"When you get back, I'd like you to work on Schmidt to keep SYMBI-62022 in the pipeline and the trial going. Call Gabby. She's covering while I'm gone, and I've got patients whom I believe are really being helped by it—and I mean *really* helped, and the President wasn't *actually* part of the trial." He pictured Dolly at her recent visit. "Your scientists have developed a drug with amazing potential. We can't let one misguided deviation from good scientific method derail its availability to patients who need it."

Marie shrugged. "I'll try, but that may depend on what POTUS has to say about it to the press after he leaves his golf course."

"Well, give it your best. If he continues to try to stay in power, we're not sure when we'll come back to the States."

Hours later, Fred opened the limo door in front of Dulles Airport's Departures' entrances. "Let me get your bags for you. Should be plenty of time to check in for your flight. Would you like me to find a luggage cart?"

"Thank you, Fred," Iris replied. "I think we can manage, but we'll miss how well you've treated us."

"Been a pleasure, Ma'am. Have a wonderful vacation." A quick bow.

"Is it a vacation, if I'm already retired?" Iris mused. "I guess so, if it gets me off the campaign trail for a while." The lines in her face, now less visible, suggested that she might be beginning to relax.

Phineas rested his arm across her shoulders. "Martha will be fine. You gave her a great start, and Marie plans to fill your political shoes while you're gone."

Marie climbed out of the limo's back seat sporting the curious track warm-up suit she'd changed into at the hotel. "Right. I've been texting with Martha. I'll check in with her when I get back. You two relax and enjoy Italy."

Iris motioned for Marie to come close for a firm hug. When they separated, Marie blinked and sniffed. "I'm expecting to see pictures before long," she said.

"Iris takes the pictures." Phineas offered her his right hand.

Marie grasped his hand firmly then reached behind his shoulder with her left hand and pressed against him like buddies or teammates do. She caught him off guard, but her gesture felt just right. She'd be a trusted friend, not someone who held anything against him. The back of his nose tingled, not sadness this time but relief.

"Mind if I start calling you Finman—when we're outside of work?" she murmured.

"I'd like that."

He let Marie go and swung his backpack over his shoulder. "We'll be back for Martha's final push—unless we decide to stay. And who knows?"

∿

In the back seat of their Milan limousine, Phineas reached over for Iris' hand and planted a kiss on her cheek, then another full on her lips. He murmured, "Italy always makes me feel romantic."

She pressed his hand between both of hers. "Hold that thought till we get to the villa. We can nap then."

"I may not need a nap. First class, Iris! I actually slept while we crossed the Atlantic." He leaned back into the roomy, luxurious leather seat and stretched his legs straight out.

Iris released his hand and started fiddling with her phone. A minute later, she announced, "I made it onto the Italian network, and I'm starting to get texts from Jacob." She studied the screen. "You should set up your phone...Oh my!"

"What did he say?"

"Marie dropped by our house wearing a crazy track warmup suit. Has a picture on it of a guy with a beet for a head." She kept scrolling and reading. "Then Nancy strengthened, and the edge of the hurricane hit Chapel Hill hard. The whole area lost power. Then the storm headed north."

Phineas pulled his phone from his pocket and found the network and the thread. "So, the house is fine. He thinks only a few small trees came down in the yard, but it's still dark there. Phew! Glad he's at the house."

"He's drawing this out. Seems to be keeping us in suspense." Iris looked stunned. "Marie rode out the storm there."

"Didn't see that coming...Maybe the hurricane trapped her there."

"Jacob says that before they lost power, they were making Bolognese sauce together from fresh-picked tomatoes. Had to finish it on the grill burner."

"Hmph. Making sauce. Is that code?"

She scrolled down her phone's screen. "He's thinking about telling Cornell to put their faculty position offer on hold for now."

"He might stay in North Carolina? Fantastic!" Ithaca would have seemed a million miles away. "And just last week, she didn't seem that interested in him."

"Well, now she knows Jacob's *not* her brother..."

Phineas left thumb began its cursed rhythmic rolling across his cell phone screen. He shoved both hands in his pants pockets, turned his attention to the countryside outside the side window, and tried to appear nonchalant.

"When were you going to tell me?" Iris asked like she'd been waiting for the right moment.

"Tell you what?"

"About your hand. You know this retired social worker has seen her share of tremors." She pressed her hand over his in the pocket.

"It's nothing. Just happens out of the blue on occasion."

"So, what do you think it is?"

"Parkinson's, obviously." The images of Iris pushing him in a wheelchair, lifting him on and off the toilet, telling him the same information over and over made him close his eyes and shake his head to try to cast those thoughts out.

"As a pulmonologist, you've seen only a very skewed group of patients with it—those with severe complications."

True.

"Parkinson's—if that's what it is—can stay mild and there can be a normal lifespan." She leaned close. "When we get back, we'll set up a consultation."

He forced a smile...then felt it grow into a real smile. She'd be there with him and for him.

⌒

The chanting and car horns outside their bedroom's balcony were getting steadily more raucous. The noise roused Phineas from the deep slumber so customary to him after extreme fatigue, similar to his catching up after a month-long stressful rotation supervising the ICU. Sunlight streaming in through the tall west facing window lit up Iris' cascading silver hair, her graceful naked back, and the sheet draped over her hips. She began to stir from the satisfying sleep that she always enjoyed after love-making; she'd told him once it wasn't mere sex, but better—lovemaking.

He appreciated how she thought of the act, and he privately celebrated every single one of them as if it was their first time.

She rolled onto her back and opened an eye. "Ummm, this bed is so comfortable" The noise grew even louder. "Phineas, is there a holiday we didn't know about?"

He sat on the edge of the bed and gazed out the window into the scenic mountain village's medieval piazza. "The streets are full—I can't understand what they're saying. Maybe there's something on TV." He stood and found the remote to the flat screen mounted on the wall across from the foot of the bed.

"Cute buns." Back on her side, she rested her head on her hand, and her elbow disappeared into the soft bedding.

"Glad you still think so, since you might see more of them in our retirement."

The screen displayed a brightly illuminated head shot of a middle-aged man in uniform. His eyebrows arched up under a blond crewcut as he dabbed at an eye. A woman shoved a microphone in his face. Italian words ran from left to right under his face. Phineas raised the volume. The man was speaking in English.

"The President ordered me to fly him in his helicopter to take him from his golf course to the White House. I explained that the barometric pressure was falling too rapidly, that the winds spawned at the edge of Hurricane Nancy would be unstable...Bottom line—I wouldn't be able to keep him safe...Traffic was stop and roll ahead of the storm. Even so, I tried to press the point—he should take a motorcade."

The pilot looked down, swallowed hard enough for Phineas to see his Adam's apple lift, then stared into the camera. "The President said he was too important to waste his time sitting in a traffic jam. Then he fired me, and his people found someone else to fly him."

A deep breath and an uncomfortable silence. Was the shaken pilot grieving or traumatized from undeserved abuse?

The camera shifted to the right. Next to the pilot, a solemn four-star general leaned close to the microphone. "Near the American Legion Bridge over I-495, a sudden burst of high winds sent the presidential helicopter into an abutment." He bowed his head. "There were no survivors."

Phineas dropped onto the foot end of the bed, his buttocks sinking into its luxurious padding. The patient he'd just saved...struck down in an instant. He expected grief but felt only peace.

The channel switched locations to a newsroom where a beautiful young woman with shiny, long black hair was speaking in Italian. He made out only "presidente" among her rapid-fire words. Her face was soon replaced by a familiar one in front of the White House.

The Vice President of the United States opened a black leather folder and set it on a lectern. Italian words began crossing the screen under his face. He looked up at the camera. His eyes were red, and the peeling and split corners of his mouth were drawn downward. A pesky soot-black house fly touched down on his perfectly groomed porcelain-white hair.

"It is with the greatest sadness that I must tell you, the American people, of the passing of your president. Let us all pray that he's now receiving the rewards he so richly deserves for all his works here on Earth." He bowed his head, and his lips silently mouthed The Lord's Prayer. Then he stared, it seemed, straight at Phineas and Iris. "The Chief Justice will now administer the Oath of Office."

Iris settled into the cozy mattress depression next to Phineas, pressed her warm skin against his, and whispered, "Our president should have paid attention when she bit him on the ass."

"She?"

"Why, Mother Nature, of course."

ABOUT THE AUTHOR

 MARK ANTHONY POWERS grew up in the small town of West Lebanon, NH. At Cornell University, he branched out into Creative Writing and Russian while majoring in engineering. After receiving his MD from Dartmouth, he went south to the University of North Carolina for an internship and residency in Internal Medicine, followed by a fellowship in Pulmonary Diseases and Critical Care Medicine.

After almost forty years in clinical practice and teaching, he retired from Duke University as an Associate Professor Emeritus of Medicine and began his exploration of other parts of his brain. Writing, gardening, IT, and magic courses were just some of the enjoyment that followed. A deep dive into beekeeping led to his presidency of the county beekeeping association and certification as a Master Beekeeper.

Two cups of coffee and two hours of writing most mornings produced the medical thrillers *A Swarm in May, Breath and Mercy, Nature's Bite*, and his forthcoming book in this series, *Culled*. To learn more or connect with Mark, please visit www.markanthonypowers.com.

Made in the USA
Columbia, SC
23 September 2022

67255142R00140